**Praise for the novels of
New York Times and *USA TODAY*
bestselling author**

shannon
stacey

"Books like this are why I read romance."
—*Smart Bitches, Trashy Books*
on *Exclusively Yours*

"This is the perfect contemporary romance!"
—*RT Book Reviews* on *Undeniably Yours*

"Sexy, sassy and immensely satisfying."
—*Fresh Fiction* on *Undeniably Yours*

"*Yours to Keep* was a wonderful,
sexy and witty installment in this series....
This was a truly magical book."
—*The Book Pushers*

"This contemporary romance
is filled with charm, wit, sophistication,
and is anything but predictable."
—*Heart to Heart, BN.com Romance Blog,*
on *Yours to Keep*

shannon stacey

exclusively *Yours*

HQN™

Recycling programs
for this product may
not exist in your area.

ISBN-13: 978-0-373-77678-8

EXCLUSIVELY YOURS

ACKNOWLEDGMENTS

"No man is an island, entire of itself..."
—John Donne, 1624

No author is an island entire of herself,
either—a fact for which I'm very grateful
every time I sit down at my computer to write.

It's a privilege and a pleasure to work with
Carina Press. Knowing I have a knowledgeable,
passionate team of professionals working with
me to ensure my books are the best they can be
makes the process of writing
a far less solitary endeavor.

And to the HQN team
for bringing the Kowalski family into print
and to more readers, thank you.

For Stuart and our boys because there's no greater joy than sitting around the campfire with you after a fun day of riding the trails. I love you all madly, even when you're muddy and smell like bug spray. For Steve and Carla, who not only give our family a place to play, but brought great friends into our lives. And thank you to my editor, Angela James, for taking a book so close to my heart and making it better.

exclusively *Yours*

CHAPTER ONE

"YOU GOT *BUSY* IN THE BACKSEAT of a '78 Ford Granada with Joseph Kowalski—only the most reclusive best-selling author since J. D. Salinger—and you don't think to tell me about it?"

Keri Daniels sucked the last dregs of her too-fruity smoothie through her straw and shrugged at her boss. "Would *you* want anybody to know?"

"That I had sex with Joseph Kowalski?"

"No, that you had sex in the backseat of a '78 Granada." Keri had no idea how Tina Deschanel had gotten the dirt on her high school indiscretions, but she knew she was in trouble.

An exceptionally well-paid reporter for a glossy weekly entertainment magazine did not withhold carnal knowledge of a celebrity on the editor in chief's most-wanted list. And having kept that juicy little detail to herself wouldn't get Keri any closer to parking her butt in an editorial chair.

Tina slipped a photograph from her purse and slid it across the table. Keri didn't look down. She was mentally compiling a short list of the people who knew she'd fogged up the windows of one of the ug-liest cars in the history of fossil fuels. Her friends.

The cop who'd knocked on the fogged-up window with a flashlight at a really inopportune moment. Her parents, since the cop was in a bad mood that night. The approximately six hundred kids attending her high school that year and anybody *they'd* told. Maybe *short list* wasn't the right term.

"That was like two decades ago," Keri pointed out, because her boss clearly expected her to say something. "Not exactly a current event. And you ambushed me with this shopping spree."

Actually, their table in the outdoor café was surrounded by enough bags to stagger a pack mule on steroids, but now Keri knew she'd merely been offered the retail therapy *before* the bad news. It shouldn't have surprised her. Tina Deschanel was a shark, and any friendly gesture should have been seen as a prelude to getting bitten in the ass.

"Ambushed?" Tina repeated, loudly enough to distract a pair of Hollywood starlets engaging in some serious public displays of affection in a blatant attempt to attract the cheap tabloid paparazzi. A rabid horde that might include Keri in the near future if she didn't handle this correctly.

"How do you think I felt?" Tina went on. "I reached out to a woman who mentioned on her blog she'd gone to high school with Joseph Kowalski. Once there was money on the table, I made her cough up some evidence, and she sent me a few photos. She was even kind enough to caption them for me."

Keri recognized a cue when it was shoved down

her throat. With one perfectly manicured nail she hooked the eight-by-ten blowup and pulled it closer.

A girl smiled at her from the photo. She wore a pink fuzzy sweater, faded second-skin jeans and pink high heels. Raccoon eyeliner made her dark brown eyes darker, frosty pink coated her lips and her hair was as big as Wisconsin.

Keri smiled back at her, remembering those curling iron and aerosol days. If the EPA had shut down their cheerleading squad back then, global warming might have been a total nonissue today.

Then she looked at the boy. He was leaning against the hideous brown car, his arms wrapped around young Keri's waist. Joe's blue eyes were as dark as the school sweatshirt he wore, and his grin managed to be both innocent and naughty at the same time. And those damn dimples—she'd been a sucker for them. His honey-brown hair was hidden by a Red Sox cap, but she didn't need to see it to remember how the strands felt sliding through her fingers.

She never failed to be amazed by how much she still missed him sometimes.

But who had they been smiling at? For the life of her, Keri couldn't remember who was standing behind the camera. She tore her gaze away from the happy couple and read the caption typed across the bottom.

Joe Kowalski and his girlfriend, Keri Daniels, a few hours before a cop busted them making out on a back road and called their parents. Rumor had it

*when Joe dropped her off, Mr. Daniels chased him
all the way home with a golf club.*

Keri snorted. "Dad only chased him to the end
of the block. Even a '78 Granada could outrun a
middle-age fat guy with a five iron."

"I fail to see the humor in this."

"You didn't see my old man chasing taillights
down the middle of the street in his bathrobe. It
wasn't very funny at the time, though."

"Focus, Keri," Tina snapped. "Do you or do you
not walk by the bulletin board in the bull pen every
day?"

"I do."

"And have you not seen the sheet marked *Spotlight Magazine's* Most Wanted every day?"

"I have."

"And did you happen to notice Joseph Kowalski has been number three for several years?" Keri
nodded, and Tina leaned across the table. "*You* are
going to get me an exclusive feature interview with
the man."

"Or…?"

Tina sat back and folded her arms across her
chest. "Don't take it to that point, Keri. Look, the
man's eleventh bestseller is going to be *the* summer
blockbuster film of the decade. More A-listers lined
up to read for that movie than line up on the red
carpet for the Oscars. And he's a total mystery man."

"I don't get why you're so dedicated to chasing
him down. He's just an author."

"Joseph Kowalski isn't just an author. He played

the media like a fiddle and became a celebrity. The splashy NY parties with that gorgeous redhead— Lauren Huckins, that was it—on his arm. Then Lauren slaps him with a multimillion dollar emotional distress suit, he pays her off with a sealed agreement and then he disappears from the map? There's a story there, and I want it. Our readers will eat him up, and *Spotlight* is going to serve him to them because you have access to him nobody else does."

"Had. I *had* access to him." Keri sighed and flipped the photo back across the table, even though she would rather have kept it to moon over later. "Eighteen years ago."

"You were his high school sweetheart. Nostalgia, darling! And rumor has it he's still single."

Keri *knew* he was still single because the Danielses and Kowalskis still lived in the same small New Hampshire town, though Mr. and Mrs. Kowalski lived in a much nicer house now. Very *much* nicer, according to Keri's mother.

"You've risen fast in this field," Tina continued, "because you have sharp instincts and a way with people, to say nothing of the fact I trusted you. But this…"

The words trailed away, but Keri heard her boss loud and clear. She was going to get this exclusive or her career with *Spotlight* was over and she could start fresh at the bottom of another magazine's totem pole. And since her career was pretty much the sum total of her life, it wasn't exactly a threat without teeth.

But seeing Joe again? The idea both intrigued her and scared the crap out of her at the same time. "He's not going to open up his insanely private life to the magazine because he and I wore out a set of shocks in high school, Tina. It was fun, but it wasn't *that* good."

Now she was flat-out lying. Joe Kowalski had set the gold standard in Keri's sex life. An ugly car, a Whitesnake tape, cheap wine and Joe still topped her personal Ten Ways to a Better Orgasm list.

Tina ran her tongue over her front teeth, and Keri had known her long enough to know her boss was about to deliver the kill shot.

"I've already reassigned your other stories," she said. It was an act of interference entirely inappropriate for Tina to do to someone of Keri's status at the magazine.

"That's unacceptable, Tina. You're overstepping your—"

"I can't overstep boundaries I don't have, Daniels. It's my magazine and your promotion to editorial depends on your getting an interview with Kowalski, plain and simple." Then she reached into her purse and passed another sheet to her. "Here's your flight information."

THE RECLUSIVE, mega-bestselling author in question was trying to decide between regular beef jerky or teriyaki flavored when he heard Keri Daniels was back in town.

Joe Kowalski nodded at the cashier, who'd actually left a customer half-rung up in an attempt to be the first to deliver the news. It wasn't the first time Keri had been back. If she'd gone eighteen years without a visit home to her parents, Janie Daniels would have flown out to L.A. and dragged her daughter home by an earlobe.

It was, however, the first time Keri had come looking for him that he knew of.

"She's been asking around for your phone number," the cashier added, watching him like a half-starved piranha. "Of course nobody will give it to her, because we know how you feel about your privacy."

And because nobody had his number, but he didn't feel a need to point that out. He was surprised it had taken Keri as long as this to get around to looking him up, especially considering just how many years Tina Deschanel had been stalking his agent.

"Maybe she's on the class reunion committee," Joe told the cashier, and her face fell. Committees didn't make for hot gossip.

Members of the media had been hounding his agent for years, but only Tina Deschanel, who took tenacious to a whole new level, was Keri Daniels's boss. Joe had been watching Keri's career from the beginning, waiting for her to sell him out, but she never had. Until now, maybe.

While he wasn't a recluse of Salinger-esque stature, Joe liked his privacy. The New England dislike of outsiders butting into their lives, combined with his own fiscal generosity—in the form of a ballpark, playgrounds, library donations or whatever else they needed—kept the locals from spilling his business. By the time he'd struck it big, classmates who'd moved away didn't remember enough about him to provide interesting fodder.

Nobody knew the details of the lawsuit settlement except the lawyers, his family and Lauren—who would be financially devastated should she choose to break her silence. And, as unlikely as it seemed, he and Keri had never been linked together in the media reports his publicist monitored. He managed to keep his private life pretty much just that, despite the hype surrounding the movie.

"You're not old enough for a class reunion," Tiffany said, batting her way-too-young eyelashes at him.

A half dozen of each, he decided, tossing bags of beef jerky into his cart. He had a lot more list than cart space left and he kicked himself for not making Terry come along. She could have pushed a second cart *and* run interference on nosy cashiers. She was good in the role, probably from years of experience.

As if on cue, the loudspeaker crackled. "Um… Tiffany, can you come back to register one, please? I have to pick up my kids in ten minutes."

The girl rolled her eyes and started back toward the front of the town's tiny market, but not before calling over her shoulder, "She's staying with her parents, but I guess you already know where they live."

Yeah, he guessed he did, too. The only question was what he was going to do about it. He and his entire family were preparing to leave town for two weeks, and it would be a shame if he missed out on whatever game Keri was playing.

Assuming it was even true. Not that she was in town, but that she wanted to give him a call. In his experience, if there wasn't enough dirt to keep a small-town grapevine bearing fruit, people would just add a heaping pile of manufactured fertilizer.

Joe gave a row of pepperoni sticks the thousand-yard stare. If Keri Daniels *was* looking for his phone number, it had to mean somebody had spilled the beans. The rabid pit bull of a woman she worked for must have discovered her star reporter was once the girl of Joe's dreams. If that was the case, he and Keri were heading for a reunion, and *this* time Keri could do the begging, just as he had before she'd run off to California.

Two hours later, after he'd unloaded his groceries at his own place, he faced his twin sister across the expanse of their mother's kitchen. Theresa Kowalski Porter was *not* a happy woman.

"You are one dumb son of a bitch."

Whereas he liked to play with words—savor them—Terry just spat them out as they popped into her head.

"I thought you were a moron for putting up with

her shit then," she said. "But now you're going back for a second helping?"

"I'm ninety-nine percent sure her boss sent her out here in order to use our history to manipulate me into giving the magazine an interview."

"Keri Daniels never needed any help when it came to manipulating people. And I don't even want to think about that other one percent on an empty stomach."

The entire Kowalski family had once held some resentment toward Keri, but Terry's had festered. Not only because his sister knew how to hold a grudge—although she certainly did—but because Keri had hurt her even before she'd gotten around to hurting Joe.

Terry and Keri had been best friends since kindergarten, despite how corny their names sounded when said together. The trouble started during their freshman year when Mr. Daniels got a big promotion. Between the new style Daddy's money bought and a developing body that just wouldn't quit, Keri had soon started circling with a new group of friends. By the beginning of sophomore year, Keri had left Terry in her social dust, and she hadn't been forgiven. Joe's relationship with Keri was the only thing that had ever come between him and his twin.

And that's why he'd come to Terry first. "Aren't you even a little curious about how she turned out?"

"No." She pulled a soda from the fridge and popped the top without offering him one—never a good sign. "She broke your heart and now, almost twenty years later, she wants to capitalize on that and sell you out to further her career. That tells me all I need to know about how she turned out, thanks."

Joe kicked out a chair and sat at the kitchen table. "It's just dinner, Terry. Dinner with somebody who used to mean a lot to both of us."

"Why are you even talking to me about this, Joseph? I could give a shit less about Keri Daniels. If you want to have dinner with her, then do it. You're an adult."

"I need you to cover for me with the family."

Terry laughed, then grabbed a list from the fridge to double-check against the army of plastic bins at her feet. "Okay, *almost* an adult."

"You know Mom's going to be all over my ass about being ready to go day after tomorrow, even though I'm the first one packed every year. If I fall off her radar for even a few hours, she'll have a fit."

"You really are a dumbass. Mom knows she's in town. Tell her you're going to dinner with the bitch who ripped your heart out of your chest and stomped on it. Do you think three jars of peanut butter are enough?"

"We're only going for two weeks. And I don't want the whole damn town to know I'm going to see her."

"Eight adults and five kids…I guess three will be enough."

"Terry." He waited until she looked up from her list. "Seven adults."

"What? Oh. Yeah." She laughed at herself, but the pain was written all over her face. "Who's the dumbass now, huh?"

"He is," Joe said, not for the first time. "Did you call that divorce lawyer my agent recommended yet?"

"I'm putting it off until the trip is over." She held up a hand to ward off the argument she knew was coming. "I never thought I'd say this, but I'd rather talk about Keri Daniels."

"Fine. If she agrees to dinner, I'm going to tell everybody I've got a meeting in Boston tomorrow night. Will you back me up?"

"Why didn't you just tell *me* that, too?" she asked, clearly exasperated now.

"I thought about it. But I kept seeing Keri a secret from you once, sis, and it hurt you when you found out. I didn't want to do it again."

She sighed and Joe tasted victory. "Okay, I'll back you up, but I still think you're a moron. How many jars of pickles did we go through last year?"

"YOU WANT ME TO DO *what?*"

Joe stretched out on the battered leather couch in his office and tried not to laugh at the tone of horrified shock in his agent's voice. "Dinner date. Reporter from *Spotlight Magazine.* You heard right."

"Did that Deschanel bitch kidnap one of the kids? Threaten your mother? I know people, Joe. I can take care of this for you."

"It's Keri. Keri Daniels."

A loaded pause. "That's great. Sure I want to do that for you, Joe, because with a big movie premiere coming up and a deadline approaching, I absolutely want your head fucked up over your high school sweetheart. And exposing yourself professionally to somebody you've exposed yourself to personally? Great idea."

"Dan. Take a breath."

"Oh, I'm taking so many breaths I'm hyperventilating. I need to put a fucking bag over my mouth. Or maybe put a bag over your head because your brains are leaking out."

"I'm pretty sure Tina Deschanel found out Keri and I dated in high school and I doubt Keri wants to do this any more than I do."

"Then don't do it. Please, for the love of my fifteen percent, don't do it."

"I'm just going to have dinner with her and then she can go back to California and tell her boss she tried."

"Then why don't *you* call her?"

Good question. One he didn't particularly care to share the pathetic answer to with Dan.

After all these years, he didn't want to be reunited with Keri by telephone. He wanted to see her face at the same time he heard her voice. Okay, if he was being honest, he wanted to know if he could see the Keri he'd loved in her.

Worst case scenario, whatever business she felt she had with him could be conducted over the phone and he wouldn't get to see her at all. It was just curiosity—for old times' sake—but he wanted to see her again.

"I'm famous," he said lightly. "I pay people to make my phone calls for me."

"Bullshit. And speaking of paying people, why are you dumping this on me? Jackie's in charge of publicity and press."

"Her head would explode."

The silence on the other end lasted so long Joe thought his agent might have hung up on him. But no such luck. "Joe, we've been together a long time and, speaking as a guy who's had your back for almost a decade and a half, I think this is even a worse idea personally than it is professionally."

"I know, but I'm going to do it anyway."

KERI SWALLOWED another mouthful of non-designer water and resisted glancing at her watch again. Maybe she'd been spoiled by a generous expense account, but meeting in a cheap chain restaurant in the city was too high a price to pay for privacy, in her opinion.

And what was with Joe having his agent contact her to set up the dinner? He couldn't pick up the phone and call her himself? Maybe his overinflated ego interfered with telephone use, so he had to use his agent as though Keri were a total stranger. As if she didn't know he had a birthmark shaped like an amoeba on his right ass cheek.

Unfortunately, her opinions didn't seem to matter. Tina had made it very clear that if Joseph Kowalski held up a hoop, Keri was to jump through it, wearing a pom-pom hat and barking like a dog if that's what it took to make the author happy.

It really burned her ass to be in this predicament, and just thinking about her boss made her temples throb. The temptation to walk out was incredibly strong but, while she knew she could walk into any magazine editor's office and come out with a job, it would set her back years in her quest to climb to the top of the masthead.

It was only an interview, after all.

There hadn't been a new press or book-jacket photo of Joe since his sixth book. That picture had pretty much looked like him, albeit without the grin and dimples. It was one of those serious and contemplative author photos and she'd hated it. But by now, especially considering the coin he was pulling down, he was probably a self-indulgent, fat, bald man with a hunched back from too much time over the keyboard.

She, on the other hand, thought she'd aged well. Nothing about her was as firm as it had been in high school, but she was still slim enough to pull off the pricey little black dress she'd chosen for tonight. Her hair, now sleek and smooth to her shoulders, was still naturally blond, though she would admit to some subtle highlighting.

"Hey, babe," a voice above her said, and just like that the sophisticated woman was gone. She was eighteen again, with big dreams, bigger hair and an itch only Joe Kowalski could scratch.

She could almost taste the Boone's Farm as she turned, braced for an old, fat Joe and finding...just Joe.

He'd aged even better than she had, the bastard. His face had matured and he had a trace of what men were allowed to call character lines, but he still had that slightly naughtier version of the boy-next-door look. Of course, he wasn't quite as lean as he used to be, but it probably wasn't noticeable to anybody who hadn't spent a significant amount of senior year running her hands over his naked body.

All in all, he resembled the boy who'd charmed her out of her pants a lot more than he did the stodgy author she'd hoped to charm into an interview.

"Hi, Joe." She'd stored up a mental cache of opening lines ranging from cute to funny to serious, and every single one seemed to have been deleted. "Thank you for coming."

He slid onto the bench seat across the booth from her. "Time's been pretty damn good to you, if you don't mind my saying so."

No, she didn't mind at all. "You, too. Interesting choice of restaurant, by the way. An eccentricity of the rich and reclusive author?"

He flashed those dimples at her and Keri stifled a groan. Why couldn't he have been fat and bald except for unattractive tufts of hair sprouting from his ears?

"I just like the all-you-can-eat salad bar," he said. "So tell me, is Tina hiding under the table? Waiting to pounce on me in the men's room?"

Keri laughed, partly because it was such a relief to have the topic out in the open. "No, she refuses to leave the city. Says her lungs can't process unpolluted air."

His smoky blue eyes were serious, even though his dimples were showing. "Terry's been expecting you to sell me out for your own advantage since I first made the *NYT* list."

Hearing his sister's name made her wince, and knowing she still held such a low opinion of Keri just made her sad. During the very rare moments she allowed herself to dwell on regrets, she really only had two. And they were both named Kowalski.

"I'm being professionally blackmailed," she admitted. "If I don't get an exclusive interview for *Spotlight* from you, I'm out of a job."

"I figured as much. Who spilled the beans?"

Keri pulled the eight-by-ten she'd managed to sneak a copy of from her bag and handed it to him. "I don't know. Do you remember who took that?"

"Alex did, remember? The night we…well, the caption's pretty thorough."

She remembered now. Alex had been a friend of Joe's, but they'd all traveled in the same circle. "But Tina said the blogger who claimed to go to school with you was a woman."

"His name's Alexis now. You wouldn't believe how much he paid for his breasts."

Keri laughed, but Joe was still looking at the photo. Judging by the way the corners of his lips twitched into a small smile and how he tilted his head, Keri figured Tina was right about the nostalgia angle.

The waitress approached their table, order pad in hand.

Joe still hadn't looked up. "Remember the night you started drinking your screwdrivers without the orange juice and did a striptease on Alex's pool table?"

"I bet the jokes about Alex's pool table having a nice rack went on forever," the waitress said, and *then* Joe looked up.

"You bet they did," he said easily, but he was blushing.

"There must be a whole new slew of jokes about Alex's rack now," Keri said, making Joe laugh.

The waitress tapped her pen on the tab. "So do you guys know what you want?"

And then he did it, just as he always had whenever he'd been asked that question—he looked straight at Keri with blatant hunger in his eyes and said, "Yes, ma'am, I do."

The shiver passed all the way from her perfectly styled hair to her Ferragamo pumps. Then she watched in silent amusement while he ordered for them both—her regular high school favorite of a medium-well bacon cheeseburger with extra pickles, fries and a side of coleslaw. There was no mention of salad, all-you-can-eat or otherwise.

When the waitress left, Keri gave him a scolding look. "That's more calories than I've consumed in the last two years, Joe."

He waved away her halfhearted objection. "Let's get down to business."

Keri didn't want to. She was too busy enjoying that sizzle of anticipation she'd always felt when Joe looked at her. Apparently those blue eyes hadn't lost their potency over the past two decades.

Joe leaned back against the booth and crossed his arms. It was probably supposed to look intimidating, but all the gesture really did was draw attention to how tan and incredibly well defined his biceps were against his white T-shirt. Typing definitely wasn't the only workout his arms got.

"Let's see if I can synopsize our situation," he said. "I never give interviews. You want an interview. No, strike that. You *need* an interview, because the rabid jackal you work for has made it clear your job is on the line. Am I close?"

The sizzle receded to a tingle. "You're in the ballpark."

"I'm not just in the ballpark, babe. I'm Josh Beckett on the mound at Fenway. If I don't give you what you need, you're hiding behind palm trees waiting for drunk pop stars to pop out of their Wonderbras."

And that pretty much killed the last of the lingering tingle. "Payback's a bitch and all that, right, Joe?"

The dimples flashed. "Isn't it?"

Keri just shrugged. She wasn't about to start putting deals on the table or making promises. After years of dealing with celebrities, she usually knew how to handle herself. But this was Joe Kowalski. He'd seen her naked and she'd broken his heart. That changed the rules.

"I'm leaving town tomorrow," he said. "I'll be gone two weeks."

The tingle flared up again, but this time it was a lot more panic and a lot less anticipation. "There's always the telephone or fax or email."

"Not where I'm going."

She laughed. "Would that be Antarctica or a grass hut in the Amazon basin?"

"I'm not even leaving the state."

Joe had sucked at cards in high school—he had no poker face—but she couldn't read him now. The instincts that had skyrocketed her to the top of the *Spotlight* food chain were giving her nothing, except the feeling he was setting her up for something she might want no part of.

The waitress brought their food, buying Keri a few more minutes to think. One thing Joe had never had was a mean streak—if there was no chance in hell of the interview happening, he wouldn't have agreed to meet her for dinner. He'd never had it in him to humiliate somebody for the sake of his own enjoyment.

Granted, the kind of checks he had to be cashing changed a person, but she'd already seen enough of him—and heard enough from her mother—to know Joe was still Joe. Just with more expensive toys.

That didn't mean he wasn't going to have her

jumping through hoops, of course. Probably an entire flaming series of them.

She bit into the bacon cheeseburger and the long-forgotten flavor exploded on her tongue. She closed her eyes and moaned, chewing slowly to fully savor the experience.

"How long has it been since you've had one of those?" Joe asked, and she opened her eyes to find him watching her.

Keri swallowed, already anticipating the next bite. "Years. Too many years."

He laughed at her, and they enjoyed some idle chitchat while they ate. She brought up the movie and he talked about it in a generic sense, but she noted how careful he was not to say anything even remotely interview-worthy.

There would be no tricking the man into revealing something that would get Tina off Keri's back.

"You know," she said, still holding half her cheeseburger, "I *really* want to enjoy this meal more, and I can't with this hanging over my head. What's it going to take?"

"I gave it some thought before I came, and I think you should come with me."

"Where?"

"To where I'm going."

Keri set the cheeseburger on the plate. "For two weeks?"

The length of time hardly mattered, since she couldn't return to California without the interview

anyway. But she'd like an idea of what she was signing up for.

"Whether you're there for two weeks or not is up
to you. For each full day you stick it out with the
Kowalskis, you get to ask me one question."

Keri, unlike Joe, did have a poker face and she
made sure it was in place while she turned his words
over in her head. "When you say the Kowalskis, you
mean…"

"The entire family." The dimples were about as
pronounced as she'd ever seen them. "Every one of
them."

Her first thought was *oh, shit.* Her second, to
wonder if *People* was hiring.

Joe reached into the back pocket of his jeans and
pulled out a folded sheet of spiral notebook paper.
"Here's a list of things you'll need. I jotted it down
in the parking lot."

Keri unfolded the paper and read the list twice,
trying to get a sense of what she was in for.

*BRING: Bug spray; jeans; T-shirts; several
sweatshirts, at least one with a hood; one
flannel shirt (mandatory); pajamas (optional);
underwear (also optional); bathing suit (preferably skimpy); more bug spray; sneakers; wa-
terproof boots; good socks; sunscreen; two
rolls of quarters.*
DO NOT BRING: cell phone; BlackBerry;

laptop; camera, either still or video; alarm clock; voice recorder; any other kind of electronic anything.

She had no clue what it meant, other than Joe wanting her half-naked and unable to text for help.

CHAPTER TWO

THE FIRST DAY OF THE ANNUAL family vacation was always hell for Terry Kowalski Porter. Her twelve days of fun and relaxation were bookended by two days of wanting to throw herself under a speeding RV.

The convoy of Kowalskis usually managed to make it up the interstate and across Route 3 in a somewhat organized fashion, but as soon as they entered the campground they scattered, leaving Terry to run her ass off helping everybody get settled in.

First, her parents, because their forty-foot luxury liner on wheels brought all campground activity to a screeching halt until it was docked. Leo Kowalski refused to let anybody else drive the baby his son had bought him, so Terry's main purpose was keeping her impatient brothers on a tight leash while Dad executed a precision eighty-point turn to back it into their site.

Then came landing pads, leveling and sewer pipes. Water hoses and electrical connections. They had the routine pretty much down by this point, but heaven forbid Leo and Mary Kowalski not have drama.

"That seem level to you, Mary?" One thing about their parents, they were *loud*.

"I'm inside, Leo! How would I know?"

"Are you listing to the left?"

Next came her middle brother, Mike, and his family, who needed three adjoining sites for their sprawl. The first site held their RV—a much smaller one than their parents'—in which Mike, Lisa and their two youngest boys slept. The site also held a multiburnered barbecue grill-slash-cooking center so massive it took all three brothers plus the oldest of Mike's sons to lift it out of the trailer.

The second site held the pop-up camper they pulled behind the RV and in which their two older boys slept. It was also here Lisa erected the complex and extensive network of clothesline strung from tree to tree until it was large enough to contain their family's wet clothes.

The third site would contain a large screenhouse and a series of tarps that served to guarantee that, no matter how hard it rained, Lisa would not be confined in her RV with her four rambunctious boys.

The youngest of the Kowalski siblings, Kevin, was the easiest to get set up. Since his divorce, he required only a small tent, a hibachi and the largest cooler money could buy. He claimed to be a camping purist, but Terry knew he didn't see any point in going whole hog when his parents were four sites over in a half-million-dollar home away from home.

Joe always rented one of the campground's cabins so he could bring his laptop and have relative comfort and privacy to write, and normally Terry would help him unload his SUV. But she didn't happen to be speaking to her twin brother just now, so she sent her nephews in her place.

The havoc the four boys would wreak on his cabin would be just the beginning of the payback Joe Kowalski would suffer.

The minute she'd heard her brother's voice on the other end of the line telling her they might need another jar of peanut butter after all, Terry knew what the dumb son of a bitch had gone and done.

As if the Kowalski family *vacation* wasn't hectic enough, he'd thrown Keri Daniels into the mix. Even worse, the rest of the family threw in behind Joe. Their parents were thrilled. Mike and Lisa couldn't spare the energy to care one way or the other, and Kevin? Terry knew Kevin well enough to know he was going to weasel his way into Keri's pants if he could, or at least use her to needle his big brother if he couldn't.

Of course, none of *them* had a twelve-year-old daughter who hated camping, hated being disconnected from IM for more than a single hour and—most of all—hated the fact her parents were separated. And of course she couldn't understand why her uncle Joe's ex-girlfriend was invited, but not her dad, who technically wasn't even an ex yet.

The same twelve-year-old daughter who was at that very moment sitting in a lounge chair, sipping Coke in front of their still-closed RV. Terry's brothers had helped her get it backed in and they'd leveled it and done the sewer and water hookups before she'd shooed them away. She and Steph had to get used to doing things for themselves now that there was no man around the house.

Unfortunately, getting her daughter to do anything at all was a challenge in itself. "Stephanie, I asked you to at least get it plugged in and open the windows."

"Dad always does that part."

"Dad's not here. And you always helped him, so I know you know how to do it."

Eye roll. "Why couldn't I stay with him?"

Terry took a deep breath, reminding herself for the umpteenth time it was about who had internet access for the next two weeks and not which parent Stephanie loved most. "Because his apartment isn't big enough and you're too old to share his damn futon with him."

"When is Uncle Joe's old girlfriend supposed to get here?"

"I don't know, Steph. Let's just get set up so we can—"

"I think that's her."

Terry turned, then muttered a word she tried, as a rule, not to say in front of her daughter.

Of course that was her. God forbid Keri Daniels should ever gain a pound or twenty or have visible roots, dammit. No, she was still thin, still gorgeous, and—unlike Terry's—none of her body parts appeared to be migrating south.

Keri was staring in horror at the trailers littering the common area, waiting for the campers and trucks that had hauled them to be situated before they were unloaded. On the trailers sat twelve four-wheelers of various sizes and colors, one of them brand-spanking-new.

Keri turned, making eye contact with Terry for the first time in decades. "What the hell are those?"

"They're four-wheelers. My dad took us riding when we were ten, or did you forget that, too?"

Keri's crimson lips pursed in disgust. "Oh, for heaven's sake. Joe must have more money than God. You people couldn't take a cruise or something?"

"Us people like four-wheeling. Besides, nothing brings a family together like a post-ride tick check."

"Tick check?" Terry had the satisfaction of seeing her best friend-turned-nemesis turn pale under her expertly applied blush. "*Tick check?* I can't do this."

"Steph, let your uncle know Keri Daniels has arrived."

"Uncle Joe, you're girlfriend's here!" the girl bellowed in the direction of the cabins.

"If I wanted it screamed across the campground, Stephanie Porter, I could have done it myself."

But in reality, she didn't feel like yelling. She felt a lot more like rolling on the grass laughing her ass off.

Miss Perfect looked like she'd just taken a flying leap into a steaming pile of cow manure, and Terry had to think the next two weeks might not be so bad after all. Payback was indeed a bitch.

WHEN KERI SAW JOE walking toward her, his hands in his pockets and his dimples visible from the moon, she couldn't even articulate all the things she wanted to say to him.

She settled for, "You are *not* checking me for ticks, Joseph Kowalski."

"Damn, babe, don't go squashing all my hopes on the first day." It was Keri who felt like an idiot, but Joe who was grinning like one. "I see you found Terry."

"I'm not riding one of those." She pointed at the trailers of ATVs.

"See that shiny new red one? That's yours, babe. And don't tell me you forgot the rules already."

As if she could. The Rules had been hand-delivered to her parents' house before she'd even gotten out of bed that morning.

(1) Only "official" answers to "official" questions may be published in Spotlight.
(2) Any mention of where we go, what we do, or any other family member but me will result in the best legal team money can buy raining all over you and your magazine like a Georgia thunderstorm.
(3) For every full day you spend with the Kowalski family, you can ask one question.
(4) For each answer I give, I get to ask you one question. Failure to answer forfeits your next question.
(5) Disclosure of any information other than

*the official interview questions and answers
to Tina Deschanel, especially the attached
MapQuest directions to your destination, will
result in a horror show you don't want any
part of. Trust me.*
*(6) Refusal to participate in any Kowalski
family activity will result in no interview.
(Unless it involves Kevin and nudity, which,
with him, may or may not include sex.)*

Keri didn't intend to get naked with *any* of the
Kowalskis. No tick checks. No sex. No skinny-
dipping. Her swimsuit was a one-piece. And pajamas were *not* optional.

That last thought stuck in her head and she looked
at the row of campers and tents with a rising sense
of alarm. "Where will I be sleeping?"

Joe was still grinning, though Terry had wandered away to help the girl who must be her daughter
hook up their camper. "Cabin, around the corner."

"A cabin?" That didn't sound too bad. "You mean
like with walls and a door and a bed?"

"And electrical outlets, even."

Keri snorted. "Those will come in handy for
all those electronic devices you made me leave at
home."

"Pull your car around and maybe we can get
you settled in before the rest of the family finds
out you're here. They all walked down to the store
to visit the campground owners and buy wood for
campfires."

Keri drove her compact rental up the narrow dirt lane and pulled in at the first cabin, parking in the shadow of Joe's massive SUV. The cabin was small, but looked sound enough, and it even had a nice little porch.

At Joe's gesture, she opened the door and stepped inside. It seemed even smaller on the inside, but it had ceiling fans and a gas fireplace, and a dinette set. Along the back were a double bed and a set of bunk beds. A cheery braided rug covered the hardwood floor.

And Joe's stuff was strewn across every surface but the bottom bunk. "What is this?"

"Our cabin. You get stuck with the bunk bed because I'm the famous author."

"You're the famous *freakin' insane* author if you think I'm sharing a cabin with you."

"The others are booked for the coming weekend. You can go home if you want, of course. I'm sure your boss would understand."

"Or you can sleep in my tent."

Keri whirled around at the sound of a second male voice. The man was incredibly tall, incredibly built, and… "Oh my God, Kevin? What the hell have they been feeding you?"

"Virgins and Budweiser, three times a day. You look great, Keri. It's been a long time."

She tried to remember how much younger Kevin was than her, Joe and Terry. Six years? Something like that. He'd been gangly and acne-prone the last time she'd seen him. He certainly wasn't anymore.

"*You* barely fit in your tent," Joe told him before Keri could think up a response, "never mind a woman, too."

"She could sleep on top of me."

"Get out," Joe said while Keri laughed. "Go grab Keri's bags out of the car before you go, though."

Kevin sighed and cast a mournful glance at Keri. "The curse of being the only Kowalski son with any muscles."

He disappeared and Keri took a moment to try to calm herself. It didn't work. Even after almost twenty years in California, she still hadn't found her center, chi, Zen or whatever the hell it was she was supposed to find.

On the one hand she had living with Joe Kowalski for fourteen days. On the other she had a career in the toilet and her living in some sublet fleabag apartment.

Then it occurred to her to wonder if pajamas were optional for Joe, too, and she had to find the switch for the ceiling fans and flip them on. It was awfully hot all of a sudden. And she wasn't sure whether a pajama-free Joe went in the *pro* or the *con* column, which *really* played hell on her Zen.

Kevin returned, setting her bags inside the door. "I intercepted the mob and turned them back. I'd say you've got fifteen minutes max before they come looking again."

Then he was gone. Keri took another useless deep breath and tried to brace herself for the minutes/days/weeks ahead. It wasn't working.

"This is so unprofessional of you," she accused Joe, who was making a big show of plumping his pillow and testing his comfortable-looking mattress.

"Right, because expecting me to expose my private life to the masses because we had sex twenty years ago is the epitome of professionalism."

Keri walked over to test her own mattress. It was what it looked like—a slab of foam on a sheet of plywood laid over two-by-four supports. Lovely. "I wouldn't do this if I had a choice, but my career means everything to me."

"No, babe, your career *is* everything to you. And we're going to remind you success doesn't equal bylines and bottom lines."

He wasn't smiling, so she wondered if he actually believed the tripe he was spewing. "So you're doing this for my own good? To save the shallow princess from her gleaming ivory tower?"

Now the dimples made an appearance. "As the good and pure-hearted prince the shallow princess stomped all over on her way up the ivory steps, I just want to see you get mud in your hair."

"So it's all just a grand scheme to humiliate me." She stood, intent on getting to her car. "You probably never intended to answer my damn questions at all."

Keri didn't get far before Joe spun her around so she ended up, as luck would have it, with her back against the footboards of the bunk bed. When he tucked one leg between hers and rested a hand on either side of her head, her traitorous body immediately recognized *the locker position* and relaxed. She even had to curl her hands into fists to keep from tucking her fingers into the front pockets of his jeans.

They'd spent every spare moment at school in just this position—she resting her back against her locker with Joe leaning over her. Inevitably a teacher would come along and bark at them. "Daniels and Kowalski, I want to see daylight between you two!"

There wasn't much daylight between them right now. And there weren't any teachers coming, either, though odds were good his family would come at some point. What she didn't know was whether they'd be horrified or encourage him.

"I didn't bring you here to humiliate you, babe."

Keri wished he'd quit calling her that, but she couldn't make him stop without drawing attention to the fact it bothered her. "Then why am I here? You could have flat out said no, or you could have scheduled the interview for two weeks out."

"But then I wouldn't get to spend the time with you."

How had she not drowned in those eyes back in high school? It was hard to focus on the words coming out of his mouth when he looked at her like that. "It's been almost twenty years, Joe."

"Exactly. You weren't just my girlfriend, you know. You were my best friend, and I want to catch up. Oprah would say I need closure."

"Like you watch Oprah." Keri's fingers were

practically itching now to tuck themselves into his front pockets, so she shoved them into her own.

"My niece does, and I'm sure if I asked her, she'd tell you that's what Oprah would say."

"I think it's about ten percent closure and ninety percent payback."

Joe grinned. "Seventy-thirty."

"Thirty-seventy."

He leaned in closer, and Keri had no room to back up. A billion thoughts seemed to fly through her head, but only two stuck. Was he going to kiss her? And why, after all these years and a few significant—albeit doomed—relationships, did she care?

It had to be nostalgia. They said a girl never forgot her first, after all. She'd had more than one dream set in the backseat of a 1978 Granada. But this was too much.

A brief flash lit up the cabin, and Joe swore so softly only somebody practically pressed up against him would hear it.

"Say cheese!"

"That would be Bobby," Joe told her before stepping away—much to her surprising dismay. Had he really meant to kiss her? "He used his allowance to buy a package of disposable cameras for the trip."

"I thought we couldn't have cameras."

"No, babe, *you* can't have a camera. *We* have cameras—disposable, film, digital, video, digital video, you name it. Hell, there's a good chance Ma's still got her old 110 in the bottom of her purse."

Keri looked at the little boy giving her a grin that would probably be as potent as his uncle's when he got older. "Hi, Bobby. Aren't I supposed to say cheese *before* you take the picture?"

"When I do it that way, people hide their faces, so I like it to be a surprise."

She smiled, but she was wondering how surprised Bobby's mother would be to find a picture of Joe pinning her against the bunk bed come up in her son's vacation pictures.

"Grammy sent me to tell you to stop hiding and get the machines unloaded so the trailers can go in the parking area. And she said Miss Keri better go say hello right now or Uncle Kevin gets her s'mores."

JOE WALKED AROUND the trailers, loosening tie-down straps while keeping an eye on Keri as she was given the quick, but probably not easy, tour of the Kowalski family tree. Considering her line of work and the fact their mothers remained friends, he was pretty sure she'd already been given a rundown on who was who, but they still made for a daunting group.

Keri knew his parents and siblings, of course, but Mike and Kevin had changed a lot in the past eighteen years. Mike's wife, Lisa, had moved up from Massachusetts right after Joe graduated, so Keri didn't know her at all. And their four boys—Joey (fifteen), Danny (twelve), Brian (nine) and Bobby (six)—never stood still long enough to pin a face to a name. Terry's girl, Stephanie, was hovering on the brink of teenage attitude. Throwing in Kevin, with his frat-boy charm, and Terry, with her decades-long grudge, made for an interesting mix.

And speaking of interesting, Joe couldn't believe Keri thought his sole aim in inviting her along was to humiliate her. So maybe *inviting* wasn't quite the right word for what he'd done, but he hadn't realized until she'd thrown that accusation at him they weren't on the same page. Hell, they weren't even in the same chapter.

Maybe he'd totally misread the vibe he'd gotten in the restaurant. He could have sworn she'd also felt the flicker that lingered from the burning inferno that used to be their chemistry, and when she agreed to the ridiculous offer he'd expected her to turn down flat, he thought she was as interested in fanning that little flame as he was. Instead she'd taken what was a half joke, half refusal gone wrong and blown it into a revenge plot of Shakespearean proportions.

And Joe was left looking and feeling like an asshole. There was no way to explain to her that the proposal he'd come up with in the car on the drive to the restaurant was nothing more than a chickenshit way of refusing the interview without outright saying no. He'd started thinking it might be fun when she'd given him the same look that had turned his head in high school, and he *really* got on board when she closed her eyes and moaned after taking a bite of the cheeseburger. When she'd agreed to the stupid plan, he'd assumed she was on board, too, and the cool and calm demeanor was a bid to not look too eager.

Now he knew it was merely stoicism in the face of anticipated emotional torture, and that royally sucked. If he backed down now he'd have no control over what she printed, plus he'd have to explain why he hadn't made it through day one, which couldn't be done without making a massive fool of himself.

"If you're going to stand around and stare at your ex-girlfriend all day, get out of the way first."

Mike's voice dragged Joe back to what he was doing—which was, apparently, standing there with a tie-down strap in his hand, mooning over Keri Daniels.

He tossed the strap to the older of his younger brothers and straddled the first machine. "Got the keys?"

Mike held up a handful, then tossed him the correct one. "You know Terry won't let anybody back out of the driveway until every key is accounted for. She'd staple them to our foreheads if she could find a staple gun strong enough to penetrate our thick skulls."

Joe fired up the ATV, backed it down the ramps and pulled it off to one side. After giving the look of death to Mike's four boys, who were watching him like turkey vultures, he climbed back onto the trailer.

"Lisa likes her," Mike said, since he was taking his own turn at watching the family drama unfold.

"Key. How can you tell?"

"Body language. We've been married sixteen

years, Joe. I can tell when she needs to take a piss at this point."

"But you can't tell how she feels about unballing your dirty socks?"

Mike took a swipe at him, but Joe hit the throttle and laughed as he unloaded Joey's machine. He glanced over at the campsites to see his namesake practically jumping up and down, so he gave him another look of death for good measure before climbing up the ramp again. Through the corner of his eye he saw Keri holding an armful of riding gear, looking utterly baffled.

"She wants to get pregnant."

Joe's head snapped around. *Pregnant?* "What the hell are you talking about?"

"Lisa wants another kid."

"Oh." That made a little more sense than what he'd initially thought, but not much. "You guys are barely surviving the four boys you have, and Lisa is actually planning to throw a party when Bobby starts first grade in the fall. Are you sure?"

Mike nodded and tossed Joe the key to Danny's ATV. "She said it straight out. Said it might be a girl this time."

"Or it could be a boy. And it ain't like twins are unheard of in the Kowalski family. Think about it, Mike. Six boys. We'd have to hire people to drive all your campers and machines here."

Mike laughed, but Joe could see the tension in him. Though two years younger, he often seemed like the oldest now, and Joe wasn't the only one to notice it lately.

"You know what you need? Let's get these suckers unloaded and go for a brothers-only ride."

"The boys will have a fit," Mike said, but his face lit up just thinking about it.

The Kowalskis rode their ATVs at a wide variety of speeds. When the little kids were on their own machines and Grammy was along, half-dead pack mules made better time. When the two youngest boys rode with their parents and Grammy was napping, the entire crew could be a little more adventurous. Sometimes *all* the children were left with Leo and Mary, allowing Joe, Kevin, Terry—and last year her husband, Evan—Mike and Lisa to go bombing through the trail system.

But the brothers-only rides, those were special, with a high pucker factor. Just Joe, Mike and Kevin—testosterone, mud, rocks and a combined twenty-one-hundred cc's of four-wheel-drive power. It was almost as good as sex, although the attrition rate was generally higher.

Mike cast a glance at his wife, scoping out her mood. "Lisa'd be pissed if the boys are underfoot while she's trying to get everything set up. Remember '04 when she made me sleep in the screenhouse?"

Joe called out his sister-in-law's name and beckoned her over. "We feel a need for speed."

Lisa was a short, fragile-looking brunette with a

tall, not-so-fragile attitude. "You are *not* going riding with all this work left to do."

Joe flashed his winningest grin, but she'd been a Kowalski wife for sixteen years and was raising four of her own. She'd built up an immunity. "Forget it."

"Keri and I will take the boys into town for pizza in a few days." She wasn't immune to bribes involving freedom. "You and Mike can sneak off and ride up to that hidden grassy spot you guys like so much. It puts color in your cheeks."

As always, the promise of sex free of juvenile interruption made her cave like a wet napkin. "One hour. And you guys pull lifeguard duty for the first trip to the pool."

"Three hours, two lifeguard duties, and we'll keep the boys out for ice cream, too."

"Two hours, all of the above, plus s'mores duty tonight."

"Done."

After Lisa walked away, Joe grinned at his brother. "Piece of cake."

"Never works for me."

"That's because you're her husband. She likes me better because she doesn't have to wash my underwear. Plus, I'm better lookin'."

Mike laughed. "You keep telling yourself that while I'm getting laid out in the woods, my friend."

"You just like it out there because the mosquito bites make your dick look bigger."

Joe ducked Mike's swing and launched Danny's machine down the ramp. Keri was watching him and he thumbed the throttle a little, making the engine rev. She tossed her hair back when she laughed, just like she had in high school, and Joe pondered his chances of a little trip to the grass clearing of his own.

Thoughts of Keri, a bed of grass and a bottle of Deep Woods Off! lotion got all jumbled in his head until he had to douse himself with a mental cold shower. Heading out for a brothers-only ride with a hard-on that wouldn't quit was a recipe for masculine disaster.

CHAPTER THREE

KERI WASN'T SURE HOW just yet, but Joe was going to pay for abandoning her. While he and his brothers went off on their brothers-only ride—whatever the hell *that* meant—she was left to fend for herself with the Kowalski clan.

Flash. "Say cheese!"

"Cheese." Keri smiled at the clothesline she was trying to knot around a tree.

By her count, it was the eleventh boring picture of her Bobby had taken since Joe's departure. "Don't use up your camera on the first day."

"You're pretty."

"Thank you."

"Aunt Terry said you probably had work done, like Daddy did on his truck at the body shop."

She glanced at Terry, who seemed *very* interested in the knot she was tying across the site. "Nope. No work done."

"She said you were probably plastic and Uncle Kevin said he'd give you a feel and let her know and then Uncle Joe punched him in the shoulder and said the only thing he'd feel is his A-S-S getting kicked if he tried."

"Robert Joseph Kowalski!" Lisa descended on the boy and started shooing him away. "Put the camera away and hit the playground, short fry."

Terry was still intent on her knot, which was kicking her ass if the redness in her face was any indication. Lisa gave Keri a sheepish grin, then went back to her own knot tying.

Keri probably would have minded the plastic comment a lot more if she wasn't feeling all warm and fuzzy about Joe's hitting Kevin for offering to feel her up. He'd been possessive like that in school—without crossing over the line into controlling—and she'd felt like a treasured princess. While she didn't feel exactly regal right now, standing on a cooler breaking fingernails in the name of a clothesline, it was kind of sweet. Not sweet enough to get his butt out of the sling, but enough to give her a little tingle.

Terry, the overachieving show-off, was done with her share of clothesline hanging, so she popped open a soda and sat on another cooler. "The guys will be back any minute, Lisa. Got your quarters ready?"

Lisa blushed and Keri was dying to be let in on the inside joke, but she couldn't bring herself to ask Terry what she meant. They'd managed to avoid direct communication for two hours now, and she figured careful planning and pure stubbornness could extend the streak to two weeks.

Then again, she didn't want to spend fourteen days with two decades of tension weighing on her, and they weren't in junior high anymore. Plus, she had two rolls of unexplained quarters in her bag. So she took a deep breath and looked right at Terry. "What are the quarters for?"

"The bathhouse showers." For a second Keri thought those terse three words were all she was going to get, but then Terry took a deep breath of her own and seemed to relax. "When the guys ride like that they get...wound up. All that testosterone and grunting, I guess. Anyway, Mike always drags Lisa off to the bathhouse as soon as he gets back."

"Tick check," Lisa muttered, but she was damn near as red as Terry had been a few minutes before.

"So...who checks Kevin and Joe for ticks in the shower?" Keri asked. *Finally* her knot seemed secure. She tugged on it and, when it didn't pull loose for the umpteenth time, jumped off her cooler.

Terry shrugged, but her dimples—which were never quite as pronounced as Joe's—made a brief appearance. "I guess they have to take matters into their own hands, so to speak."

Keri went from warm and fuzzy to hot and bothered just like that. Back when she and Joe were doing everything but *it,* he'd shown her how he took matters into his own hands, so to speak, and that wasn't an image a girl forgot.

Only now the image morphed into an older Joe, naked and soapy and...

Holy crap, it was hot again all of a sudden. If she'd known being around Joe would be like suffering from menopause, she might have rethought her career path. Or at least packed some herbal tea or something.

"Don't you even think about it, Keri Daniels."

Keri could almost see the fork in the road of maturity rising before her. She could take the high road and assure Terry her interest in Joe was strictly professional, or she could take the low road, which she had no doubt was the path Terry would be traveling on for the next two weeks.

"Oh, I'm thinking about it, Theresa Kowalski."

"Her last name is Porter," a voice called from a camper, and all three women jumped. While it was impossible to overlook the four boys playing some demented cross between football and basketball on the playground, Keri had forgotten about Steph. Oops. Hopefully she was a little more discreet than her younger cousin.

Terry was glaring at Keri, no doubt trying to warn her away from Joe without saying the words out loud. Fat chance of that, since they'd be sharing a cabin every night, with his pajama status still to be determined.

"I should fire up the grill and throw on some dogs," Lisa said with the air of somebody desperately trying to smooth over a rocky patch in a conversation.

"No sense in that until after the guys get back," Terry pointed out. "Especially since Mike will have some excuse for needing your help in the bathhouse."

"Gross!" Stephanie yelled. "FYI, I'm putting my headphones on now."

Lisa waited a few seconds, then grinned at Terry. "Don't even use that tone with me. You and Evan spent more time in the bathhouse than anybody."

Terry's smile slipped a little and even Keri could tell Lisa was giving herself a mental slap upside the head. Her mom had given Keri the details she knew over a hurried breakfast that morning, but there weren't many.

Evan Porter had left his wife three months before, moving into a tiny studio apartment over the Laundromat. Nobody seemed to know why, but there'd been no hint of another woman. Or another man, for that matter.

"Don't the RVs have bathrooms?" she asked, feeling some pressure to fill the conversational pothole.

Both women laughed, but it was Lisa who said, "I'll take your lifeguard duty at the pool for three days if you can have sex with a Kowalski man in that shower without knocking the camper right off its levelers."

"I'll hide your bug spray if you even try to have sex with my brother in the RV—or anywhere else for that matter," Terry said, and the way Lisa gasped made Keri think it was a dire threat indeed. "Go ahead, Keri, laugh at me. But once the sun starts going down you'd duct tape your own thighs closed for a bottle of Deep Woods Off! Trust me."

"Since she'd be the only woman for ten miles not reeking of DEET, she'd have guys trying to gnaw their way through the duct tape within minutes," Lisa countered.

Keri was blessedly saved from having to comment on that interesting visual by the restrained rumble of approaching ATVs. There was an obey-or-die speed limit in the campground, but as soon as the three Kowalski brothers rounded into view— putting sedately along—Keri could see they'd done some serious hell-raising somewhere. Men and machines both were covered in dirt and mud, and about the only clean thing she could see were three grins' worth of white teeth.

Joe expected her to subject herself to *that?*

Their arrival brought the boys swarming back from the playground, while Stephanie, Leo and Mary emerged from campers.

"Finally, I get to have some lunch," Leo yelled.

Though it had been far too long since she'd last seen him, Keri's adoration of Leo Kowalski was total and unabashed. He was a deceptively short and wiry man, but she knew he could probably bench-press one of those four-wheelers if he got stubborn about it. He'd worn his hair in a gray crew cut for as long as she could remember, and he was the source of the pretty blue eyes. Mary, who had become the quintessential grammy, gave the kids their dimples.

Many years before, Keri had been terrified of Leo Kowalski. Her own father was a quiet sort— other than the five-iron incident—and Leo was like a firecracker of energy with a built-in megaphone.

She didn't know what to make of the man, who very loudly threatened his children with such dire consequences as having their asses kicked up around their ears and trips behind the woodshed. Of course, neither Keri nor the Kowalski kids knew what a woodshed was and he'd never laid a hand on them in anger, but that didn't make the promises any less foreboding. She'd discovered after only a few visits it was Mary and her wooden spoon a kid really had to watch out for.

But what Keri liked most about Leo and Mary right then was the fact they'd greeted her as if it had been eighteen hours, not years, since they'd seen her. No melodrama, resentments, admonishments or exuberance. They were just…normal.

Unlike the rest of them. Joe, Mike and Kevin were shouting over each other to tell the family about their ride. There were words like *off-camber, high-sided* and *roost* being thrown around, which could have been German for all she knew, but the gist of it was they'd ridden to the edge of breaking their idiot necks, but had come home in one piece.

Now they were filthy, starving and—judging by the smoking way Joe kept looking at her over his nephews' heads—as wound up, so to speak, as the women said they'd be.

Sure enough, Mike was beckoning to Lisa. "Hold off on lunch for a few minutes so I can shower this mud off. You should come check me for ticks, too."

"Lucky bastards," Kevin muttered before heading to his tent for a change of clothes.

Keri wasn't sure what was up with the plural *bastards* until she saw Joe moving toward her. Other than his hair and a raccoon mask of white where his goggles had rested, every inch of Joe looked as though he'd taken a mud bath and skipped the rinse.

"Don't you even think about touching me," she warned.

"I think there's a tick on my back, so you should come to the bathhouse and check me over."

She could tell by his expression the only thing keeping him from claiming the tick was in his pants was the presence of the kids. "Nice try, Kowalski. As filthy as you are, a tick couldn't find your skin with MapQuest and a GPS."

He sighed. "I guess I'll have to make do on my own."

Again with the freakin' hot flashes. She watched him jump on his four-wheeler and head for the cabin, trying like hell to kill the visual of Joe making do on his own.

When he passed by a few minutes later with a duffel bag tossed on the ATV's front rack, she was still trying. She watched him turn up toward the bathhouse, seriously reconsidering her refusal. There couldn't be an interview if she let Joseph Kowalski die of some tick-borne disease, could there?

Then came the realization that everybody else was watching her watch Joe, followed closely by the thought that he was heading to the bathhouse, not because the cabin's shower was too small, but because it didn't have one. Or a toilet. What if she had to go pee in the middle of the night?

Flash. "Say cheese!"

KERI WATCHED TERRY slip nine-year-old Brian a dollar and shook her head. Ten bucks he'd be the first one to get melted marshmallow in her hair if she didn't keep an eye on him.

It was s'mores time and she watched Leo and all the women place their chairs well outside of the campfire perimeter because the guys had apparently promised Lisa they'd help the kids tonight. Even though Keri had breasts, she was exempt because of her status as Joe's flaming hoop-jumping lapdog.

But she was ready for this. During an assignment at a summer camp for underprivileged kids founded by an A-lister early in her career, Keri had mastered the art of the perfect s'more.

The key was in the organization and careful preparation. First, a square graham cracker had to be set on the picnic table with a smaller square of chocolate centered on top of it. Another graham cracker set next to it. Only then should the marshmallow be toasted to a perfect golden brown. Set it on top of the chocolate, along one edge of the cracker, put the other cracker on top, exert slight pressure and then drag the stick out in the direction of the opposite edge, thereby spreading the gooey marshmallow along the chocolate. Count to ten, then eat. A perfect s'more.

"Everybody got a stick?" Kevin asked.

In case the chorus of cheers wasn't enough, the five kids offered visual proof in the form of a flurry of wildly waving sticks. Keri flinched when Danny's threatened to take off the tip of her nose.

Kevin ripped open the bag of marshmallows and Bobby squealed with delight. Before Keri could point out it was time for neither sticks nor marshmallows yet the kids had presented their sticks like musketeer swords and their uncle shoved a marshmallow on the end of each one.

She could only watch in horror as, after throwing elbows for position, the kids converged on the fire. Joe, Mike and Kevin circled constantly, adjusting stick heights and pointing out when one needed to be turned. Bobby's burst into flames and only Mike's reflexes kept him from jerking the stick and winging the flaming marshmallow into the air.

Suddenly sticks pointed at her from every direction, marshmallows varying from light beige to charcoal-black drooping from the ends.

"You're not ready!" Stephanie shrieked, just as Bobby's overcooked glop let go of the stick and dropped onto the toe of Keri's sneaker.

"I need a cracker!"

"Where's the chocolate?"

"Uncle Joe, she doesn't even know how to make a s'more!"

Keri scrambled, dispensing crackers and chocolate as fast as she could while Bobby's burnt marshmallow bonded with her shoelaces. By the time

Brian was shoving his in his mouth, Joey was roasting his second marshmallow.

Thirty minutes later, when Lisa finally called a halt to the sugar consumption, Keri was exhausted, sticky and feeling slightly nauseated by the s'mores each of the kids had made special just for her. She'd tried accidentally dropping Stephanie's on the ground and kicking it under the picnic table, but the girl had seen her and, not wanting her to be sad, promptly made her another.

And Brian, the little twerp, had definitely earned his dollar. He was responsible for the marshmallow gluing Keri's hair to her left ear, the smear of chocolate down the leg of her jeans and the graham cracker crumbs he'd managed to dump down her back while giving her a thank-you hug.

As soon as the last mouthful was gulped down, the kids disappeared to the playground, leaving the grown-ups to deal with the fallout. Keri was about to drop into a chair, but Joe grabbed her by the elbow and held her up.

"You've got marshmallow on your ass," he said, and she could tell by the damn dimples that it was killing him not to laugh in her face.

"That was the most demented display of s'mores making I've ever seen," she hissed, resisting the urge to kick him in the shin.

"You've got chocolate on your lip."

Before she could react his finger was there, the tip dipping into the hollow of her mouth and then gliding across her lower lip. She shivered, unable to look away as Joe brought that finger to his mouth and sucked the chocolate off the end.

The faint suction sound made her insides quiver and she had a hell of a time swallowing. He was sure taking his time about it, and a glimpse of tongue flicking away the last of the chocolate spiked her body temperature.

A moan almost escaped her throat and Keri dug her fingernails into her palms. What was wrong with her? Her body was acting as though she hadn't had sex in...

How long had it been? Months? Years, even? No, it couldn't have been years since she'd had sex. That would be sad. The last time had been Scott, colleague with benefits until he'd moved to New York. That had been...thirty-one months ago.

She hadn't had sex in thirty-one months.

"Get a room," Kevin told them as he shoved Joe out of his way. He picked up an empty Hershey's bar wrapper and walked away.

The trance broken, Keri turned her back on her tormentor and busied herself gathering the graham crackers strewn across the picnic table. Thank goodness for Kevin, or who knew what her traitorous body might have coerced her into doing.

Clearly she needed to avoid being alone with Joe. Sure, that was problematic with them sharing a cabin and sleeping only a few feet from each other. But she could make sure his family was always around during the day and then feign sleep as soon as they retired to the cabin at night.

Being alone with Joe Kowalski was going to get her in trouble. Only this time giving in to his charm could get her in trouble with Tina, who was a lot scarier than her dad, even without a five iron.

WAY TOO MANY LONG and torturous hours later, Joe finally found himself alone with Keri. Unfortunately, she was wearing pajamas that buttoned clear up to her eyebrows and was tossing and turning like a princess in a pea-riddled bunk. Every once in a while she'd emit one of those female sighs that said she was annoyed and he wasn't going to get any sleep until he acknowledged it.

Not that he'd been anticipating a good night's sleep anyway. Arranging to have Keri Daniels spend the night in a bed only six feet from his own wasn't one of his brighter ideas. Arranging to have her sleep six feet away for *thirteen* nights was just downright moronic.

Keri sighed again. The sighs were getting louder, and he knew why.

"The more you think about it," Joe said, "the more you'll have to go."

She picked up her head and punched her pillow into a ball. "I didn't have anything to drink for hours."

"I noticed, but now you're thinking about it and you aren't thinking quietly."

"Fine." He heard her throw back her covers and then stumble toward the door.

"The flashlight's on the floor to the right of the door."

There were some fumbling noises, and the flashlight clicked on. She managed to shine it in his eyes twice while slipping her shoes on and heading out the door.

She was gone all of twenty seconds.

"Oh my God," Keri yelped, slamming the door behind her. "There are eyes out there."

Yup, sleep really was just a pipe dream tonight. "Furry woodland creatures, babe."

"I think it was a raccoon." It was hard not to laugh at her when she twisted the dead bolt.

"Look on the bright side—if the raccoon's hanging out at our site, the skunks and bears are probably visiting somebody else."

"How can you find this funny?"

"I'm not the one who's gotta take a leak."

Four D cells' worth of light burned into his retinas when Keri turned the flashlight on him. "I can't sleep until I've gone to the bathhouse, Kowalski. And if I don't sleep, you don't sleep."

That much was obvious, so Joe swung his legs over the edge and stood. Unlike Keri, he wasn't wearing pajamas that buttoned to his eyebrows and he laughed when the flashlight beam ran down over his black boxer briefs before whipping back to the door. He pulled on his sweatpants and shoved his bare feet into his sneakers. After a brief hesitation, he pulled a shirt over his head. While his bare chest was still buff enough to attract the females, up here they'd all be of the buzzing, biting variety.

"Let's go," he said, and he wasn't surprised when she made him go out the door first. Without relinquishing the flashlight, of course.

There were a couple of low fires burning in the campground as they made their way to the bathhouse, but all was mostly quiet. The Kowalskis always arrived on a Monday so they could be all set up and get a few rides in before the place filled up. Joe reached over and took the flashlight out of Keri's hand so he could turn it off.

"I can't see," she protested.

"Just be still a second and let your eyes adjust."

"If I stand in one place too long the bugs will hang an all-you-can-eat buffet sign on me."

He chuckled softly and started walking again. "You used to love being outside with me at night."

"I used to strip on pool tables to Guns N' Roses, too," Keri said, "but times change. People change."

Joe would have liked to deny he'd changed all that much, but it probably wouldn't have been true. He'd been a gung-ho boy who'd made good on his dreams, only to end up jaded and still looking for... something. But even though Keri had changed a lot more than he had, just being with her made him remember being young.

"It doesn't get dark like this at home," Keri whispered, and he was reminded how far her home was from his.

"Bright lights in the big city," he muttered, thankful their arrival at the bathhouse derailed any further discussion about Los Angeles.

Keri was in there a few minutes, then emerged with a sheepish smile. "Thank you. I think I can sleep now."

"Or we could go make out on the seesaw," he said, just to make her laugh.

It worked. "Terry said she'd hide my bug spray until I duct tape my thighs together if I try making out with you."

Keri stumbled on a rock and Joe instinctively took her hand to steady her. After she regained her balance, he just sort of kept it. "How did that happen to come up in conversation?"

She turned her head and he could see the gleam of her teeth when she smiled. "It was right after Lisa offered three days of lifeguard duty if you and I can have sex in her RV's shower without knocking it off its levelers."

Joe stopped, still holding her hand. "Why the hell was anybody talking about us having sex? Not that it's a bad thing, but...why?"

"Mostly to annoy Terry." But she looked away when she said it.

"Three days, huh?"

She tried to pull away, but he yanked her back, so she poked a finger at his chest instead. "Forget it, Kowalski. Sitting by the pool happens to be one of my more finely honed skills."

"You've never been poolside with my nephews."

So he wasn't the only one in the campground

mentally combining the words *Joe, Keri* and *sex.* Interesting.

Then he spotted his sister. Across the dark playground, Terry sat in one of the swings, drawing in the dirt with the toes of her sneakers.

"Hey, I'm going to talk to Terry for a sec. Take the flashlight and go on ahead."

He could see the urge to protest cross Keri's face, but then she looked across the playground, too. "Fine, but if I get mauled by a bear, you're going to feel like an asshole in the morning."

Joe waited until the flashlight beam—moving at a very fast clip—rounded the corner toward the cabins, then made his way to the swing set. He took the swing next to her, careful to hold it still. Damn things made him carsick for some reason.

"I thought it would be easier away from the house," Terry said without looking up from her dirt scribbles. "But I can't sleep without his snoring, and the quiet here only makes it worse."

"Everybody will understand if you pack it up and head home, you know."

She snorted. "And leave you all here to fend for yourselves?"

The old conversational high-wire—how to remind her they were all reasonably competent adults without minimizing the work she put into the family. "A temporary diet of hot dogs and marshmallows won't kill anybody."

When she didn't even crack a smile, Joe started mentally combining the words *Evan, head* and *base-*

ball bat. His soon-to-be-ex brother-in-law was a good guy he'd always considered a friend, but Joe was in big-brother mode—even if he was only nine minutes older.

"I thought he'd come running right back," Terry said. "But he didn't, and now... He said he was leaving because there had to be more—something *better*—and now he lives alone in a basic closet over a freakin' Laundromat."

"I know it seems like forever, but it's only been three months. You guys can still work it out if you both want it."

"Why should I try, when he could flush thirteen years down the toilet because I wouldn't have a quickie on the kitchen table?"

That was a part of the story Joe hadn't yet heard. "No offense, but I don't think that fancy brass-and-glass set of yours would stand up to it."

"That's what I told him, and that I'm not serving up cornflakes on his ass prints. He was gone forty minutes later."

"A guy doesn't walk out on his family because he ain't getting lucky on the kitchen table. You know there has to be more to it than that."

Terry sighed and looked up at the stars. "He said now that our daughter's older and out with her friends so much, he wanted to work on being Evan and Terry more, instead of just Stephanie's parents. He wanted more spontaneity, and he said I treat him more like a second child than a husband."

Now Joe was crossing that conversational high-wire again, only this time he was blindfolded and slightly intoxicated. She did, after all, excel in family micromanagement and treated them all like children at times. This was the woman who asked him every single year if he'd packed enough underwear for the trip. But again, now was not the time to even hint at siding with Evan.

"It was probably some midlife meltdown," he said, "and he just doesn't have the balls to come crawling back."

"Maybe." She sniffed and shrugged her shoulders, and the subject was closed. "What are you doing with her, Joe?"

He didn't need to ask who she meant. "I don't know, sis. It started out as some weird mix of curiosity, revenge and nostalgia, but now... Sometimes she's a total stranger and sometimes she's the Keri I loved. And the chemistry's still pretty damn potent."

"She's going to leave again, the second she has what she wants from you, and don't forget it. She's not any better than Lauren."

That was a low blow, but not a surprise. Terry didn't like feeling shitty alone. But dragging his ex-almost-fiancée into the pity party was just bitchy. "She's nothing like Lauren. Keri's not hiding what she wants from me or why she's here. And I know she'll be gone as soon as she has her interview. I'm just enjoying her company until then."

Terry turned to make eye contact with him again. "I didn't like the guy you became after she left the first time, and I still don't think you should be around her."

"For chrissake, Terry, you're acting like a mother hen."

As soon as the words left his mouth he wished he could take them back. It wasn't the first time he'd ever said them to her, but he couldn't have chosen a worse time.

"Fine, Joe," she said in a low voice. "Get your heart broken again. We can be a matched set."

Then she crossed the playground to her camper without looking back.

KERI WAS, REGRETTABLY, already awake and mentally updating her résumé with the covers over her head when Joe slapped her on the ass.

"Rise and shine, babe. Breakfast is at eight and by eight-fifteen Kevin's licking the last crumbs off the plates."

"I don't care." She had just passed the worst night of her life, and a pancake wasn't going to help.

"I'm heading over. If you're not there in a few minutes, Ma's going to send the boys after you. Just FYI."

When the cabin door opened and closed, Keri groaned and pulled the covers down. Camping sucked.

When a subdued Joe had returned to the cabin last night, he'd promptly fallen into a sound sleep. She, on the other hand, had tossed and turned on her foam slab—kept awake by a silence broken only by Joe's unfamiliar snoring and what had sounded suspiciously like a rabid, ferocious raccoon trying to jimmy the dead bolt on the cabin door.

Agreeing to this asinine blackmail scheme had been a mistake.

Looking in the mirror was a bigger one. Even feeling as crappy as she did hadn't prepared her for how bad she looked.

And she had no sink. No shower. And no toilet.

Yes, camping really sucked, except for the opportunity to bury Joe's body out in the wilderness where nobody would ever find it.

Keri threw everything she needed for a trip to the bathhouse into one of the plastic shopping bags Joe left lying around, then donned a hooded, zip-up sweatshirt. After pulling the hood as far over her really bad hair as possible, she opened the door.

Flash. "Say cheese!"

No. Strangling. Children. "You and I are going to have a little talk about privacy, Bobby."

"Aunt Terry said to tell you I'm the parazappy."

"That's *paparazzi,* and I'm not them. I'm a journalist, so you can tell Aunt Terry to…" Just in the nick of time, her thought-to-speech filter woke up and smelled the coffee. "Never mind."

"You were a lot prettier yesterday."

"And you were a lot more charming."

He just grinned his uncle's grin at her. "Grammy said the food's going fast and you don't want to go riding on an empty stomach."

"I don't want to go riding at all," she said, but Bobby was already running down the dirt road.

She managed to shower fast enough to snatch a pancake and the last two strips of bacon out from under Kevin's nose. The caffeine flowed freely from the coffeemaker connected by extension cord to Lisa's RV, thank God, and she was almost feeling human when the boys started dragging gear out of the totes in the screenhouse.

"I…have a headache," Keri lied weakly.

Joe took her coffee mug away and tugged her to her feet. "You can ride with me today, to get a feel for it."

"I'd rather not."

"You didn't go flatlander on me, did you, girl?" Leo demanded in that booming voice of his. Terry snickered.

Keri may have spent half her life in California, but she was no damn flatlander and said so.

Terry tossed her a helmet, which she managed to catch without breaking a nail. "Prove it."

Joe grinned and leaned into her personal space to whisper, "Just wrap yourself around me and hold on tight, babe. You'll be fine."

"Where's the duct tape?" Terry yelled, and this time it was Lisa who snickered.

Keri shivered when Joe's breath tickled her ear. Between the newly triggered hot flashes and the imminent threats of mud in her hair and duct-taped thighs, she was anything *but* fine.

CHAPTER FOUR

"I FEEL LIKE MR. MAGOO."

Joe smiled and worked at buckling the chin strap of Keri's helmet. "It's only a slight resemblance."

Her eyes narrowed behind the oversize protective lens of her goggles. "How slight?"

"Very. Trust me, babe, I never found Mr. Magoo anywhere near as hot as you look right now."

"In this?"

Absolutely in that. The jeans and boots were tame enough, but there was something about seeing her decked out in riding gear that got his motor running. The pink-and-white jersey hugged her curves before disappearing into the waist of her jeans, where her pink-gloved hands rested to show her annoyance. The pink-and-silver helmet covered her head and the lower half of her face, with the goggles helping obscure her features.

But her eyes and body language let him know she didn't realize just how much she looked like one of the models posing on ATVs in magazine ads. He thought she looked sexy as hell.

"Just so you know, the muddier I get, the more intrusive my questions will be."

"Just remember I get to ask one for every one I answer, and I'm a guy. Just imagine how intrusive my questions could be."

Joe finally managed to get her buckle snug, then slapped the side of her helmet. "Oh, sorry about that. I'm used to helping the boys. It's a guy thing."

"It's a little claustrophobic in here," she said, tugging down on the front of the helmet.

"It goes away when you're moving and getting some air flow. Let's go, babe."

"Why do we have to be in front? I'd rather be in the back where nobody can hear me scream."

"Usually Terry's first so she can set the pace, while I'm stuck in the back eating dust and making sure nobody's LFD."

"LFD?"

"Oh, left for dead." She stopped walking and when he looked back, her eyes were almost as wide as her goggles. "It's just an expression. I just make sure nobody stops to take a leak or have a drink or something alone. But it's dusty as hell, and since this is your first time, you get to be in front."

"Great, now Terry can hate me for making her eat dust, too."

"Kevin will ride drag today. Usually he sticks close to Pop, but we'll be taking it easy today. Plus it rained a little during the night, so it won't be bad."

"But, shouldn't—"

"You're procrastinating. Quit talking and get on."

He watched her climb aboard the ATV and settle herself onto the passenger box he'd installed just for her. It gave her a nice cushioned seat with a backrest, instead of having to sit on the rear rack, but she didn't look all that appreciative. Instead she looked as if she was scooting her way to the gallows, like a sexy, pink-clad, condemned woman.

Two hours later, *sexy* was no longer the adjective that came to mind when he thought of Keri Daniels. Stubborn, maybe. Pain in the ass? Definitely, if it could be counted as one adjective.

At her first glimpse of the hill up to the Bear Paw scenic picnic area, she'd let go of her handholds and wrapped her arms around his waist, pressing her body against his back. It wasn't as sexy as he'd imagined, though, because every time he tried to hit the throttle, Keri gave him the Heimlich.

"Relax, babe. It's not that steep."

"There are ruts. And a big rock!"

He tried for a soothing voice, but it wasn't easy with both of them in helmets. "It's not as bad as it looks. I promise."

He eased into the throttle and she screamed, squeezing him so hard he almost lost his breakfast. With a sigh, he flagged the others around. One by one the family went by, most of them laughing as they did.

Joe tapped Keri's knee and pointed as Bobby went around them on his little 50cc machine. His nephew, aware he had an audience, took the hill as though an Olympic gold medal was waiting at the top. Keri's grip relaxed as she watched him, and Joe took a deep breath.

Then Terry stopped. If Keri wasn't clinging to him like a freshly dried sweater, he'd have been tempted to jump over and stuff a sock in his sister's mouth, but he was helpless to stop whatever verbal jab she was about to deliver.

"Ma made her blond brownies," Terry told Keri. "But they're at the top."

Then she took off in a fishtail of dust and gravel, powering up the hill.

"That bitch," Keri said. "She knows those were my favorite. But when I said they were to die for, I didn't really mean it literally."

"Come on, babe. You just watched the kids go up it just fine. Who do you think taught them to ride?"

"Mike."

Ouch. "Oh, ye of little faith. No blond brownies for you."

"Isn't there another way up?"

"Nope. But hey, if you tough it out, I'll let you sleep in the big bed tonight."

That got her attention. He could tell by the way her head swung around, her helmet visor smacking the back of his helmet. Again. "If we don't die going up this hill, you'll let me sleep in the bed?"

"Absolutely."

She was quiet for a second, then transferred her death grip back to the box handles. "Okay. Whether I'm in the bed or in intensive care, at least I won't have to sleep on that damn bunk tonight."

If he'd been alone, Joe would have punched it, banking the corners and launching off rocks, but instead he drove sedately up the smooth inside of the trail, like his mother had. By the time they reached the top, gear and people had scattered everywhere while Ma and Terry unpacked the coolers.

He pulled up next to Kevin's machine and killed the engine. Keri managed to knee him in the kidney and elbow him in the side of the head as she climbed off, but after narrowly avoiding hiking the quarter of a mile up the hill, he didn't mind. After pulling off his goggles, gloves and helmet, he set them on the front rack and turned to help Keri.

She'd beat him to it. Standing there with her hair mussed and dust coating her face, helmet tucked under her arm, she took his breath away. Her eyes were lit up and the smile meant either she was that thrilled to still be alive or she'd actually had a good time.

"I get a brownie *and* the bed," she said.

Like an idiot, Joe reached out and cupped the back of her neck and kissed her.

Flash. "Say cheese!"

"Any chance he's taking a picture of Kevin?" she murmured against his mouth.

Joe pulled back. "Since Kevin's not doing anything but staring at us like a moron, probably not."

"Joseph, stop kissing that girl and get the hibachi set up!" his father yelled from across the clearing.

Every head turned in their direction, and the blush glowed through the smudges of dirt on Keri's face.

"If Terry hides my bug spray," she said, "you're buying me more."

Joe went to unstrap the little grill from his father's front rack while Keri walked to the edge of the picnic area. The view from the top of the mountain was amazing—they could see across the river into Vermont—and he wished he'd brought her up here for the first time alone.

Preferably late at night, when the moon was full, the woods were quiet and Keri was wearing very little clothing. They could spread a blanket over the grass. Make love under the stars.

Better yet, they could make love on the ATV. It was an idea that had had him sleeping on his back for a while last night. Joe looked at his machine, pondering the best position for—

Whack. "Not in front of your mother."

"I wasn't doing anything," Joe protested, rubbing the sore spot. When his pop cuffed somebody in the back of the head, he didn't do it half-assed.

"Since you ain't got a math book handy, you carry that grill in front of you and think about cold showers."

Nothing got by the old man, so Joe did as he was told, taking the hibachi over to the flat slab of granite they always used for their cookouts.

Kevin slapped a box of hot dogs down on the rock. "What the hell was that?"

"A kiss. It's something guys like me do with girls we like. But don't worry, someday you'll find one drunk enough to let you try it."

"Funny. But in case you haven't noticed, our

sister's bitchy enough without you making out with public enemy number one in front of her."

"Keri's not public enemy number one. That would be Lauren. Then Tina, Keri's boss. She's definitely number two. Evan's pretty high on the list right now, but he's only been on there three months. I guess I'd put Keri in a solid tie for the third slot."

Kevin snorted and walked away. Joe didn't blame him. All the stupid banter in the world couldn't cover up the fact he'd just kissed Keri Daniels in front of his whole freaking family.

What the hell was he thinking?

TERRY HAD THE BLOND BROWNIE in her hand, ready to offer it like a high-calorie olive branch, when Joe kissed Keri.

It crumbled in her hand.

The only thing keeping her from tossing the whole bag of the blonde, brother-kissing bimbo's favorite dessert to the crows was the fact her mother had baked them. While the RV had a nicer-than-most kitchen, baking was still no easy feat.

She turned away, shoving brownie pieces into her mouth. She'd stopped at the bottom of the hill with full intention to say something mean—maybe something about the machine rolling over backward. But the fear on Keri's face had been so profound she couldn't bring herself to say it. Now she wished she had.

"What's wrong, Mom?"

Terry swallowed brownie and tried to smile at Steph. "Nothing, why?"

"I don't get why it bothers you so much if Uncle Joe hooks up with Keri again."

"They're not *hooking up.* And what part of nothing didn't you understand?"

"You were making the same face you made when Dad came home to pack his stuff."

She shoved the mangled remains of the brownie into her mouth just to buy herself a second to think. "After they broke up, Uncle Joe was pretty unhappy for a long time. I don't want him to go through that again is all."

"Maybe they just weren't ready, but now that they've grown up and done other stuff, they'll realize they love each other, after all."

How had Terry given birth to a hopeless romantic? "She has a life and a big-shot career in Los Angeles. She's not staying, and if they hook up, as you call it, he's going to end up hurt again."

"Whatever," Steph said, and Terry said a silent prayer of thanks for the teenage attention span.

She watched her daughter walk over to where the boys had set up a makeshift racketless game of badminton. It didn't surprise her at all that one of her nephews traveled with a battered birdie. Between the four of them, they could produce almost any bizarre item on demand.

By throwing herself into preparing a barbecue in a clearing on the side of a mountain, Terry managed to avoid standing in one place long enough for anybody to initiate a conversation. And she didn't miss the fact that Keri was managing to do the same.

No matter how much her family wanted to welcome Keri back into the fold, Terry couldn't be open-minded about it. She was Joe's twin—nobody empathized with him as keenly as she did. Maybe they'd forgotten the days—*years*—Joe had locked himself in his office with his computer and a case of beer.

In the beginning, he'd tried to feed her some bullshit about the alcohol breaking down the wall between the logical and the creative sides of his brain. In reality, all it did was break down his relationship with his family.

She'd never forget the day Joe quit drinking. He'd taken a swing at Kevin—not in a brotherly way, but a real, rage-driven swing that had busted his nose. That was the end of it. He'd quit cold turkey and never looked back, even during the darkest days of the Lauren incident.

But Terry was afraid Keri was Joe's Achilles' heel, and she didn't want a rerun of that particular episode.

"Have you figured out how you're going to come between them this time yet?" her mother asked. She was standing next to her, her hands full of condiment packets.

Was she always this freaking transparent? "I didn't come between them the first time. Keri did. And she's no good for him, Ma. You know that."

"What I *know* is that you feel like your life is out

of control, so you're going to control your brother's." She dumped the packets in the center of the picnic table.

Dozens of bitter retorts backed up in Terry's throat, but she swallowed them all. "Maybe."

"Or maybe you're more worried about her leaving *you* again than Joe."

Or maybe Ma needed to spend a little less time watching those Dr. Self-Improvement du Jour shows.

"Have you and Evan made an appointment with a counselor yet?"

Speaking of self-improvement. "No. I'm calling a divorce lawyer when I get home."

"Not that I know *anything* about making a marriage stick after all these years, but you could try talking to him before you divorce him."

"*He's* divorcing *me,* Ma."

"Not if you talk it out."

Sure, because a woman couldn't hear *I'd rather be alone than married to you* often enough. "Maybe we could have talked about it if he'd told me he was unhappy. We could have tried counseling. He chose to walk out the door instead."

"You should—"

"Stop," Terry snapped. "Please, Ma. Can't I just enjoy the scenery like everybody else?"

When her mother put out her arms, Terry had no choice but to surrender to the maternal gesture.

"It just makes me sad," she said quietly against Terry's cheek, "that you won't fight for him. I *know* you love him."

And she did. But she didn't have the strength to drag Evan home and then spend the rest of her life wondering every single day if that would be the day he left her again.

"Sometimes love's not enough."

KERI HAD GONE TWENTY-FOUR hours without phone, email or texting for the first time in as long as she could remember. Probably years. As wired for communication as she usually was, she'd expected to be going through some kind of withdrawal—some shaking, maybe twitching fingers. Phantom texting.

Instead she felt relaxed. Relieved. She could understand fasting a little better if this was how people felt after going food-free for a day.

Detoxed.

The low pitch of Joe's voice drew her attention to where he stood talking to Kevin. They were talking about something on Kevin's ATV, and she watched them through the corner of her eye, trying not to be obvious.

A skill Joe obviously hadn't mastered. Kissing her in front of his family? What was that about? Hell, he shouldn't have been kissing her at all. Not that she really minded, but still.

What did it mean? The man had spent an entire night alone with her in a secluded cabin and kept his hands to himself. Now, with his mother and Terry in the audience, he felt a pressing need to plant one on her?

If she'd thought it strange that her body instinctively remembered the locker position, it was down-right disturbing to learn her libido had a memory like an elephant when it came to Joe's kisses.

As soon as his lips had touched hers, her neck had tingled in anticipation of his mouth moving south. Then her nipples got all perky because they were the next step on the journey.

After that…well, the warm-and-fuzzies kept moving on down until Bobby's camera had interrupted. But all through the burned hot dogs and chip crumbs, her mind kept wandering back to making love with Joe.

It had taken a few tries to get it right, but practicing hadn't exactly been a hardship. Whitesnake blaring from the Granada's speakers. The sweet tang of Boone's Farm on Joe's lips. Their laughter when an elbow or a foot hit the car horn.

And then, the doing of *it.* How every single time he would *always* pause at some point and, with the restraint causing his muscles to twitch, he would stare down into her face and say, "I love you, babe."

"Stop staring at my brother's ass."

Busted. Unable to do a damn thing about the flush blooming on her neck and cheeks, Keri glared at her former best friend. "Where's my brownie?"

"I ate it while you were making out with Joe in front of his nieces and nephews. Oh, and our *parents.*"

"Ah, the darling of the Drama Club takes center stage again." She'd made out with Joe and one kiss was *not* his definition of making out. "Are you going to take cheap shots at me the whole time?"

Terry shrugged. "You can leave anytime."

"I have a job to do." And if she didn't do it, she'd have no job at all.

Terry rolled her eyes and walked away, which was fine by her.

"Pack it up!" Leo bellowed, and everybody moved.

When everything had been bungee-corded back onto the four wheelers, it was time to don their gear. Thankfully, Keri managed to get her helmet buckled herself, so she was spared Joe's knuckles brushing her jaw.

She climbed up onto her seat, then held her breath as Joe settled between her thighs.

"Hold on, babe!"

Keri gripped the handholds molded into the passenger box, but once they started down the hill, she started sliding. It wasn't the first time since they'd left the campground she found herself pressed up against him, crotch to ass and breasts to back, but it was different this time.

He'd kissed her. Kissing, which would, if left unchecked, lead to more kissing, then necking, and then…

The machine leveled out at the bottom of the hill and she scooted her way back into her seat. It didn't help. There just wasn't enough room to get the kind of space she was looking for.

Determined to distract herself before she did something stupid, like forget his family was behind them and go for the reach-around, Keri tried to concentrate on the scenery.

Trees. More trees.

Oh look!

A tree.

Then he hit a bump and the machine bounced, bucking her right back to where she'd started—plastered up against Joe. Her helmet smacked his—again—and she let go of the handles to wrap her arms around him, her palms pressed against the flat of his stomach.

The ATV stopped so fast their bodies jerked and Joe did some kind of sideways hop to get off the machine. "You want to drive?"

"No."

"Slide forward. It'll be fun."

With a pronounced sense of foreboding, she did as he said. Anything had to be better than having his ass between her thighs.

BY THE TIME JOE REALIZED just how bad a mistake he'd made, it was too late to do anything about it.

He'd needed Keri's thighs to stop squeezing his hips and her hands to stop hanging out mere inches above the fly of his jeans. In a panic, he'd decided to put her in front of him.

Really. *Bad.* Idea.

If he'd taken thirty seconds to consider the ramifications of *her* ass resting between *his* thighs, he might have just given her the machine and walked all the way back to the campground.

"What do I do?" she asked, and he tried to focus on the fact he'd just made himself a passenger on seven hundred pounds of machine the driver didn't know how to operate.

"Uh…push on the throttle with your thumb, but—"

Their helmets smacked as the ATV surged forward so fast she almost wheelied. Keri made a choked yelping sound while he yelled at her to stop over the roar of the engine and grabbed the handholds so she didn't dump him off the back.

Just as suddenly, the machine stopped and he yanked his head to the side to save them both another whack to the helmet. "You didn't let me finish. I was going to say *gently.*"

Laughter and whistles from the back of the pack made her stiffen against him. "I can't do this."

Joe turned and waved the others by, not missing Terry's dark glare at the side of Keri's helmet, or the kids' snickers.

Kevin, who was riding drag, pulled up alongside them and stopped. "You want me to hang back?"

"No, we're just gonna take it slow." When his brother gave him a *yeah, right* look, obviously not referring to their speedometer, Joe ignored him. "See you back there."

He gave the rest of the family a good head start, mostly to let the dust settle, then set about trying to guide her through driving while maintaining as little physical contact as possible.

She got the hang of it pretty quickly, though, and

once the fear of injury passed, his mind was free to take their proximity, add the fact they were alone, and come up with the sum total of trouble.

Ever since that impromptu, very public kiss, he'd been thinking about doing it again. Maybe with a little more finesse and a lot fewer spectators. The question was whether or not Keri would let him. The first time had been a sneak attack, but she hadn't slapped his face or cursed him out afterward.

When they came to a well-shaded intersection, Keri pulled the machine to the side of the trail and shut it off. "My thumb hurts."

He laughed while she climbed off and removed her goggles. "That's normal. Everybody's does at first, but then you get used to it."

When she slipped off her helmet, he could see how much she'd enjoyed herself.

He hadn't been exaggerating in the restaurant when he'd told her time had been pretty damn good to her. Decked out in that little black dress with killer heels and her makeup just so, she'd been a hot number. But out here in the woods with trail dust smudging her face and helmet hair and a big-ass grin, she was the most beautiful woman he'd ever seen.

It was dangerous, looking for the young Keri who'd loved him in her eyes, but he could see her. Inside the polished stranger lurked the girl he'd wanted to spend the rest of his life with.

"Can I drive all the way back?" she asked, and he stifled a groan.

All the way back to the campground with her shifting her weight between his legs? *Oh, hell no.* He'd never make it without coming in his pants like a teenager. "Sure."

Since the cooler packed with water bottles had gone on ahead with the family, they stood around for a couple of minutes while Joe thought about working up the nerve to kiss her again.

"Why did you kiss me?" she asked suddenly, her gaze like an interrogator's spotlight on his face.

"Glitch in the space-time continuum, I guess. Old habits die hard and all that." *Chickenshit.*

"Okay." She nodded, but he didn't think she looked as relieved as she was going for. "Because, you know, we're not teenagers anymore. And we're practically strangers."

"Sure." He was practically a stranger who knew just where to touch her to make her squirm and beg for him to… *Dammit.* "You ready to head back?"

He had to get away from her, even for a few minutes. There was no way in hell he was going to survive two weeks of this.

CHAPTER FIVE

KERI HAD BARELY MANAGED to catch her breath after the ride before she found herself roped into lifeguard duty. Something to do with Joe making a promise to Lisa in exchange for Mike going out with his brothers.

Of all the Kowalski activities Joe would no doubt coerce her into, she anticipated enjoying this one the most. Back home the landscape was littered with swimming pools, but Tina didn't pay her to lounge poolside.

She was pretty sure she had everything. A folding chair lifted from Lisa's campsite. A flimsy yet festive wrap to accent her black tank suit. Towel, water bottle and the paperback legal thriller she'd picked up at LAX. With her hair pulled back in an elastic band and sunscreen liberally applied, she was ready.

Joe stood and gave her a low wolf whistle when she stepped out onto the porch. "Damn, babe."

"Save it, Kowalski." But she still felt the blush. Recovering from the day's close contact was taking longer than she'd thought. "And stop calling me babe. We're not teenagers anymore."

"Can't help it. I see you and think *babe.* Always have."

Sure, he'd always called her babe, but that was back before she was trying—and failing—to keep some kind of professional distance between them. "Can you at least not call me that in front of your family?"

"Can I call you babe when we're alone?"

"Can I stop you?"

He shrugged. "Probably not."

It was the best deal she was going to get and, truth be told, she didn't mind it quite as much as she let on. "Fine."

"If you want to head down, the kids will be waiting at the pool's gate because they're not allowed to go in until an adult shows up. I'll be down after I get changed. You might want to rethink the book, though."

"I'm going to sit by the pool, relax, read my book and watch the kids swim."

"Don't say I didn't warn you."

Fifteen minutes later, the paperback had swelled to *War and Peace* proportions, her chair was upside down, she was involuntarily in the pool, and Steph was using Keri's sopping-wet wrap to snap the back of Danny's thighs.

She'd given up trying to keep track of who wasn't supposed to be running, who wasn't supposed to be diving and who wasn't supposed to be drowning whom.

There was shouting, shoving, splashing, screeching and it was impossible to keep all five of them in her line of vision at one time.

Keri hauled herself onto the side of the pool just in time to hear, "Fore!" The shout was followed by a splash and mini-tidal wave.

"No diving!" she shouted. "No running, no screaming and, for God's sake, Brian, let your brother come up for air!"

She heard Joe's laugh before she saw him, and turned to see him and his brothers coming toward the gate. While normally she might take a second to appreciate the sight of three tall, rugged Kowalski men in nothing but swim trunks, her libido was as frazzled as the rest of her.

"I thought you weren't going in," Joe called.

"I wasn't. But then Joey tried to drag Brian into something called the tandem cannonball of doom, which didn't sound good. So I went over to break it up and one of the other demon spawn—no offense, Mike—ran by and bumped into me. I tripped and ended up in something called the triple cannonball of doom, which is *not* as fun as it sounds." She paused to take a breath. "And that was *after* my book got wet."

Joe was laughing so hard she was surprised he could breathe, but Mike put two fingers in his mouth and gave a shrill whistle.

In the blink of an eye, all five kids were sitting on the edge of the pool, innocence blanketing their devious little faces.

"Two through six," he called to the kids. "Go."

It took Keri a few seconds to realize they were mumbling the multiplication table. "Does that really work?"

"You bet. Two through six is a warning. Seven through ten's pretty serious. Rarely do we need eleven and twelve."

"If this is their usual punishment, they must be *great* at math."

Mike grinned. "Straight A's across the board, every one of them. Well, not Bobby yet, but he got all E's in kindergarten."

"You're kidding." Keri used her hand to wipe water from her face since her towel had already been doused. "Evil *and* smart. Scary."

She took advantage of the lull to right her chair and hang her wrap and towel over the fence. Her book she set in a sunny spot to dry. She'd just reached a good part, dammit.

"Six times twelve is seventy-two!" the kids yelled in unison.

"Take it easy on Keri," Joe warned. "She's soft."

Without thinking, she planted her feet and shoved him in the pool. The shouting, shoving, splashing and screeching resumed. It wasn't quite as bad until Kevin tried to get her into a tandem cannonball of doom. The ensuing underwater wrestling match between Joe and his brother got the kids *really* wound up, until Mike had to resort to whistling again.

Finally, wet and exhausted and with a tinge of sunburn, it was time for Keri to drag her worse-for-wear belongings back up the dirt road. She made it as far as Lisa's site before she unfolded her chair and dropped into it.

"You have my undying respect and admiration," she told the boys' mother, who only rolled her eyes and opened the grill. "Seriously. I don't know how you do it."

"They were loving, adorable babies. Sucked me in while they were young."

Keri smiled and let her eyes drift closed. She should get up and head to the cabin. Take a shower and get dressed. Find some bottled water. But it was cool in the shade and Lisa was humming and she couldn't bring herself to move. Just a few more minutes.

THE LAST THING TERRY WANTED to see when she came around the corner of Lisa's RV was Keri Daniels, bathing-suit-clad, eyes closed and gracefully draped in a folding chair.

She knew from countless childhood sleepovers Keri snored like crazy, so she didn't think she was asleep. Then again, maybe they fixed those kinds of flaws out there in California. Adenoid removal or something. Terry managed—barely—to refrain from kicking Keri's chair on her way by. Rational or not, Terry felt that Keri had become the face of all the crap screwing up her life. She couldn't take her frustrations out on her family and Evan was too far away, but she could channel that discontent into her feelings about the woman who was playing her brother for a fool. Again.

Letting the princess rest, Terry threw herself into helping Lisa make supper for the crowd. Family members trickled in and at some point she looked up to find Keri in deep conversation with Danny. Mike's twelve-year-old was nodding solemnly at every word she said, as though she were some kind of damn oracle.

"Think you can help with salads, Keri, or you afraid you'll break a nail?" Everybody turned to look at Terry, and she wasn't surprised. That had come across a little bitchier than she'd intended. "They're in Ma's fridge."

"All you had to do was tell me you needed a hand," Keri said calmly, which, of course, made Terry look even more irrational. "I was getting ready to offer, anyway. Just wanted to finish my conversation with Danny."

"Won't be long then, since you ditch friendships like dirty socks."

Keri froze for a second, and then her eyes narrowed. "Oh, that's it! I call bullsh…crap, Theresa Kowalski."

"Porter," Steph chimed.

"Don't even try to deny it, Keri Daniels. Once Whatsherface with the blond hair and big boobs let you sit at her lunch table, that was the end of our friendship."

"That was Keri," Kevin interrupted.

"What?" they asked together.

"Keri had the blond hair and big boobs. Whatsherface was a brunette."

"Whatever," Terry snapped before turning back to Keri. "The point is, you dropped me like a flaming bag of dog shit for a girl whose name we can't even remember."

"Courtney Carlson," Kevin said.

"That's right." Keri frowned at him. "How do you remember that? You were behind us in school."

"Her yearbook photos, especially the cheerleading candids. Sometimes I'd—" he paused, obviously remembering Steph's presence "—have them nearby while checking myself for ticks."

Terry gave him a quelling look of death before turning back to the blonde in question.

"I tried," Keri said. "I'd call you to invite you somewhere and you always got bitchy. Said you were busy and I should have fun with my *new* friends. Eventually I quit trying."

Heat climbed Terry's neck and knowing they could see it pissed her off even more. "You chose them over me."

"They were fun and you had a hair across your ass so at some point, yeah, hanging out with them instead of you was inevitable, don't you think?"

"*Girls!* Enough."

Once Mary Kowalski said something was enough, that something was over, so everybody went back to doing what they'd been doing, except Keri, who managed to surreptitiously flip Terry the bird before heading off to Ma's camper.

The laugh that bubbled up surprised Terry, and she squashed it the best she could. She could remem-

ber back when they were young, she had been the
first to dare the gesture. Privately, of course. Just
practicing. It took a while for Keri to work up the
courage, and she'd had the misfortune to be near a
mirror. Joe caught sight of Keri's finger and yelled
for Ma, who let them know unequivocally that was
enough of *that*.

They'd had so many good times together. Most
of her childhood memories included Keri, the two
of them giggling and playing with Barbie dolls and
tormenting Joe.

But she could also remember how much it had
hurt seeing Keri hanging out with new friends.
And, yes, maybe Terry had driven Keri away before
Keri could dump her, thinking it would hurt less.
Or maybe the friendship had simply run its natural
course.

Terry was shy, though, and losing her best friend
had hurt, no matter whose fault it was. Keri sitting with the in-crowd at lunch, with her awesome
hair, and clothes that hadn't come from Kmart had
seemed like an unforgivable sin.

Almost twenty years ago. Even Terry had to
admit Keri hadn't done anything to merit being
treated like crap since she'd arrived. Joe had told
Terry that Keri was upfront about what she was
looking for, and that she'd agreed to every one of his
stipulations. As for the kiss, Joe was the one doing
the pursuing. Her brother was an attractive guy and
Terry couldn't really blame Keri for not trying too
hard to get away, past history or no.

Which meant—*crap*—she owed Keri an apology.

Maybe later, when she didn't have an audience. Of course, if it had been Stephanie, Terry would have made her apologize in front of everybody. You do the crime in public, you do the time in public.

But one of the few benefits of being the adult was the freedom to break your own rules.

Terry managed to keep her mouth shut through supper, even once Stephanie had done the math and came up with Keri Daniels plus *Spotlight Magazine* equaled firsthand knowledge of celebrity gossip. Have you ever met "fill in the blank" became the question of the evening, and the number of yeses turned her daughter into as big a fan of Keri as Joe was.

"Ohmigod, Mom, did you hear that?" Steph exclaimed when Keri was done telling her the story of having wine spilled on her by one of the hottest leading men in Hollywood.

"Yup. That's funny. And at least he could afford the dry cleaning bill," she said lightly, and she could almost feel the tension pop like a balloon. Her mother's look of maternal approval took care of any doubt that they'd been expecting her to say something nasty.

It hadn't been easy, though. Stephanie had been a bundle of preteen angst and attitude lately and seeing her drink up Keri's company made Terry feel as if she was sitting alone at the wrong lunch table again.

Keri launched into another tale of celebrity embarrassment and Terry tuned her out, as well as Stephanie's totally enraptured responses.

She turned her attention instead to Mike and Lisa, who were barely managing to hide the fact they weren't really speaking to each other a whole lot. If possible, there seemed to be even more tension between them than between her and Keri.

The family grapevine had clued her in to the fact Lisa had responded to Mike's suggestion that he was ready to face a vasectomy with the proposal they think about having another baby first. Not surprisingly, Mike hadn't reacted well.

Depression settled over Terry like a fog. They all seemed to be falling apart. Even Kevin was nursing the heartbreak of a divorce, though he refused to talk about it. Now Mike and Lisa, the seemingly perfect couple, had hit a rocky patch, and there was nothing Terry could do to help them through it.

Hell, she couldn't even save her own marriage. What made her think she had a chance in hell of helping anybody else?

KERI THREW HERSELF diagonally across the big bed with a satisfied sigh. No foam slab for her tonight. No creaking plywood. And no fear of jerking upright out of a sound sleep and knocking herself out on the top bunk should that raccoon figure out the dead bolt.

Pajama-clad and fresh from a run to the bathhouse, she was ready to crash for the night.

She grabbed a T-shirt and comb Joe'd left on the

bed and tossed them over to the bottom bunk. Then she stretched out on her back, managing to take up the entire bed.

"Comfy?"

Joe didn't sound nearly as thrilled about the new sleeping arrangement as she was. "Very, thank you."

"Gonna take your shoes off?"

"Maybe." Later. She was exhausted and, for right now, she wasn't moving.

The plywood groaned as Joe tested his weight on it. "I should have left you at the bottom of the hill and made you walk up."

"Be quiet. I'm trying to go to sleep before I have to pee again."

"You haven't asked me a question yet."

"What are you— Oh!" Shit! How could she have forgotten the interview? She blamed the marinated steak tips. And Mary's potato salad. And the best corn on the cob ever. She was in a food stupor even her killer ambition couldn't penetrate, and it was a good thing Tina couldn't see her.

Cursing her boss and that second helping of potato salad, Keri rolled herself to her side and sat up on the edge of the bed. Joe was stretched out on the bunk, his hands tucked behind his head and his feet flat against the footboard. He was a tight fit and she wondered whether or not she should feel guilty, but payback went both ways.

Just to get it over with so she could sleep, Keri grabbed a bottle of water and her steno pad. Although it was dry in the cabin, she wouldn't drink a lot, because that could lead to a middle-of-the-night sprint through the dark.

Sitting on the side of the big, comfy bed, she opened the notebook to her first question. "So how did a nice guy like you end up writing sick, twisted thrillers?"

He turned his head to frown at her. "What the hell kind of question is that?"

"A legitimate one."

"You called me sick and twisted."

"No, I called your books sick and twisted."

"But I write them."

"Hence the question. What kind of demented muse comes up with stories like that?"

He looked back at the bottom of the top bunk. "Actually, this girl I once knew is my muse. We were in love, and I had this dream of writing profound literary works that earned critical acclaim and fancy prizes. Then the girl ripped my heart out of my chest and stuck a California or Bust sign through it."

Keri rolled her eyes and tapped the eraser of her mechanical pencil against her steno pad. "Oh please."

"So I got drunk and wrote a book about a chick named Carrie Danielson who's tormented by a revenge demon summoned by her devastated ex-boyfriend."

"Yes, I read it. I wasn't impressed."

"That's when I discovered sick and twisted was fun to write. Pays well, too."

"Joe, I can't print that."

"Why? It's the truth."

"One, your mother would whack me with her spoon. And two, people will go digging and find out who the so-called Carrie Danielson is."

"Some women would be flattered to be the muse of a popular author."

"Some women didn't get to read themselves getting a machete manicure."

The dimple on the cheek facing her popped into view. "Okay, that was a little harsh."

"And the scene where the revenge demon possesses the hero's car and chases her until she jumps off the bridge into the freezing water to escape it?"

"One of my favorites, actually."

"I would have burned the whole damn thing if I wasn't fundamentally opposed to desecrating books. I bet your family got a real kick out of it, though."

"Terry sure did."

"Fine, but I still don't want to print that. Do you really want your fans to know you wrote your first book drunk?"

"I wrote my first *four* books drunk. Your leaving hit me pretty hard, and there were a few years when whiskey, murder and mayhem were my world."

"I haven't seen you drink at all since we got here."

"I quit when my family started liking me even less than I liked myself. That was a tough year. My third book hit the *New York Times* list and my fourth book had already been turned in, but my fifth was actually rejected. I had to learn to write without the booze."

"Jesus, Joe, we were kids. Did you really think we were going to live happily ever after?"

"Yeah, babe. I really did."

And so had she. Or she'd hoped, anyway. But Joe's future consisted of staying close to his family and tapping away on his keyboard. Keri wanted her future to include travel and maybe some wealth, and definitely some killer shoes.

By the dawning of graduation day, she'd known two things. Joe wasn't leaving New Hampshire, and she was. Watching him give his valedictory speech, with its overwhelming theme of home and family, had cemented it.

"It wasn't going to happen for us, Joe. You had everything you wanted already. I didn't even know what I wanted yet."

"I did have everything I wanted until you left." The slow emergence of his naughty dimples made her melt, but only on the inside where he couldn't see it. "But now you're back."

Oh, boy, when he said it like that, it almost sounded like a good thing. Rather than risk going down that mental path, she clipped her pencil to the notepad and ignored his last comment. She had to focus on the job.

"Your turn, Kowalski. One question." She cracked the cap on the bottle of water and took a long sip.

"Have you ever faked an orgasm?"

And she choked on the water. "What? You can't ask me that!"

"You're the one who negotiated the terms. Or

rather, *didn't*. Are you refusing to answer the question?"

She almost said yes. She wasn't in the habit of discussing her orgasms, faux or otherwise, with anybody. She didn't even keep a journal.

"You can refuse to answer, of course, but then you won't get to ask me one tomorrow," he reminded her, as if she could have forgotten.

Refusing might almost be worth it, but she was barely going to have enough usable content to get Tina off her ass as it was. "Yes, I have faked orgasms in the past."

His eyes widened. "How far in the past? Did you ever fake with me?"

He looked so horrified at the idea, she had to laugh. That made him look even more stricken, which made her laugh harder.

"It's not funny, Daniels. Did you ever fake an orgasm with me?"

"Your one question for the evening has been asked and answered, Kowalski. Feel free to save that for tomorrow." She set the bottle on the nightstand and crawled under the covers. "If you're sure you *really* want to know."

CHAPTER SIX

KERI SURVIVED HER FIRST SOLO outing on the machine Joe had brought for her, though she'd had her doubts a few times.

It was smaller than Joe's, which she'd driven the day before, and it didn't lunge as badly if she hit the throttle a little too hard. And they'd given her a few minutes of driving it around the campground before they hit the trails.

Fortunately, the kids had all stayed back at the campground with Leo and Mary, despite the boys' loud objections, so she didn't have to worry about being shown up by a little squirt on an undersized ATV. And at the last minute, Lisa had claimed a headache and stayed behind, which made no sense to Keri. The four Kowalski boys were far from the cure for a headache.

Joe took his time on the ride, having her follow in his tracks through the rough spots. Twice she balked at a hill, making him walk back down and drive her machine up. Mostly, though, she enjoyed herself.

They stopped for a snack in a shady spot next to a pond, and Keri stretched her fingers and wiggled her thumb, trying to keep the stiffness at bay. With the machines off it was quiet in a way she could never find in Los Angeles, even within the walls of her apartment. In the distance a loon dove underwater, looking for fish.

"Pretty, isn't it?" Terry asked, and Keri realized all the men had disappeared. Probably to mark their territory by pissing on trees, an ability she'd never envied until now.

"It's definitely quiet."

"Come out early enough and you'll see some moose."

"The four-wheelers don't scare them off?" She wasn't sure why Terry was making small talk with her all of a sudden, but she'd go with it.

"Moose aren't afraid of anything. And the ones out here get used to it."

Keri downed half a bottle of water, hoping she'd sweat it out and not have to pee before they got back to the campground, as the silence grew awkward.

"I'm sorry about yesterday," Terry said, all in a rush as if she'd had to force the words out. "The crack about you breaking a nail, I mean. It was un-called for."

Wow. "Thank you. Apology accepted."

"Just like that?"

"I don't want to fight with you the whole time I'm here. I'm sorry we grew apart and I'm sorry about things not working out with Joe, but that was a long time ago. We're adults now and your brother knows why I'm here, and he knows I'm leaving when the time's up."

Terry looked as if she wanted to say more, but Kevin walked out of the woods, looking relieved, which ticked Keri off to no end. She had dirt on her face and really bad helmet hair, but she wasn't so far removed from civilization she'd be hanging her bare ass over a log any time soon.

Mike and Joe reappeared, too, and they all sat on the grassy bank of the pond, munching on peanut butter crackers. An unfortunate choice, Keri thought, since she had to drink more water. Her poor bladder would never make it.

"So the whole world knows what Joe does," she said after washing down the peanut butter, "but what about the rest of you?"

"I'm a bean counter," Mike said. "Mostly Joe's beans, but I have other clients, too. I specialize in authors. Lisa's mainly a stay-at-home mom, but she chips in with the paperwork come tax time."

"I do whatever his editor, agent, publicist and accountant don't," Terry told her. "I take care of his website. Moderate his forum and chat list. Presort his emails. Help hammer out plot problems at two in the morning."

"Her official title is personal assistant to Joseph Kowalski," Joe said with a chuckle, "but she's really the glue that holds it all together."

Keri nodded, then turned to Kevin. "How about you? Do you work for the family business, too?"

"No. I was a cop with Boston P.D. until two years ago, when I bought a sports bar in Concord."

"Little too young to retire, weren't you? Oh! You didn't get hurt, did you? Shot or something?"

"No, I didn't get shot."

Kevin's jaw was clenched and Keri's instincts told her there was a nice, juicy story there, but she only hesitated a second before changing the subject. "I think it's cool Danny wants to be a writer like his uncle."

Joe laughed. "Not exactly like his uncle. He's got a more serious, literary bent. Wants to write short stories and work his way up to the great American literary masterpiece."

They all chatted for a few more minutes, then set out for the campground. On the way, Keri, who was well on her way to becoming addicted to four-wheeling, saw two rabbits, a tiny snake and what she thought might be a fox's ass disappearing into the woods. She also got hung up on a rock buried by mud—what the guys called high-sided—requiring Joe to come to her rescue. But, other than that, it was a great ride.

The evening, however, sounded as though it was going to be a lot more treacherous than rocks and stumps and the occasional mud puddle.

Once they were back in the cabin, Joe told her he'd also promised they'd take the kids out for pizza, and this was the night.

"Why tonight?" she wanted to know. While she wasn't going to admit it, riding a four-wheeler required an entirely different set of muscles than sitting at a desk or walking in heels, and she was sore.

"You should ration out the activities—save something for next week."

"Because I can use the bribe again if I get it out of the way now."

"Why do you have to do this again?"

"Mike got to ride with Kevin and me for two hours in exchange for two lifeguard duties, taking the boys out for pizza and ice cream, and s'mores duty the first night."

An experience she might never recover from. Melted marshmallow was a bitch and the Kowalski kids knew how to fling it around like silly string. "Taking advantage of the plight of an overwhelmed mother for your own benefit isn't very nice."

"You've already done a lifeguard duty and s'mores with me. You really think *she's* the one being taken advantage of?"

Good point. Considering what those kids could do with marshmallow, she wasn't sure she wanted to see what they could accomplish with pizza sauce.

"I'm going to take a shower," she told him. And probably another when they got back to get the strewn toppings out of her hair.

"You should let me check you for ticks."

She paused in the act of digging through her bag for quarters. "Oh, no you don't."

He pulled one of the chairs away from the table. "Sit. At least let me do your hair."

"I was wearing a helmet."

"Not during rest stops, you weren't. Sit."

It was on the tip of her tongue to tell him there

was no way in hell she was letting him run his fingers through her hair, but then her scalp tightened.

What if, right that very second, a nasty little tick was rummaging around in her hair, looking for the perfect spot to sink his fangs into her skin? She shuddered, shaking her head a little, but the creepy-crawly feeling didn't abate. If anything, it got worse.

"Okay, fine, but make it quick." She wasn't sure how long she could take his hands stroking her, even if he claimed he was looking for bugs.

Her butt had barely hit the chair when Joe's hands plunged into her hair, his fingertips massaging her scalp. She sighed and relaxed against the chair as the creepy-crawly feeling faded.

After a few minutes he pushed her head forward a little so his thumbs could rub the back of her neck. She was fairly sure it wasn't a popular tick hangout, but it felt good. Very good. Definitely too good to protest.

"Got your question all ready for tonight?" he asked, but her brain was turning to totally relaxed mush.

"Hmm?" was all she could manage.

"Your interview question? You know, the questions that are supposedly going to save your career?"

"Mmm-hmm." She knew which questions he meant. It was just that, right then and as long as Joe had his hands on her, she didn't care.

IF KERI DIDN'T QUIT with the little moaning noises, Joe was going to prematurely blow his load as he had the first night Keri finally let him take off her bra and touch her nipples.

It had been embarrassing enough at the time, but a reenactment now would be nothing short of mortifying. Time to stop touching her.

With a bone-deep reluctance, he let his hands drop and stepped back from the chair. "No ticks."

She rolled her head, making more damn sex noises. "I could let you do that all night long."

That wasn't exactly what he wanted to do to her all night long, so he let that invitation pass. "I'm gonna round up the kids while you shower."

He was out the door before she could say anything else that his libido would warp with its sexual slant.

The last thing he wanted to do at that moment was face the horde of Kowalski kids, so he turned left on the dirt road, walking toward the woods and away from the center of the campground.

If his subconscious had been trying to punish Keri for dumping him in favor of high-rise littered pastures, it had seriously backfired. He was the one suffering.

The overwhelming—and surprising—want he felt for her was knocking him on his ass.

Sure, he'd thought about her a lot over the years. Her mom and his were close friends, so Keri came up in conversation. And she worked for a woman one skipped dose away from being his own personal stalker.

But it wasn't as if he hadn't moved on. There had

been plenty of women, some of whom he'd almost believed might be the one. And Lauren...

He wouldn't have guessed those little pangs of nostalgia he'd felt whenever he thought of Keri were actually buried feelings waiting to slap him upside the head the first time he saw her again.

The low rumble of an ATV signaled incoming, and Joe moved to the side of the road to let it pass.

It pulled up beside him instead. "Hangin' out with all your friends?"

He flipped Kevin the bird and kept walking. Sadly, his brother didn't catch the hint and idled along beside him.

"Saw Keri headed for the bathhouse. Looked like she was in a better mood than you."

No shit. She didn't have the fly of her jeans chafing the erection that wouldn't die. "Good for her."

"Ouch. Wanna talk about it?"

Joe gave up and stood still. "Nothing to talk about."

Kevin killed his engine and crossed his arms. "You can't bullshit a bullshitter, my friend."

"What the hell was I thinking?"

"Hot. Alone. Cabin."

Joe snorted, wishing it were that simple, but a part of him had been playing *what-if* as soon as he'd heard she was looking for him. The *hot* had come after. "She's here for work."

"Maybe you repressed the memory, but you kissed her in front of the whole family. She didn't exactly knee you in the balls for it."

Worse. She'd given him the *let's be reasonable adults* talk. And had made it sound reasonable. His brain had got the message, but so far the memo hadn't made it below the waist. "We're taking the kids out for pizza tonight."

"Ding! Nice change of subject. And, no, I don't wanna tag along."

"I don't remember inviting you."

"Just you, your high school sweetheart and a pack of kids. Cozy."

It would be good. Since he wouldn't put the moves on her in front of the kids, even in his current state of sexual starvation, maybe he could regain his footing. Being forced to keep his hands to himself might give him a chance to remind himself she was just using their past to further her career.

So far that had yet to trump *hot. Alone. Cabin.*

"You've got that glazed look you get when you fall in a plot hole," Kevin said.

He'd fallen in some kind of hole, all right. And it was time to climb out before his libido dug it any deeper.

He slapped his brother on the shoulder. "I'm going to round up the kids. Catch you later."

Not surprisingly, Joe found Steph slumped in a chair under their camper's awning, earbuds in place and eyes closed.

He pulled her right earbud out by the wire. "Hey, kiddo."

"Hey, Uncle Joe."

"Keri and I are taking all the kids into town for pizza. You in?"

"Nah. I'll just hang out here."

Even taking into account preteen attitude and maybe even the onset of feminine crankiness, which he did *not* want to consider, Steph seemed out of sorts. "It's not like you to pass up pizza. There might even be ice cream."

Steph shrugged. "Not hungry."

Now he knew something was wrong. Steph's last name might be Porter, but she was a Kowalski and Kowalskis never missed a meal. "What's buggin' you?"

A one-shoulder shrug this time, for variety. "Nothin'."

"Pants on fire?"

"Whatever."

If she were one of his nephews, Joe would roughhouse her into submission, but she'd turned the corner into that awkward phase where he couldn't drag her onto his lap and tickle her until she begged for mercy.

Of course, if she were one of the boys, they wouldn't be in this situation to start with. They were pretty vocal about everything, including anything weighing on their minds.

"I heard Mom crying today."

Shit.

"She thought we were all at the store, but I forgot my money so I came back. She was in her bedroom with the door closed and she was crying."

"It's a hard time for your mom, honey. For *all* of you."

"It makes me mad at my dad," she said in a little voice that reminded him of the little girl who *had* crawled onto her uncle's lap, looking for comfort after a scrape with her cousins.

Joe satisfied himself with crouching in front of her, his hands on her knees. "You're going to have a lot of mixed-up feelings, Steph, and they're all normal."

She shrugged again, but it was as though the weight of the world rested on her shoulders, making the gesture slow-motion. "I love them both."

"And they both love you. You don't ever have to choose sides." He longed for the bygone days when a magic kiss could heal any boo-boo. "No matter how things turn out, it will get better. The emotional up-heaval will settle and you'll find a new normal."

When she sighed and managed a small smile, Joe stood again. He was getting too old to crouch down like that for long. "You sure pizza and ice cream won't make you feel better?"

"I just wanna hang out and enjoy time alone. Maybe I'll get to go in the pool without any brats trying to drown me."

He leaned down and kissed the top of her head, then gave her hair a tousle. When she squealed and slapped at his hand, Joe laughed and went off in search of the brats.

Twenty minutes later, he was driving north with four rambunctious boys and Keri.

Keri, who smelled like soap and shampoo and the tropical flowers of her skin- and mosquito-friendly herbal insect repellent. No doubt she'd go for the DEET-heavy stuff within five minutes of getting back, but for now it was hard not to be distracted by the fresh, feminine scent wafting his way.

Okay, time to get a grip, Kowalski. On himself, not her.

She'd broken his heart. She was using him to get ahead at work. She lived as far away as possible without leaving the contiguous states.

She laughed at something one of the boys said.

Hot. Alone. Cabin.

THE PIZZA PLACE wasn't packed, so they were able to shove two tables together and seat all six. Then the fun began.

One boy refused to eat pizza without pepperoni, and one refused to eat pizza with pepperoni. One wanted mushrooms, another gagged. No anchovies, two for sausage, one for hamburger and a unanimous no to black olives. Joe let them carry on for a few minutes and then ordered a large pepperoni, a large cheese and a large half mushroom, half sausage.

When Keri put her order in for a salad, five pairs of Kowalski eyes stared at her in disbelief.

"Salad?" they echoed as one.

"Vegetables are good for you."

Joe just shook his head and turned back to the counter. "We'll also have a small Hawaiian pizza with half the sauce and twice the pineapple."

Keri's mouth started watering and her tear ducts nearly followed suit. Did the fact a man she hadn't seen in nearly twenty years knew her better than anyone else speak to her being a social hermit, or had he really loved her that much?

Tilting pinball machines kept the boys' squabbling to a minimum and Joe went through enough quarters to buy a decent used car before their number was finally called. Between the two of them, they managed to get the boys seated and began dispensing slices.

"Mine's supposed to have pepperoni."

"Ew, a mushroom touched mine!"

"You're supposed to blow on it, not spit."

"Danny's has more cheese than mine."

"Look at this."

"Oh, dude, that's so gross!"

As Keri finally bit into her first slice, she wondered how Lisa managed to get through each day with her sobriety intact. Even having just two of the boys would have driven Keri to drink. A lot. And their uncle Joe wasn't helping, with the hyperactivity of either the boys or her hormones.

The way he kept looking at her, his eyes filled with humor, the occasional apology, and a little something else when the boys weren't looking, warmed her insides in a way the spicy sauce couldn't touch.

Is this what it would have been like if she hadn't left? Joe and their kids sharing really bad knock-knock jokes over pizza, the promise of a private, late-night dessert in his eyes? Love, laughter and five pizza sauce-smeared pairs of jeans in the laundry?

Or would she have resented every day of mopping up muddy floors and potty-training misfires until she couldn't stand it—or him—anymore? Would their marriage have survived his name being splashed across bestseller lists while hers graced permission slips and the electric bill?

"Be right back." Joe pushed his chair back and stood.

"What? Where are you going?" And why wasn't he taking the kids with him?

He laughed at her. "I'll be right back. Promise."

He'd left her alone with them once and look what had happened—the destruction of a perfectly good book, among other things. She knew nothing about kids. Nobody in her life had children, or if they did, they were tucked away somewhere with high-priced au pairs or illegal nannies.

"He's probably going to check his messages or call his agent," Danny told her.

"Oh. From a pay phone?"

"His cell."

"He told me there isn't any reception up here." Lying rat bastard.

Brian laughed. "If you go behind the pizza place and stand up on top of the picnic table closest to the Dumpster and face east and the weather's good, you can get two bars."

Which would be helpful if she hadn't been forced

to leave her cell phone at her parents' house. As much as she wanted to see Joe standing on a picnic table to get reception and then cajole him into letting her climb up and access her voice mail remotely, she couldn't risk leaving the kids alone. So far they seemed orderly enough, but God only knew what they'd do with no supervision.

Bobby suddenly leaned forward and pinned her with an intense look. "Who's better, Wolverine or the Incredible Hulk?"

The other three boys stilled and Keri got the impression this ranked high on their list of very important questions. "Wonder Woman."

It was as if she'd set off a stink bomb in their midst. Eyes rolling. Groaning. Hands covering their faces. Gagging.

"You should go on a date with Uncle Kevin," Bobby said.

It took her a second to realize he'd said Kevin and not Joe. "Why is that?"

"He knows lots about Wonder Woman," Joey explained. "He says girls like it when you think Wonder Woman's cool and they'll go on dates with you."

Keri laughed and it was at that moment Joe slid back into his seat. "What's so funny?"

Bobby clapped his hands. "Keri's going on a date with Uncle Kevin!"

Joe didn't laugh.

CHAPTER SEVEN

BACK AT THE CAMPGROUND, Terry watched with a sinking feeling in her stomach as Mike and Kevin rode out alone.

Usually when somebody took the boys, the dust hadn't even settled from their departure before Mike and Lisa snuck off for some alone time. But this time Lisa sat by herself under her awning, staring off into space, as her husband took off with his brother. Not good.

Stephanie was floating, happily cousin-free, around the pool under her grandmother's watchful eye, so Terry grabbed a soda and joined her sister-in-law in the shade. "I wonder if Keri's developed a nervous tic yet."

Lisa laughed. "They're a handful, that's for sure. They love hanging with their uncle Joe, though, so they shouldn't get too rowdy."

"How come you didn't go out with the guys?"

"Didn't feel like it. And Mike needed to blow off some steam, I think."

"Rough patch?" As if she didn't already know.

Lisa nodded, looking anywhere but at Terry. "Is it so wrong to want another baby?"

Insane was probably a better word than *wrong*. The boys were well-behaved when required—at school, in public, et cetera—but all together they really were a handful. They dominated Mike and Lisa's lives and, as parents, they were just starting to get a little breathing room.

"What's really going on with you, hon?" she asked. "A few months ago you were planning to throw a drunken bash the morning Bobby started first grade. Now you're thinking about another one?"

"I…I miss having a baby around."

"I love you to death, but you are *so* lying."

Lisa looked for a second as if she was going to lose her s'mores, but then she sighed and looked down at her feet. "Mike only married me because I was pregnant with Joey."

Terry opened her mouth to deny it, but closed it again. Empty denials of an unfortunate truth weren't going to help her sister-in-law get through this. "It might have started out that way, but he loves you, Lisa."

"He's never had a choice, has he? You know as well as I do he'd never put a little one through a divorce."

"So, now that Bobby's old enough to go to school and have a halfway intelligent conversation, you think Mike is going to leave you? That's a shitty reason to have a baby."

"You have no idea how it feels to wonder every single day if your husband would have married you if you didn't get pregnant."

"No, I don't, but having another child isn't the solution. It's not like you can keep doing it. Eventually you're going to run out of eggs, you know."

As intended, the comment made Lisa smile, but it didn't last long. "Mike works out of his home office a couple days a week now, and we barely talk."

"Hate to state the obvious, but maybe he's working."

"He takes breaks. Sometimes we even go out for breakfast after dropping Bobby at school and it's hell trying to come up with something to talk about so we don't look pathetic sitting there, staring over each other's shoulders."

"Every parent goes through that. As the kids' lives stop revolving around you and vice versa, there's an empty spot. You and Mike need to find something to do together to fill it up."

"Is that what happened with you and Evan?"

Smacked in the face by the marital advice boomerang. "You'd have to ask him."

She wished she knew. That whole sex on the kitchen table thing was just a symptom of a bigger issue, but that issue was almost impossible to wrap her head around.

Did Evan really believe that, since Steph was old enough to hang at a friend's house or go to a slumber party, Terry was free of responsibility? Whether Steph was home or not, she still had a job and a house to keep up, and all the things people asked of her because she worked from home and therefore was always *available*.

She could do spontaneous if it meant catching a movie on an evening Steph was out. But if his idea of spontaneity was playing Discovery Channel on the same piece of furniture she served food on, he was welcome to not let the door hit him in the ass on his way out.

Which it hadn't, of course, because she'd stood there like an idiot, holding it open, while her brain tried to comprehend that, yes, he really was leaving her.

"Mike hasn't been happy since I mentioned having another baby," Lisa said, drawing Terry's attention back to her sister-in-law's woes. "If I try to talk to him about it, he walks away."

"You can't make him want another baby. And, let's be honest, you don't want another one, either."

Lisa set her lips in a stubborn line. "No, I think I do. Maybe it'll be a girl."

"You said that the last two times."

That was one of the shorter moments of self-awareness Terry had witnessed, except maybe Joe's when it came to Keri Daniels. Lisa had practically admitted she only wanted another baby to keep Mike from divorcing her, but now she'd returned to making herself really believe her biological clock had a few ticks left in it.

The irony was that Lisa was going to drive her husband away while trying to keep him. Unlike Terry, who had just driven hers away, period.

"Let's play adult Scrabble," she said, ready for

both of them to quit drowning in their sorrows for a few minutes.

Lisa whooped and went for the board while Terry dragged the big cooler over to serve as a table. The rules were simple—standard Scrabble scoring, along with a bonus double word score for any word they couldn't say in front of the kids. Any word they couldn't even bring themselves to say aloud at all earned a bonus triple word score. Generally the less sober they were, the fewer triple word scores they bagged.

Despite their lack of alcoholic intake, they were giggling like schoolgirls twenty minutes later when a nasty bit of slang cut across a four-letter verb and neither of them could spit out the words.

It felt good, and Terry let all her worries melt away as she focused on hunting down a *D* to host the *I, C* and *K* in her rack.

JOE MANAGED TO HOLD IT IN for the walk down to the ice-cream stand. As each boy was handed a cone and sent off to the picnic table, he kept his mouth shut.

But while they stood waiting for their banana splits, he couldn't stop it. "A date with Kevin?"

She smiled and he kicked himself for letting her know the idea of her and his brother maybe hooking up tied him in knots. "He's a big Wonder Woman fan."

He couldn't believe that was still working for Kevin, even when delivered by juvenile proxy. "I like Wonder Woman."

"Really?" Keri paused to take her sundae as it was passed through the window. "What's her real name?"

Joe choked, trying to run every comic book debate the kids had ever had through his mind on fast-forward. "Uh...Anna Marie?"

She laughed. "That's Rogue, but nice try."

Dammit. He might have paid more attention if he'd known he'd have to pass a quiz in order to keep his girl.

Not that Keri was his girl, but she had been once, and that meant Kevin couldn't have her. Ever. "My brother wouldn't go on a date with you anyway. There's a code."

She only gave him an enigmatic smile and walked away to join the boys. He wasn't sure what that look was supposed to mean, but if she thought she was going on a date with any Kowalski but Joe, she had another think coming.

Once he got his own banana split, he paused at the napkin dispenser for at least a dozen extra napkins, glancing over to the picnic table to estimate the cleanup.

The older three boys were laughing as Bobby gave Keri a taste of his ice cream, managing to smear chocolate and jimmies on her chin. She laughed, too, and Joe's heart fisted in his chest.

They should have had kids.

Keri was supposed to stay. They were supposed to go to UNH together. They were supposed to get married. Have babies. Their own kids to fight over pizza toppings and comic book heroes.

Instead she'd transferred to Berkeley and dumped him so abruptly he'd just stood there, wondering what the hell had just hit him.

"Uncle Joe, you're dripping!"

He shook off the melancholy and joined the sticky crowd at the picnic table. The boys had left the bench across from Keri open, leaving him no choice but to sit there. Their feet touched. Legs brushed. Her tongue kept flicking out to catch stray whipped cream.

It was brutal, but he forced himself to join the raging Marvel versus DC debate. "You sure know a lot about superheroes for a girl."

His nephews all agreed she did, but Keri shrugged. "I don't know if you've noticed, but Hollywood's been having a bit of a love affair with comic books lately. There's a lot of buzz. And…"

"And?"

"Superheroes are cool." She smiled, and then the tip of her tongue dipped into the corner of her mouth after a tiny speck of hot fudge and he forgot what they were talking about. "I wonder how Kevin feels about Supergirl."

Oh, that's right. Superheroes, which somehow equaled Keri going out with Kevin. Not gonna happen.

Once the boys had all weighed in with their less-than-glowing opinions of Superman's Kryptonian cousin, Joe sent them into the bathroom to clean up. "Wash your faces and do all the way to your elbows."

As they went, moaning and groaning the entire way, Joe mopped up the picnic table the best he could and discarded the mass of sticky napkins.

All the while trying to ignore Keri sucking the tips of her fingers clean. The faint *pops* of suction as she pulled each fingertip from her mouth. The hot tingle creeping over his skin he wanted to attribute to an ice-cream sugar rush.

Ignoring it all.

Until she let loose one of those deeply contented sighs that, in his experience, women gave after good chocolate or a better orgasm.

After shoving the napkins in a trash can, Joe sat on the bench next to Keri, straddling it so he was facing her.

"Kevin might know Wonder Woman," he said, resting his hand on the small of her back, "but he doesn't know you."

"Joe, that was just a—"

"He doesn't know how you like to be touched." He trailed his fingers up her spine until he reached the base of her neck. "He doesn't know to run his tongue over this spot right here and then blow on it."

She didn't say anything, but he could feel the slight trembling in her body. No matter what might come out of her mouth, Joe knew her body remembered what sex had been like between them.

Intense. Fun. Explosive. Hot. It had been everything he'd ever imagined or wanted.

And then she'd left.

He'd damn well better remember she was going to leave again, too. As soon as she'd gotten what she'd come here for.

Joe almost fell off the bench when Keri put her hand on his leg, her fingers curling toward that sensitive spot at the back of his knee.

"Don't forget," she whispered, "I know all your hot spots, too."

The top of his head was going to blow clean off. "I bet you've forgotten a few."

"I haven't forgotten anything about you."

Before he could gather his composure enough to dare her to prove it, his nephews and their impeccable sense of timing exploded out of the bathroom.

"Uncle Joe," Bobby yelled. "Brian got ice cream in his hair and then Danny and Joey said they were going to give him a swirly to wash it out and Brian tried to kick Joey in the pee-pee and—"

Joe held up his hand for silence. His blood hadn't yet made the return trip to above his waist and he couldn't focus on sibling hijinks. "Did you leave a mess in the bathroom?"

All four boys shook their heads and Joe believed them. Lisa had taught them to clean up after themselves—in public, at least.

"If we hurry up," Joey said, "we can go swimming before it gets dark."

"I like swimming in the dark," Keri said, and Joe's erection leapfrogged from a little uncomfortable to downright painful.

He and Keri had gone swimming in the dark once. He'd taken her with the black water enveloping their naked bodies, cooling their overheated flesh. It was the only time in his life he hadn't used a condom and just the memory of that sweet friction made him ache.

Joe watched Keri chatting with the boys while she threw her garbage away, and he wondered how things might have turned out if he'd gotten her pregnant that night at the lake.

Hell, combining *Keri* plus *baby* was an even worse idea than *hot* and *alone* and *cabin,* but during the walk back to his truck, the thought poked at his subconscious like a tongue at a sore tooth.

NOT SURPRISINGLY, Keri's favorite time of the day was after the kids had gone to bed, leaving the adults to sit around the campfire.

They used Mike and Lisa's fire ring so the kids weren't left unattended, and the camp chairs made a cozy ring around the blaze. Keri, snuggled into her oversize flannel shirt, invariably ended up next to Joe, as though they were as much a couple as the others.

"So he's up to his handlebars in icy muck and he thinks I'm going to wade out and hook on to his machine." Kevin was telling a story involving Mike, a winter ride and an iced-over swampy area that wasn't quite as iced-over as they'd thought. It was pretty obvious everybody but Keri had heard the tale before, but they all listened as though it was the first time. "Since I was behind him and I wasn't gonna get wet, I had to pull out my winch and toss it out to him a thousand times before he caught the damn thing."

Keri took a sip of the most delicious hot chocolate she'd ever had, courtesy of Lisa, and snuggled a little deeper into her chair. Because it was chillier than usual, the chairs were close together, making the ring tighter around the fire, and her arm brushed Joe's as she set her paper cup back in the cup holder.

He threaded his fingers through hers and, with their arms propped on the arms of the chairs, it would be obvious to anybody who looked they were holding hands.

Right now the focus was still on Kevin. "Then it takes him fifteen minutes of crawling around to get the winch hooked on without him getting wet. So he gives me the thumbs-up and—"

"That wasn't a thumbs-up," Mike interjected. "I whacked my hand and was flexing my fingers."

Joe's thumb was making little circles in the palm of Keri's hand at that moment, making it a little hard to concentrate on the story.

"So I started winching him in," Kevin said, "but he wasn't ready and we didn't know there was a log under the ice. The front of his machine comes up and Mike goes flying off the back. *Splash!*"

They were still laughing when the rain started falling—big, fat drops that signaled a downpour was imminent.

Joe used the hand he'd been holding to haul Keri

out of her chair as everybody yelled good-nights and began to scatter. Terry and Lisa dragged most of the chairs under the tarps, and Keri rescued her hot chocolate seconds before Joe tossed the others onto the pile.

Even though they moved at an almost-jog, they were soaked by the time they reached their site. Keri laughed as the sky really opened up when they still had the last ten feet to the cabin yet to cover.

When was the last time she'd ventured out in the rain without an umbrella? Years. She gave too much of her income to the salon to let Mother Nature ruin their hard work.

Joe held open the screen door and Keri went in first, stepping to one side to let him in. They both stood dripping on the hardwood floor, neither apparently willing to step onto the braided rug. Water dripped from her hair and ran down her face, and she shivered. Now that the fun of running through the rain was over, she was uncomfortably aware of her jeans and flannel shirt plastered to her skin.

"We should get naked and huddle together to preserve our body heat," Joe said. "Don't wanna die of hypothermia."

"Or I could change into my pajamas, crawl under the covers and finish my hot chocolate."

"Nudity and friction's a lot more effective. I read it in a book."

He was creeping closer, so she poked him with her elbow. "It was eighty degrees today."

He heaved an exaggerated sigh. "Saw you shiver. Was worth a shot."

"Might have worked if I was actually hypothermic and we weren't in a cabin."

He kicked off his sneakers before grabbing a beach towel from the back of a chair and tossing it to her. Then he gathered the bottom of his sweatshirt and the T-shirt under it, and yanked them both up and over his head.

The wet fabric hung up on his head, though, giving Keri plenty of time to admire his naked torso. His muscles flexed as he twisted, pulling at the sweatshirt, and there was no farmer's tan to be seen. An evenly bronzed expanse of skin meant he spent more than a little time running around outside shirtless. Lucky neighbors.

When he finally got the tops off and started unzipping the bottom, Keri turned her back and buried her head in the towel before he could catch her ogling his abs…or his glutes.

After giving her hair a good scrubbing, she emerged from the towel just in time to see him bend over and rummage through his duffel bag. The hot flash cut through the chill, but it left a shiver in its wake.

Black boxer briefs should be illegal. And didn't the man own any other, less flattering colors? Puce? Periwinkle? Even a plain old pair of tighty-whities didn't look good from that angle.

But Joe's ass and black boxer briefs equaled a

warm flush she was surprised didn't steam the rain-water right out of her flannel.

Much to her disappointment, he found the old University of New Hampshire sweatpants he'd been digging around for and slipped them on. Then she got to watch the muscles in his back one more time as he pulled a dry T-shirt over his head.

When he turned around, she tried to look as if she hadn't been staring, but probably didn't do a very convincing job.

"You gonna stand around all night in wet clothes?" he asked.

"How much time do you spend at the gym?" The question popped out of her mouth before she realized how much that would give away.

He shrugged. "I have a gym at home. Not a very hardball question, ace."

When she realized what he meant, she threw the towel at him. "That wasn't my interview question and you know it."

"Sounded like a question."

"A conversational question, not a professional one. You're trying to weasel your way around your own rules."

He flashed his dimples at her. "Guilty."

The dampness of her clothing was growing more uncomfortable by the second, but she had no doubt Joe was going to be an ass about her changing her clothes.

"I suppose you want me to turn around," he said, as though he'd read her mind.

"I don't trust you."

"Sorry, babe, but I'm not gonna go stand out in the rain while you change." Then the bastard sat in one of the straight-back chairs, stretched his legs out and folded his arms as though he intended to watch a show.

Two could play at the game of hot flashes and achy places one didn't mention in polite company.

She very slowly undid the top two buttons of the flannel shirt. When his body tensed and his gaze zeroed in on the third button, Keri almost smiled.

"My question for tonight…" she mused, tapping her fingernail on the button a couple of times before sliding it free of the hole and then the next. "Is the whole reclusive author thing just a long-term publicity stunt?"

"Huh?" was all Joe said as she slipped the flannel off her shoulders to reveal a T-shirt damp enough to show off a hint of the black lace underneath.

What the hell was she doing? She wasn't eighteen anymore and she sure as hell didn't look like she was. She wasn't the one with a home gym, either, which wasn't so much of an issue if she kept her clothes on.

But Joe was a breast man and hers still filled out the very expensive black bras she liked to splurge on once in a while.

"What I mean—" she slowly pulled the T-shirt free from the waist of her jeans "—is have you engineered interest in your books by being a mystery man?"

She slipped the damp T-shirt over her head and tossed it onto his pile of wet clothes. Joe made an incoherent sound she didn't think was his official answer.

She started tugging at the button of her jeans, then paused. "For instance, there are people who think the myth of J. D. Salinger was far more interesting than any of his work and if he hadn't been a famous recluse, his books would have faded into obscurity."

Just as Joe opened his mouth, as though to respond, Keri popped the button, dragged the zipper down and started shimmying the jeans over her hips.

His Adam's apple wasn't the only thing bobbing, in spite of the restraint of boxer briefs and sweatpants.

After kicking her pants off to the side, Keri walked to her bags and presented Joe with the same view he'd given her, taking her sweet time rummaging through her clothes. "In other words, would you be just another midlister if you didn't make people want to know more about Joseph Kowalski?"

After snagging her favorite pair of yoga pants, she straightened and turned, only to find herself nose-to-wings with his Aerosmith T-shirt.

"Quite the interview technique you've got, Daniels."

She'd have to look up to see his face, but she didn't dare tip her head back while in the close-enough-to-kiss zone. If that happened, while he was sporting quite the impressive erection and she was wearing nothing but a couple scraps of black lace, who knew where they'd end up.

"Does it usually work for you?" He crowded her a little more.

She really wanted to throw some witty rejoinder his way, but her brain was stuttering, stuck on *want*. "Depends on how many slices of Hawaiian pizza I've had, I guess."

When his hands rested on her hips for a second before sliding their way up her sides, Keri closed her eyes and dug deep for some resolve. Dug deep, and kept on digging.

"You've got nothing to worry about there, babe." Fortunately—she guessed—his hands went back to her hips rather than moving around to cup her breasts. That would really play hell on the resolve she was still digging for.

"Flattery won't get you out of answering the question," she told him.

"And your ass, sweet as it is, won't distract me from noticing how insulting your question was."

"I prefer *probative*."

His fingertips were ever so slowly sneaking their way under the elastic at her waist. "Speaking of probing…"

Keri laughed and darted to the left, taking her yoga pants with her. "Oh, no you don't."

"What?" His expression was all innocence. "We're talking about questions."

"With your hands down my pants?"

"Helps me think."

It took a few awkward, sideways hops that drew his attention right back to her breasts, but she managed to pull on the yoga pants. Rather than try to get past him again for a T-shirt, she grabbed her hoodie from the hook by the door and pulled it on over her bra.

"We talked about this already," she told him from out of arm's reach. "We are *not* having sex."

He heaved an exaggerated sigh. "I was hoping the striptease meant you'd changed your mind."

"If it was a striptease, I would have borrowed a pole from Kevin's tent."

"I'd pay to see that. I'd pay *a lot* to see that."

"I already have a job. I ask questions, you answer them, and my scary boss pays me."

"Then I get to ask *you* a question."

Keri rolled her eyes. "I haven't forgotten your stupid rules. But you haven't answered my question yet."

"No, my desire for privacy isn't some elaborate publicity stunt. I think the only person on the planet who actually gives a damn about my not doing book tours or interviews is your boss, who I totally believe would stalk me in person if she lived close enough."

She couldn't deny that. "So why such a recluse?"

For the first time real annoyance clouded his features. "I'm not a goddamn recluse. I do my job, which is to write books. Most readers could give a shit less about me as long as my books continue to scare the crap out of them."

"Most authors try to build a relationship with their readers."

"My words are my relationship with them. We do virtual signings for charity and I answer legitimate emails from real readers. They're not entitled to any more of my personal life than that."

"Tina thinks your disappearance from the public eye has to do with the emotional distress suit you settled with Lauren Huckins."

If she was trying to douse the flames flickering between them, she couldn't have found a better glass of ice water. His eyes hardened and his mouth formed a grim, dimple-free line.

"Your question for the day's been asked and answered," he said. "And you were already informed Lauren's not on the table for discussion."

Keri bit back the curses on the tip of her tongue. She was better than this and hadn't had a subject so completely close up on her since her rookie years.

Before she could wrap her mind around the best way to salvage the situation, Joe pulled a dry sweatshirt over his head, shoved his feet into his sneakers and went out the door. It slammed closed with a resounding bang.

"Well, *hell,*" she said to the empty cabin.

CHAPTER EIGHT

JOE PULLED THE HOOD of his sweatshirt over his head and set off in the rain with no destination in mind.

He was pretty sure he was being an ass, though he wasn't positive. Sure, her question had been a little insulting and she'd tread dangerously close to the verboten subject of Lauren. But he'd known when he'd invited—or blackmailed—her that digging around in people's dirty laundry was not only what she did, but that she was good at it.

No matter how good she looked in skimpy black lace—and holy morning wood, did she look good in skimpy black lace—Keri was there to do a job, and that job was to find skeletons in his closet. Getting pissed off when she did the thing she'd told him right up front she was there to do probably made him an ass.

He paused at the junction of dirt roads, pondering a direction. With the rain still falling at a steady clip, nobody was out and about so he'd have to knock on somebody's door if he wanted company.

Kevin's tent wasn't big enough for both of them unless they spooned. His parents were probably already snoring in their matching rocking recliners. In the mood he was already in, it was probably a good idea to avoid Terry, Mike and Lisa.

Damn. With no place to go, he just shoved his hands in his sweatshirt's kangaroo pocket and stood there.

"It's raining."

He hadn't heard Keri come up behind him, but she was next to him now, rain dripping off the bill of the baseball cap she'd donned. "At this rate, we're going to run out of dry clothes."

"May as well take a walk now that we're already soaked."

"Okay." He headed off to the right, but he didn't take her hand in his as he had earlier.

"I'm sorry I mentioned Lauren," she said after a minute or two of uncomfortable silence. "I kind of segued from my question to conversation without a clear stop and start point."

"Just doing your job."

"Yes and no. Yes, I have professional obligations but, no, not everything I ask you is for *Spotlight Magazine*. It's just…I've never interviewed somebody I have a personal relationship with before. It's awkward."

"And I've never been interviewed by an ex-girlfriend a few black scraps away from naked before." Even in the dark, he could tell she was flustered.

"I only did that because you did it to me," she said. "Parade around almost naked, I mean. I wanted to…"

"Wanted to what?" he prompted when she let the statement die off.

She said the words all in a rush. "I wanted to see if it would affect you the same way it affected me."

They had just turned the corner into a dark, secluded part of the campground, so hopefully nobody would notice his suddenly bowlegged walk. "If it made you want me to bend you over the end of the bed, then, yeah."

"That would be about the same, then." He could hear her reluctance to admit it. "We talked about this. It's not a good idea."

"Just so you know, I imagined you naked all through that conversation."

"I'm serious, Joe."

"So am I."

When she stopped walking, he looked back to see her standing with her arms folded, glaring at him. He grinned and walked back to her. "Sorry, babe. Truth, though."

"Do you see how our past history already screws with how I do my job? Imagine how it would be if we had sex in the present day."

"Oh, I do. A lot. Every five minutes or so."

"I meant, imagine how blurred the line between personal and professional would become if we start sleeping together. I'm not sure I could finish the article." Which meant she'd lose her job—a good job she'd worked hard for.

"Is there a definitive place your objectivity starts slipping? Kissing? Can we make out a little?"

"If we start making out a little, we won't stop."

"Probably not." He stepped closer and lifted her chin with his fingertips.

She didn't stop him, so he lowered his mouth to hers, capturing a raindrop on her lip with the tip of his tongue before going in for the kiss.

Because he already knew it wasn't leading to anything but a restless night, he kept it short and sweet. Or he meant to, but Keri wrapped her arms around his neck and her ball cap came off and the kiss didn't end until they had to catch their breath.

He blew out a breath and wiped some rain off his face. "How's your objectivity holding up?"

"It's a little…warm and tingly."

"We should go back before we drown out here." Back to the cabin where they'd have to change out of their wet clothes…again. He wasn't sure he could survive another glimpse of the black lace.

"Yeah, and you still get to ask me a question," she reminded him with a wry smile.

If he opened his mouth, the questions would roll off his tongue. Had she ever regretted leaving him behind? If he crawled into bed with her, would she shut him down? If not, would she hate him in the morning?

"You're not going to ask me if I ever faked an orgasm with you?" she teased.

Oh, hell no. He didn't even want to open that door. He hadn't exactly been a smooth operator their first few times around that block. "I'm saving that question for a night I can't think of a better one."

Her smile gleamed through the darkness. "Chicken."

Absolutely. "Okay, here's a question. You had any work done?"

"Oh, you mean like Mike had done on his truck at the body shop?"

"Heard about that conversation, did you?"

"Yeah, Bobby filled me in."

"Tact and discretion aren't a part of that kid's playbook yet."

"I've discovered that. And no, I've had no work done. Everything's still one hundred percent me."

"It's customary to offer a squeeze to determine if breasts are real or not, you know. Don't you watch TV?"

She laughed and shoved the retrieved ball cap back on her head. "Nice try, Kowalski. You'll have to take my word for it."

It was worth a shot. "Since we're out, let's hit the bathhouse. And when we get back, I expect you to behave like a lady and turn your back while I change."

She laughed, as he'd expected, and the tension was broken. The tension between them, anyway. The tension inside of him would only build with every passing minute he didn't allow himself to coax her into throwing her professional ethics to the wind and getting naked and sweaty with him.

Once that happened, she'd be upset with herself and upset with him and things would get really awkward between them. In the meantime, he'd just have to continue being extremely careful when zipping his fly.

THE SUN SNEAKING THROUGH the cracks in her curtains and poking at Terry's eyelids made her mumble an exceptionally bad word and yank the blanket up over her head.

Sometime during the night it had stopped raining, and that meant her excuse to take refuge in her camper, pretending to read a book, was shot. The family would descend on breakfast like a plague of locusts, devouring everything in sight, before heading out on the trails. Overnight rain meant no dust and big puddles—great riding conditions—which was cause for amped-up energy levels. Terry didn't have any more energy to give.

Tears welled up in her eyes and spilled onto her pillow, just as they had every morning she'd woken up alone.

She'd tried to convince herself she'd be okay. Rebelliously sleeping diagonally across the center of the bed, just because she could. A frilly pink bed-in-a-bag set she didn't even like, but put on the bed anyway, just because she could.

Sometimes it worked well enough that she didn't cry herself to sleep, but every morning when the time came to face the day alone, at least a few tears came. She'd even had to retreat to her bedroom a few times since they'd arrived, when being surrounded by happy—or at least not broken-up—families was too much.

"You smell like dirty, wet dog butt!"

And her nephews were awake.

It was time to wash her face and brush her teeth

so the fake smile she plastered on would be minty fresh. It was a role she'd gotten pretty good at acting out over the past three months—that of a middle-age woman who was handling the demise of her marriage with dignity and strength.

Nobody had seen her lying on the cold tile of her bathroom floor after crying so long and so hard she'd been sick. Nobody knew she'd had to pull her car over on the way to the grocery store when the thought occurred to her that Evan needed deodorant, followed by the fresh realization it wasn't her problem anymore. He would have to buy his own because he'd left her.

"Oh, yeah? Well, you smell like sweaty balls!"

"Robert Joseph Kowalski!"

Terry sighed and mopped at her tears with a corner of her blanket. Time to get up and face being one more day closer to calling a divorce lawyer.

When she finally emerged from the camper, it was to find the locusts in full plague and her mother giving her the all-knowing, maternal once-over. She'd have to avoid being caught alone with the woman, because she didn't have it in her today to discuss any possibility of reconciliation with Evan.

She couldn't say the words out loud. *He just doesn't love me anymore and I can't make him.*

The familiar routine of feeding a horde of Kowalskis helped restore her equilibrium somewhat, but she was aware of a growing desire to slap Keri Daniels upside the head with the pancake skillet.

She thought she'd made peace with the woman,

but watching her chat with Kevin and Joe so easily, their conversation punctuated with carefree laughter, was slowly killing her inside.

Of course Keri was fun. The woman had no responsibilities other than taking care of her own damn self. She didn't even own a pet.

They wouldn't find her so easy to kick back with if she had to nag them about dirty laundry and full trash bags and a garage so stuffed with junk she couldn't park her car in it. Terry would be fun, too, if she didn't have to run a household and do her job and stay on top of Stephanie's goings-on and everything else that needed doing in the course of a single day.

"Setting somebody on fire with your eyeballs only works in the movies, Theresa," her mother said.

Terry looked around, only to find herself stranded at the coffeemaker alone with her mother. Lisa was at the picnic table with the boys, fixing their plates, and everybody else was eating. *Crap.*

"I don't know what you're talking about, Ma."

"Don't lie to me, girl. I see how you're looking at her and it's not fair. She's not the reason you're unhappy. That's your own stubbornness."

Was it a generational thing? "I didn't leave him. He left me, so why do you keep blaming me for it?"

"I'm not blaming you. I'm disappointed that you won't try to talk to him about it. Whatever's wrong can be fixed."

"I can't…make him love me, Ma." The hitch in her chest made her voice break and she focused on spooning sugar into her coffee so she didn't totally break down.

"You just need to—"

"Stop." Terry dropped the spoon with a clatter as her hands balled into fists. "I can't do this here, Ma. Do you want me to fall apart in front of everybody? Do you want my daughter, who's barely getting through this herself, to see me turn into a blubbering mess?"

"Of course not, honey, it's just that—"

She walked away. It was all she could do. She walked around Mike and Lisa's camper and straight to her own. She locked the door, sank down on the floor and cried.

JOE WASN'T SURE EXACTLY what was going on, but he did his part to make sure the kids were too distracted to notice something was amiss with the adult crowd. Even Keri had jumped in, offering up a Hollywood story that had Steph so engrossed she didn't notice her mother was AWOL.

It took him a few minutes, but he finally managed to corner his mother alone. "What happened, Ma?"

"She refuses to even consider working things out with Evan. Sometimes marriage is hard and you have to work at it, but they're not supposed to be disposable."

"You need to leave her alone about it. She's got that to go home to, so she doesn't need it thrown in her face the whole time she's on vacation."

"Watch your tone, Joseph. I'm still the mother in

this family, even if none of my rotten children think I know anything about life." She folded her arms and gave him the same stubborn look she complained about in her daughter. "She's unhappy and you know how she is. She's going to make somebody else unhappy, too, and it's not fair that she's going to take out her temper on Keri."

He shrugged, raising his hands in a *whaddya gonna do* gesture. "Keri can take care of herself. If there's one thing I know about her and Terry, it's not to get in the middle of them. If she gets sick of Terry's shi…attitude, she'll let her know. As for Evan, they'll talk when they're ready."

"It's been three months already." A shimmer of tears gleamed in his mother's eyes. "The longer it goes on, the harder it will be for them to work things out."

"You can't force it. All you're doing is making Terry more unhappy, and all the pushing in the world won't make her do something she's not ready to do."

"You're stubborn like that, too," she said, slapping his arm. "All of you. You get it from your father."

Joe grinned and wrapped his mother in a hug. "Just leave her be for a while, okay?"

After she nodded, albeit reluctantly and with a dramatic sigh, Joe wandered back to the action. The younger boys were dragging everybody's gear out of the bins, while the older two were, under Kevin's supervision, starting everybody's machines and lining them up.

"You guys don't even let breakfast settle, do you?" Keri asked from right behind him.

He turned, and then smiled at the sour expression on her face. "Daylight's wasting."

"You're all sick, sick people."

"Are you riding with me today or going solo?" Oh please, he thought, let her be in the mood to ride her own machine. If one scorching kiss in the rain was enough to keep him awake for hours, mentally re-writing the ending of that episode, another day spent with her thighs hugging his ass would kill him.

"I'm going to ride my own. Since your parents are going, I shouldn't be…what did you call it? LFD?"

He chuckled. "I'd never leave you for dead, babe."

During the course of sorting thirteen helmets and goggles and twenty-six gloves, Terry rejoined the group. She was putting on one helluva show, but Joe was sure even somebody who wasn't her twin could see she was acting.

She looked fragile. Brittle, even.

But she geared up with the rest of the family and they set off. After a lot of discussion, they decided to put Keri in line behind Terry because their machines were of a similar size. That way, Keri could watch her and take the same path. Joe would ride behind Keri, which meant, since her ATV didn't have a pas-senger seat or cargo bag mounted on the rear rack, that he had an unobstructed view of her ass.

He enjoyed—and suffered—that choice bit of scenery for almost six miles before it all went to shit.

Terry drove into a sloppy, muddy-looking puddle

and, instead of sticking toward the edges, she drove deep into the center. And high-sided herself. Hidden by the soup, a rock or a hard-packed mound of mud had hung up her ATV, lifting the wheels just enough to rob them of traction. She wasn't getting loose without help.

He'd pulled up too close to Keri's machine, so he couldn't get around her unless she moved forward.

"Come give me a push," Terry yelled over her shoulder and his stomach knotted up when he realized she was talking to Keri. Not gonna end well.

Before he could get her attention, Keri drove into the puddle.

Joe panicked, knowing he had maybe thirty seconds to choose between Keri and his sister. On the one hand, keeping his mouth shut wasn't going to endear him any to the woman he was trying like hell to endear into his bed. On the other hand, she was going back to L.A. soon and Terry, who could be mean as a rabid wolverine, would still live two blocks from him.

Besides, Terry and Keri had called a truce… hadn't they?

Keri tentatively drove her ATV through the slop. The kids had all pulled up behind Joe, followed by Lisa and then Mike, and they all jumped off to watch the show.

"Keep coming," Terry instructed. "Just bump into the back of mine and knock me loose."

When Keri was a few feet behind her, Joe had a

change of heart and opened his mouth, but it was too late.

Terry held the front brake and punched the throttle, causing the rear wheels to spin like crazy. Pluming up behind her came a massive, brown rooster tail of soupy muck, perfectly timed to douse Keri.

"Say cheese!" Bobby screeched.

"Oh, *shit*," the three adults not in the middle of the muddle puddle said.

CHAPTER NINE

THE SHOCK TOOK KERI'S BREATH away long enough
to keep her from screaming like a little girl, but it
took her mind a few seconds to catch up and realize
she'd just been practically drowned in a waterfall of
muddy water. *Cold* muddy water.

It dripped off her helmet visor and plastered her
riding jersey to her skin. She couldn't see through
her goggles and she raised her hand to wipe her
mouth only to find her glove saturated, too.

She peeled it off to wipe the grit from her mouth
and then yanked her goggles off. Terry was laughing.

She could hear the cacophony of Kowalski kids
behind her, and through her peripheral vision she
could see Bobby jumping up and down with his
camera. Great. One for the family scrapbook.

"What the hell, Terry?" Joe bellowed, and his reaction made one thing clear—Terry had showered
her in muddy water on purpose. That bitch.

So much for their tenuous peace. Daring a look
over her shoulder, she saw most of her audience
enjoying various degrees of amusement, but Joe
looked mad.

When he noticed her looking at him, he waved his hand. "Put it in Reverse and back out."

She'd back out, all right. Out of the mud and through the woods and back to the campground she'd go. Then she'd load up the rental car and drive straight to the airport. By nightfall she could be back in Los Angeles, where she belonged.

A facial. A massage. Real chai. No fucking crazy-ass people making her life miserable for their own amusement.

By the time she got her machine backed out of the slop, the mob had quieted a little and she could see amusement gathering at the corners of Joe's mouth. "This is *not* funny."

Despite his best efforts, his dimples made an appearance. "Sorry, babe, but it kinda is. Think of it as a rite of passage. A christening."

"I think of it as your sister being a vindictive bitch."

"That, too. Pull off to the side so I can get around you."

She had to pull way over to the side because Joe's four-wheeler was a lot bigger than hers, with huge, deep-treaded tires. Then he was able to pass her and head into the puddle.

"Be nice, Joe!" Terry had turned around, watching his approach, and Keri was gratified to see she wasn't laughing anymore.

There were disappointed sound effects from the crowd when Joe crept up behind Terry, nicely lined his front bumper up with her machine and pushed, knocking it loose. She started forward and Keri sulked, wiping more mud off her face.

Suddenly, Mary shouted, "Joseph Michael Kowalski, don't you—"

The rest of whatever she had to say was drowned out by the roar of Joe's ATV as he pegged the throttle and threw his body sideways, yanking the machine into a circle. The aggressive tires churned up, not just a plume, but a tidal wave of mud from the bottom of the puddle. It all washed over Terry with a splat Keri wished she could hear. She did hear Terry's screech of outrage, though. Probably everybody in the northern part of the state did.

A roar of approval rose from the crowd, but it choked off pretty quickly when Terry jumped off her ATV and turned to give the look of death to her twin brother. Keri didn't even try to hide her enjoyment and when Danny put up his hand, she gave him an enthusiastic high-five.

"You jerk," Terry screamed over her shoulder.

"Payback's a bitch, ain't it?"

And Keri had no doubt the payback wasn't over yet. No question Terry would blame her for this, even though Joe had done the deed, and at some point find a way to exact revenge.

Totally worth it, though, to see her former best friend looking as though she'd been dipped in year-old chocolate.

"That is enough," Mary declared over the din, and that was the end of that.

By the time they got the rest of the family around

or through the puddle, Kevin had turned back to see
what the holdup was. He glanced between Terry and
Keri and laughed. "Mud wrestling? If one of you
wasn't my sister, this would be a wonderful thing."

"Shut up," they said in unison.

Joe's ATV had aftermarket mirrors mounted on it,
and Keri made the mistake of taking a peek. Except
for the void left by the goggles, her entire face was
speckled with bits of mud and everything from the
helmet's chinstrap down was plain nasty. Then Lisa
insisted on showing her the same scene, only this
time on the viewing screen of her digital camera.

Keri barely recognized herself. Tina certainly
wouldn't have recognized her, and neither would
anybody else she knew in California.

Joe stepped up close and asked in a low voice,
"You okay, babe?"

"Do I look okay? Really? I'm covered in shit, my
face is filthy. Look at my fingernails, Joe. Do I look
okay to you?"

"So, you'll take a shower when we get back. No
big deal."

"No big deal. Do you have any idea how much I
spend on facials and manicures? It's a *very* big deal,
thank you very much. This isn't me. None of this is
me."

"I think you look cute with mud on your face."

She snorted. "Of course you do."

"I'd even kiss you with mud on your face."

"Don't you dare." She poked him in the chest.

"You are not kissing me in front of your family again."

"Later?"

"How did we segue from my crisis to you worrying about whether you'll get any action later?"

"Dirty face. Dirty thoughts. I'm a guy—it all ties together pretty naturally for me."

She slapped her gloves together, trying without much success to knock some of the wet mud off. "When I get back to L.A., the first thing I'm going to do is have every pore in my body steam-cleaned. And it'll be a long damn time before I schedule another mud bath."

"Bet you can't wait to get home," he said, and she looked up from her gloves at the tightness in his voice. His eyes weren't sparkling with amusement now.

Why? Because she was talking about Los Angeles? Because she'd mentioned going home? She'd made it very clear she didn't even want to come back to New Hampshire to see him, never mind stay.

"I can't leave until I've asked all my questions," she pointed out, purposely keeping her tone on the playful side. "I don't give up that easy."

"Neither do I." She wasn't sure exactly what he meant by that and she didn't have the guts to ask.

TERRY WAS STUCK. She'd ducked into Mike and Lisa's pop-up camper to drop off some clothes belonging to Joey and Danny that Lisa had left in the dryer behind the bathhouse, and almost as soon as she'd closed the door behind her, Mike and Lisa had returned to their site.

Arguing.

Indecision had kept her quiet just long enough so making her presence inside the camper known would be awkward and embarrassing, and now she had to sit on the cushioned bench until her brother and his wife wrapped it up.

"Michael, all I said was that I could use a little help picking up after the boys before you go anywhere."

"No, you had to get snide and tell everybody it must be nice to be me and be able to run around with the guys while my wife did all the work."

Terry sighed and very, very slowly, so as not to make the camper shift, she leaned over and rested her head on the end of the bunk. Hopefully somebody else would show up and break up the spat soon, because this was an issue without resolution. She should know. She and Evan had fought that fight more than once when Stephanie was a baby, and they'd only had one kid.

"I wasn't lying, was I?"

"If you're so goddamned unhappy about the kids leaving their stuff laying around, why the hell do you keep talking about having another one?"

Oh, crap. Now she could listen to her sister-in-law feed her husband more bullshit pie about wanting a baby girl. If only she'd spoken up as soon as she'd heard their voices, she could be long gone.

"I don't even know why I bring up babies, since

making them actually requires having sex once in a while."

Oh, ouch. Terry tried to tune them out by thinking about something else. Anything else.

After she put the boys' laundry away, she'd planned to take a walk up to the cabin. Now that everybody had made good use of the showers, she wanted to see if Keri was over being pissed off yet. Terry had no desire to walk on eggshells when Joe was around, too. Way too much conflict for a vacation.

Apparently Mike agreed. "I didn't come all the way up here to spend two weeks fighting with you, Lisa. And I'm sorry about the sex thing, but every time I think about it lately, I think about starting all over again with another baby."

"Forget it. I don't want to fight, either. I have to go get laundry out of the dryer. Go…hang out with Kevin or something."

"Do you need help carrying the laundry down?"

Say yes, Terry thought. She knew it was Mike's way of trying to ease the tension between them. It was an olive branch, puny though it was.

"No, I've got it."

"Okay. Well…I'll be back in a while, then."

Terry lifted her head and peeked out, able to watch them both walk away. When they were out of sight, she hopped out of the pop-up and went back to her RV. She needed a drink before she went to scope out the drama situation at the cabin.

Stephanie was stretched out on the couch, watch-

ing a movie Terry knew she'd already seen at least a
dozen times. She didn't even look up when the door
opened.

"We didn't come up here to sit around and watch
TV, Steph. It's not raining and it's not cold, so you
should be outside."

"Doing what?"

Good question. "Go for a walk or something. Go
see what the—"

"Boys are doing? No thanks."

Terry sighed and resisted the urge to beat her head
against the doorjamb. The rules were pretty clear—
the television was supposed to be off unless it was
raining, after dark, or too chilly to play on the playground.

But what, exactly, was there to do on the playground? Swing? She wasn't a little girl anymore. She
was entering those in-between years when she was
too old to play with the kids, but not old enough to
enjoy the simple pleasure of sitting in a chair doing
absolutely nothing.

Last year, she'd run with the boys, playing dodge-
ball and tetherball, hunting for frogs by the pond
and exploring the woods. But now, whether it was
her age or her gender or her general attitude about
life, she was keeping herself separate. Fight it or let
it go?

"I'm going to walk up and see Uncle Joe. You
wanna go?"

"Not really. You're just going to be mean to Keri,
anyway."

"That's not fair. If it had been anybody but me who did it to anybody but Keri, everybody would have thought it was hilarious. But because I did it to her, everybody assumes I was being a b...mean."

"Are you and Dad getting divorced?"

"Steph." Conversational whiplash. And how much family crap did one woman have to deal with in a day? "We've been separated three months. You're old enough to figure out that probably means we're going to talk about divorce."

"When?"

"Probably when we get back. There's no sense in putting it off much longer."

The combination of little girl tears in eyes that looked just like Evan's was like a punch to Terry's gut. She went to the fridge and grabbed a bottle of water, then popped a couple of aspirin while she was thinking of it. The way the day was going, a stress headache was almost inevitable. Might as well deal with the tightness in her neck and shoulders before the pain hit.

"I know I'm breaking the rules, Mom, but I don't really wanna hang out with anybody right now."

It was the plea for understanding in her daughter's voice—free of any teenage attitude—that broke her. So what if she spent the day watching TV? She was on vacation, too, and it's not like the rest of the family was exactly a barrel of laughs at the moment.

She bent down and kissed Steph's forehead. "It's okay, sweetie. I'm going to head up to the cabin for a while, okay?"

"Okay. Be nice to Keri, though."

Terry ignored that last bit and stepped outside, only to run into Lisa. "Hey. Whatcha up to?"

"Did you grab the laundry out of the dryer?"

"Yeah, a while ago." She felt bad making it sound like a longer while than it really had been. "It looked like Joey and Danny's, so I stuck it in the pop-up."

"Oh, thanks. I thought I was going crazy. Then I was afraid somebody took it, but I can't imagine anybody who'd want underwear my boys wore, freshly washed or not."

"I'm heading up to the cabin. Wanna take a walk?"

"I think I've had enough of Kowalski men right now. Where's Steph?"

"She's watching a movie. She's not feeling very sociable today, so I'm letting it slide. Everything okay?" she asked, even though she knew it wasn't.

"Sure," Lisa replied in a very fake voice with a very fake smile. "I think I'm going to get my book and sit in the shade for a while. Pop's got the boys fishing at the pond, so I might have a few minutes of peace."

"I'll be back in a while, then, and we can start figuring out supper."

"Sounds good. Oh, and be nice to Keri, okay?"

Jeez, what was with people today?

KERI WAS STRETCHED OUT on Joe's bed, watching him tap away on his laptop. She was trying to leave him alone—she'd even spent a few minutes working herself—but boredom was setting in.

The short-lived attempt at working had only served to depress her. Every time she looked at the questions and answers so far and tried to work them into a compelling—or at least mildly interesting— article, it became increasingly obvious the hard-hitting journalist inside her was enjoying the vacation, while only the fluff writer she'd once been was showing up for work.

Wouldn't it be a kick in the ass to go through the Kowalski version of hell week times two, only to end up turning in a puff piece that got her fired anyway?

"What happened to Kevin?" she asked when she couldn't stand the silence anymore. Even though she couldn't use the information in her article, maybe she could fake her muse into thinking they were ac-tually working. "To make him leave the police de-partment, I mean."

Joe clicked, presumably on the save button, and turned to look at her. "You know Kev. Perfect guy to run a sports bar, don't you think?"

He was hiding something. Something big if her gut was right, and it almost always was. "Off the record, Joe. Besides the fact I agreed to your stupid rules, you know me well enough to know I'd never deliberately hurt your family."

"People change a lot in twenty years, babe."

"Bullshit. You never would have let me come here if you didn't trust me to respect their privacy."

He grinned at her, his dimples flashing. "Got me there."

"It's just natural curiosity about the people I'm hanging out with. Nothing more sinister than that. And I haven't said anything to Terry about her husband, even when she was being bitchy, have I?"

"Fine, but if you even look at Kevin with pity in your eyes, he'll know I told you. And he never even told me the whole story. I've got a friend who works for the Boston P.D. and he filled me in on a lot of it."

"Jesus, Joe, do you want me to sign a confidentiality agreement?"

"Okay, fine. Kevin worked his ass off for the department, but never got ahead. Always got the shitty shifts in bad neighborhoods. He forgot something one day and stopped at home. Found out his captain had been banging his wife for God knows how long. Kev beat the holy fuck out of him."

"Oh my God," Keri breathed. "Did they arrest him?"

"The captain's married to the daughter of a political heavy hitter, so he was publicity shy, to say the least. Kevin left the department and filed for divorce. That was the end of it."

"Poor guy."

"No sympathy! I mean it, Keri. Just leave it alone."

They heard the footsteps on the porch before the knock on the door, and Keri sighed and flopped back on the pillow. Knowing his family, her boredom—

otherwise known as peace and quiet—was about to come to an end.

"It's open," Joe called, and Keri rolled her eyes when Terry entered. "Hey, sis."

"Hey. Not much happening, so I thought I'd wander over and see what's going on. You working?"

"A little bit," he said, causing Keri to feel a pang of guilt.

He'd be getting a lot more work done if she'd gone wandering for something else to do, rather than asking nosy questions about his family. But what was she supposed to do? She didn't fish—not even the catch-and-release kind—and, the last time she'd walked to the bathroom, she hadn't seen Stephanie anywhere, so hanging with her was out. Lisa had been in the big RV with Mary, and Keri certainly wasn't about to seek out Terry. Though it seemed Terry had found her anyway.

"Sorry about the whole roosting thing," Terry said to her. "It was just too good a shot to pass up."

Since it had turned out Terry's laundry had been a lot more horrific than Keri's at the end of the day, Keri could afford to be magnanimous. "Looking back, it was actually kind of funny, even though Joe won't teach me how to do that."

The other woman smiled. "Hold your front brake and punch it."

"He won't tell me which one is the front brake."

Joe cleared his throat. "Not surprising, since I ride behind you."

"Well, I'm going to go visit Ma for a few minutes," Terry said, her hand on the door. "I just wanted to make sure there were no hard feelings."

"None," Keri assured her, and it was mostly true. She couldn't resist one last shot, though. "Joe said to think of it as a welcome-to-the-family kind of christening."

The lemon-sucking face ruined the fake smile Terry offered up before going out the door and letting it slam behind her.

Joe laughed. "You said that just to piss her off."

"I was going for mildly annoyed, but pissed works just as well."

When he stood and stretched, reaching up over his head and twisting his back, Keri looked away. The correlation between the hot flashes and Joe's muscles flexing was too coincidental to ignore, and she was going to have to do a better job of not subjecting herself to the visual torture if she was going to make it through the time she had left without throwing herself at him.

"Mike and Kevin were talking about going for a ride in a while," he said. "You know, like just the guys. Would you be okay with that?"

"What's it costing you—or *us*—this time?"

When he lifted the hem of his T-shirt and scratched his stomach, she turned her attention to the urgent matter of freeing the bedspread of any trace of fuzz.

"Whaddya mean?" he asked.

"The last time you went out alone with your brothers, I almost got drowned in the pool and then got to go on a dinner date with your nephews. A dinner date involving pizza sauce *and* hot fudge, I might add."

"They were on their very best behavior," he pointed out.

Rather than admit she'd actually enjoyed that outing, she forged on. "Oh, and let's not leave out the s'mores. I've had a lot of gunk put in my hair over years of salon treatments, but never marshmallow."

He leaned his shoulder against the bunk bed frame and crossed his arms. "I wouldn't mind revisiting the hot fudge. Without the kids this time."

Damn him. She could feel the heat radiating across her face and neck, which meant he could see it. Well, two could play at that game. "With extra whipped cream?"

Score! She didn't miss the subtle little dance meant to ease the pressure on a growing erection trapped by zipped denim.

"You're killin' me, babe."

"And we're barely halfway there."

CHAPTER TEN

THE NEXT DAY, Terry found herself battling an overwhelming urge to talk to Keri about Evan. It annoyed the hell out of her, because a truce did not a BFF—as her daughter called them—make. And though the truce had more or less survived the mud incident intact, why the need to confide in a woman she wasn't sure she even liked?

She supposed there was a logical reason for it. It would be nice to have somebody to talk to who wasn't family. They'd been supportive, but they held back a little because Evan had been family a long time. Her brothers considered him a friend, and they were all keenly aware that, no matter what, he was Steph's father forever.

There was also the matter of them pulling their punches with her. Though they meant well, the other Kowalskis were more concerned about her feelings than with helping her see the issues in a clearer light. But there was a good chance somebody who didn't like her very much would be a little more honest.

But confide in Keri Daniels?

As luck would have it, a mere hour after deciding against sharing her personal life with her former best friend, Terry found herself alone with her.

It was hot, so Mike and Lisa had taken the kids, including Steph, to the pool. Joe was writing and Kevin had gone riding with a group of guys who'd arrived with a tent for the weekend. And her parents were in their RV, pretending to watch TV with their eyes closed.

By the time everybody had gone their separate ways and the clutter was cleared away, she and Keri were the only ones left.

"Did you ever get married?" Terry asked before she could change her mind or the other woman could come up with a good excuse to disappear.

Keri looked startled by the question, but she dropped into a camp chair. "No. I've been focused on my career, I guess."

Terry lit a fire starter and threw a couple of logs in the pit before pulling her own chair close. It was a little warm for a daytime fire, but it gave them both something to look at. "I went the other way and focused a little too much on my family, I guess."

"Is that what he said when he left?"

At least Keri got where Terry was heading with the conversation and didn't make her spell it out. "I was too busy mother-henning him to death to be fun and spontaneous."

Keri didn't make any sympathetic *poor you* noises or cluck her tongue. She snorted. "Unless you guys skipped the dating and engagement phases and went right for the till-death-do-us-part, he can't claim he didn't know what he was in for. You were born a mother hen."

"I was not."

"Remember the time you locked my Barbie in your bathroom so she couldn't leave Malibu Ken for G.I. Joe?"

"G.I. Joe was too violent for her. And I never would have relented if Pop hadn't had tacos for dinner."

"Or the time you held up our entire class on the way to the playground because my shoe was untied."

"You were clumsy and if you tripped, you were going to take us all down like dominoes."

Keri threw back her head and laughed, and Terry surprised herself by joining in. It felt good.

"Or the battle of the Christmas nutcrackers," Keri gasped between peals of laughter.

That had been extreme, even for her, Terry had to admit. Her mother had a staggering collection of wooden nutcracking soldiers she displayed all over the family room during the holiday season. If there was open shelf space on Thanksgiving Day, there was a nutcracker in it before the leftover turkey was gone. One year Terry got it into her head they should be arranged in a parade around the room by height. Soldiers were an orderly bunch, after all.

So had begun a two-week-long battle between seven-year-old Terry and her mother. Terry would line them up. Ma would mess them up. Even the threat of being on Santa's naughty list couldn't sway

Terry in her determination to keep the soldier nut-crackers in order.

Keri managed to stop laughing long enough to wipe the tears from her eyes. "I'll never forget when your mom called my mom, and from her reaction I thought somebody had died at your house. I still can't believe you superglued them down."

It was probably at least another five minutes before they sobered enough to continue their conversation, and Terry could practically feel the tension melting away. That's what she'd been missing in her life—a really good girlfriend who wasn't related to her by blood or marriage.

Not that Keri could really fit that role, even if she wasn't leaving soon, but she was a pretty decent temporary substitute.

"You know," Keri said when the last hiccup of laughter had passed, "he's probably just going through some kind of midlife crisis."

"I've heard that theory. And I think it's a cop-out, like PMS."

The fire was burning fully now, and Keri backed her chair up a few inches. "Let's play a game. I read all the glossy women's magazines, and I'm a total quiz whore. So tell me the five most frequent things you say to Steph."

Terry didn't see where this was going, but she didn't want to burst the camaraderie bubble. "Okay, let's see. I love you. Have a great day. Take your shoes off. Is your homework done? And…sweet dreams."

"Now tell me the five most frequent things you said to your husband. And be honest."

All Terry had to do was close her eyes and picture Evan, and the words rolled off her tongue. "Take off your shoes. Did you take the garbage out? Dinner's at five-thirty. The lawn needs to be mowed. And, how hard is it to unroll a sock?"

She dropped her face into her hands and sighed. "I wouldn't want to be married to me, either."

"Does he seem happier now? Is he seeing anybody?"

"He doesn't seem any happier when I talk to him, but I've been a little…bitchy. And if he was seeing anybody, I'd have heard about it. I think."

"You should go call him."

Terry laughed again. "I've barely said ten words to the man in three months and you think I should call him? Are you insane? What the hell would I say, even if he was home, which he's not because he's at work."

"Even better. When you get his machine just tell him you've been thinking about him and you miss him and you'd like to have coffee when you get home. Since he can't call you back, the anticipation will build until he's dying to see you."

"He left me, Keri. I don't know how I'm supposed to forgive him for that."

"People sometimes hurt the ones they love trying to protect themselves from being hurt. Love means second chances sometimes."

"Like Joe's giving you?"

All traces of amusement vanished from Keri's face. "My being here isn't about second chances. It's about doing my job, and we happen to be enjoying one another's company while I do."

"It really screwed him up when you left the first time."

"He told me. But it's not going to happen this time because he knows up front I'm leaving."

But Terry wasn't so sure. She could read her brother like nobody else, and he wasn't just killing time. He was ready to forgive, forget and pick up where they'd left off. To take a second chance and run with it. Well, dammit, if he could do it, so could she.

"I'm going to call him." Terry jumped out of her chair before she could change her mind. It wasn't as if Evan had been begging to come home. "But please don't tell anybody."

"Cross my heart and get no pie."

Terry froze. "Oh, God, I haven't heard that in years. I can't believe you remember that."

"I remember how much your mother hated hearing *hope to die,* so she didn't let us have any strawberry-rhubarb pie that night. That was worse than death and it rhymed, so it was good enough for us."

The moment of shared history cheered Terry as she walked to the campground store, careful to take the longer route so as not to be seen from the pool area. That was just asking to have requests for sodas, ice cream and candy bars shouted at her.

After dropping quarters into the pay phone, Terry

punched in her husband's new phone number and waited through four rings.

"Hi, this is Evan."

"And Steph on the weekends!" her daughter chimed in.

"Leave a message after the beep."

Beep.

"Hi, it's me. I...I just wanted to say I miss you."

Then she slammed down the receiver, heat burning up her neck into her face. What had she done?

AFTER SPENDING AN ENTIRE half hour crafting one spectacularly shitty paragraph, Joe saved the document and shut down his laptop.

He hadn't seen Keri in a while. Long enough, actually, that he was spending more time wondering what she was up to than wondering how his protagonist was supposed to deal with the fact a malevolent—and invisible—presence was trying to molest his wife.

Almost as disturbing as the fact his protagonist was screwed because the author had no idea what he should do, was spotting Terry and Keri sitting at a campfire, laughing like long-lost best friends. It was a little disconcerting because, unless they were rehashing childhood memories, the only thing they had in common was him. And they both had more than their fair share of amusing stories about him.

Rather than risk walking into a matinee of his more embarrassing moments, he veered away from them, looking for company. Kevin's ATV wasn't parked on his site, so he'd probably hit the trails with whomever he could find to go with him. From the sounds of it, the juvenile horde was at the pool, so he made his way down there, skirting the campground to stay out of sight of the two women he really hoped were mending old broken fences.

"Uncle Joe!" Bobby shouted, and Joe waved when they all turned to look. "Watch me!"

Joe leaned against the chain-link fence—as long as he didn't step inside the gate he wasn't fair game—and watched his nephew dive to the bottom of the pool and retrieve one of the glowing sticks Mike was tossing in.

"Awesome!" he yelled when Bobby surfaced, and the boy grinned before diving down again.

"Thought you were working." Mike walked over and leaned on the other side of the fence.

"Head's not in it right now."

"I can hear Terry and Keri laughing up there. Do I want to know what's going on?"

Joe shook his head. "I don't know. I gave them a wide berth."

"Better than being at each other's throats, I guess. You going in?"

"I'm too lazy to change into my suit and then back again. You guys riding later?"

Mike sighed. "Probably not. Lisa thinks it's too hot for the boys to wear all the gear and shit. And I have to stick around or I'll be spending the rest of the trip sleeping in the screenhouse again."

Joe laughed, attracting Lisa's attention. She

waved from the far end of the enclosure, where she was supervising the older boys' trips down to the bottom of the deep end. He waved and she gave him a smile.

"Get yourself in trouble again?"

Mike bent over to gather the glow sticks the boys were tossing at his feet and chucked the whole bunch back into the pool. "Not *again*. More like a chronic *still*. You've got it good, man. You can do whatever the hell you want to."

That was right. He *could* do whatever the hell he wanted. Because there was nobody to give a shit. Maybe Mike wasn't free to hit the trails for a few hours, but he also had somebody else to talk to besides the mirror when he had a bad day. When he was worried or blue or had great news he was bursting to share.

Joe could sleep sideways on his damn bed if he wanted, because there was nobody warm to curl up against. He could eat whatever he wanted, because there was nobody to share a meal with. He could leave the toilet seat up and his socks on the floor and crank the tunes as high as he wanted.

"Yup," he said, reaching over the fence to slap his brother on the shoulder. "I've got it good. I'm going to grab some grub, then get back to work again."

In the store he found a couple of steamed hot dogs, a snack-size bag of chips and his sister, who must have snuck down the other path while he was talking to Mike. She had a fistful of candy bars and was checking out the beer cooler. "Hey, sis."

She spun around as though he'd caught her in the act of shoplifting. "Joe! What are you doing here?"

He lifted his hand, thinking the hot dogs spoke for themselves. "What's wrong?"

Color brightened her cheeks. "Nothing. Why?"

"Chocolate and wine coolers? Who do you think you're talking to here?"

"It's hot. I want a candy bar and a cold drink. Get off my back."

She was lying, of course. A chocolate bar and a drink most women outgrew in high school were her favorite stress-busters, and she usually didn't break them out unless she was really upset about something.

"Heard you and Keri laughing a few minutes ago. What was so funny?"

She shrugged and grabbed a four-pack out of the cooler before closing it with her hip. "Remember the nutcrackers?"

"Oh, jeez." What a holiday season that had been. "Should we grab something for her?"

"I'm going to get a couple more things and then go hang out with Steph. Watch some chick flicks or something."

Joe raised an eyebrow, but didn't press. Terry's no-television rule was one of the founding tenets of the annual Kowalski family camping trip. Only Mother Nature trumped that rule and only because the four boys were a bit much when confined by bad weather.

"I'll probably go find Keri, then," he told her,

showing the cashier what he'd picked out so it could go on the tab. "Catch you later."

He didn't have to look too hard for Keri. She was walking toward him wearing her black bathing suit with the pretty wraparound thing over it. The knot of fabric holding it on accentuated the swinging of her hips, like a pocket watch that sucked him in and stole his free will.

"Hey, babe," he managed to say when she got close enough. "Wanna hot dog?"

"Nope. I'm going to cool off and hang with the kids for a while."

"Voluntarily?"

God, her smile made his balls ache. "Yes, voluntarily. Are you going back to work?"

"Uh, yeah," he said, because what else was he going to say? *No, I'm going to dip my blue balls into the icy cold water and try to keep my hands off you in front of the children.*

"Have fun," she told him as she walked by him and through the pool gate.

Yup. A fun-filled afternoon of staring at the blinking cursor, trying not to think about the way that swimsuit made her legs go on forever. Or how those legs would feel wrapped around his waist.

It was a hot, slow walk back to the cabin.

"THAT'S DAD'S TRUCK!"

Terry didn't look up from the book she was reading. "I'm sure it looks like it, but it's not."

"Well, Dad's driving it."

That certainly got her attention. She turned her head just in time to see Evan throw his truck in Park and get out. His four-wheeler was in the back of the pickup, camping gear bungee-corded to its racks.

She'd only called him four hours ago, for chrissake.

"Hello, ladies," her maybe almost-ex-husband said.

Evan wasn't as tall as her brothers and there was no doubt he'd been well fed going into middle age, but she didn't find him any less attractive than she had the day they'd met. His dirty-blond hair was getting a little shaggy and she couldn't help but wonder if he even knew the name of the barber shop where *she'd* always scheduled his appointments.

"What are you doing here?" she asked, trying to sound disinterested and failing by a mile.

"I missed you, too." He winked at her, then turned to their daughter. "And I couldn't miss my weekend time with Stephie."

Funny how missing one weekend had been okay with him before Terry had made that stupid call. Terry didn't know what to say. How could he just show up with no warning after what he'd done?

"I'm on site four," he continued. "Your brothers can all get a good laugh watching me try to put up my tent. Unless you're going to help me."

"I'm sure it came with instructions," she snapped. How dare he put her in this position just because she'd been stupid enough to confess her feelings to his answering machine in a misguided, Keri-fueled moment?

"You gonna help me?" he asked their daughter, who absolutely beamed. Funny how an almost teenage girl who couldn't plug an RV cord into an electrical outlet was suddenly the Bob Vila of tents.

Twenty minutes later, Terry's palms bore red crescent fingernail marks. They were doing it wrong. They hadn't stretched the tent out enough before pegging the corners, plus Steph didn't drive the pegs in nearly far enough. And how the hell did they expect to get any of it right when they'd let the directions blow into a cluster of blackberry bushes?

Not her problem. The man would rather be alone than married to her? They'd see how much he liked being alone when his tent collapsed on him in the middle of the night and he couldn't find the zipper.

When two arms came around her shoulders from behind, she knew it was Joe and leaned back against his chest as he asked, "What's going on here?"

"Keri Daniels is going on here."

"Evan came to see Keri?"

"No. Your girlfriend talked me into calling his answering machine while he was at work and telling him I miss him." Dumbest idea ever.

"This is a good thing, then. You called. He came."

She snorted. "He said he didn't want to miss his weekend with Steph."

"You want me to go over there and kick his ass?"

Joe could always make her laugh. "That tent's doing a good enough job already."

His arms tightened around her and he rested his chin on her shoulder. "Don't freeze him out this weekend, Terry. I know he hurt you, but from a man's point of view, his coming up here is pretty huge."

They watched as Kevin and Mike approached site number four, both of them chuckling and shaking their heads, while Terry fumed. Now they'd take over the operation and Evan would be spared the humiliation of calling for help at two in the morning.

"Cut 'em some slack," Joe said, probably feeling the tension in her shoulders. "He was our family for thirteen years, too. You're our sister, but he's our friend. It's not fair of you to expect us to give him the cold shoulder when he's right here, smack-dab in the middle of things."

"How do you expect me to deal with all this?"

"Talk to him. Seriously, his being here means there's a chance you can work this out."

"Gee, did Ma write that script for you?"

"Strangely enough, the people who love you all feel pretty much the same about this. Wonder why that is."

"Because you're all pains in my ass."

Joe gave her another squeeze, then let her go. "Let him see what you're feeling, sis. Let him know you're hurt."

She had no intention of going crying to Evan. He was the one who'd left. And she wasn't about to let him know it was destroying her inside.

CHAPTER ELEVEN

"HOW MUCH DOES SHE HATE ME right now?" Keri whispered to Joe, who was helping her wrap potatoes in tinfoil for baking in the campfire coals.

"I wouldn't pull up behind her in any mud puddles for a while."

"How was I supposed to know Evan would drive all the way up here? The plan was for him to have to wait for her to come home, so he'd be practically drooling with anticipation by the time he got to see her. Instead, *she's* foaming at the mouth."

"She'll get over it." When she laughed, he rolled his eyes. "Okay, she can hold a grudge. But, trust me, this is the best thing that's happened to her in three months. She just doesn't realize it yet."

"You're not done with those potatoes yet?" Mary snatched the roll of aluminum foil away from Joe. "You go help your father. You two are gabbing more than you're working and we'll be having baked potatoes for midnight snack at this rate."

Since neither of them was eager to argue with a woman wielding a roll of heavy-duty aluminum foil, Joe shrugged and went off to find Leo, and Keri poked holes in the potatoes with a fork a little bit faster.

"I hear Evan being here is all your fault." Mary tore off a square of foil to wrap around the potato Keri handed her.

How was it her fault? "That seems to be the rumor."

"Good. I don't know how you did it, but it's good that he's here. Maybe that will prove to Theresa they can talk this out and put it all behind them."

"All I did was tell her she should call him and tell him she missed him. The driving up here and surprising her part was all him."

And Terry was not happy about it. She was currently sitting in the shade stripping the hell out of fresh ears of corn. Husk was flying and everybody was giving her space. A lot of space.

"Talking it out would require her actually talking to him," Keri pointed out.

Mary shrugged. "She will. Later, when it's quiet and the entire family isn't hanging around."

If Keri stepped a little to the left, she could see across the campground to site four, where Evan and Stephanie were involved in their own dinner preparations. But while the Kowalskis were going for an all-out barbecue feast, the Porters were roasting hot dogs over the fire with sticks.

Keri was jealous. Slaving away over dinner wasn't her idea of a vacation and the fact that she was doing it outside didn't make it a grand adventure. It just made it harder to wash her hands.

"I'd like to see everybody settled," Mary continued. "Theresa and Evan. You and Joe."

"Umm..." Flustered, she dropped the potato and it rolled, which at least gave her the opportunity to crawl under the picnic table and fish it out, giving her a few seconds to think.

What, exactly, did Joe's mother think she was doing here? Keri knew he'd told his family she was here to write an article about him and that he'd left out the charming blackmail aspect of the story. But there was no mistaking Mary's intent—she'd paired them off as couples. Terry and Evan. She and Joe.

She ran the potato under the water spigot and then stabbed it a few times with the fork before handing it to Mary. "Things are very settled between Joe and I. When you guys go home, I'm going back to Los Angeles, where I'll write my article and get my promotion."

"We'll see," Mary said with an enigmatic smile Keri was afraid to analyze too much. She wrapped the last potato and set down the aluminum foil. "Go help Theresa with the corn, sweetie."

Great. Cornhusking and a healthy dose of attitude. Just what her day needed. But she did as she was told and dragged a chair over to what looked like bushels of ears of corn. Not that she knew what a bushel looked like, but it was a lot.

"I've got this," Terry snapped.

"Your mother told me to help you. Take it up with her."

When she didn't, Keri picked up an ear of corn

and tried to do to it what Terry was doing to hers. It wasn't as easy as it looked, though, and the sticky stuff that was like hair was clinging to the corn and then clinging to her.

"You can buy corn on the cob already prepped, you know," she said, not even trying to hide her irritation.

"It's not as good that way."

She was about to say she was one sticky piece of corn string away from joining Evan and Steph in roasting hot dogs on sticks, then closed her mouth. Probably not the right time to imply Evan was doing something in a better way than his pissed-off wife.

"I can't believe he came up here," Terry muttered at the ear of corn she was mauling.

Keri wasn't sure if she was actually talking to the corn, or if the comment was directed at her, but it was an opening. "Don't you think it's a good thing? You called and he came running. Literally."

"No." She snapped the ends of the corn off with frighteningly little effort. "I don't think it's a good thing. What is it going to help, him being over there cooking like a freakin' caveman?"

"He'd be over here if you weren't being such a bitch."

For a second, she thought Terry was going to chuck an ear of corn at her. But then the mask slipped—just for a second—and Keri saw not anger or annoyance, but total devastation.

"Things were said that can't ever be taken back," Terry said quietly, but then she resumed ripping into the corn. "What the hell would you know about it, anyway?"

"About as much as I do about corn on the cob," she replied, knowing she'd pushed Terry as far as she could for the moment.

They were on the last ears when Joe walked up behind Keri and rested his hands on her shoulders. "Ma said to hurry up or—"

"We'll be having corn on the cob for midnight snack," they finished together.

Keri managed a laugh, but she was hyperaware of Joe's fingers curling over her shoulders. And hyperaware of his mother milling around the site, probably nursing her glow of maternal satisfaction thinking Joe was one step closer to being *settled*.

Keri tried shrugging him off, but he didn't take the hint, so, short of reaching up and physically removing his hands, there was nothing she could do. And, Mary aside, she didn't really want to.

She was only vaguely aware of Joe talking about what was happening with the steaks and chicken breasts, but very aware of his thumbs making small circles, drawing closer and closer to the base of her neck.

What was unsettling was how natural—how couplelike—the gesture was. She had no doubt he was doing it subconsciously, with a lack of awareness that made her fear he was thinking along the same lines as his mother.

But then his right thumb hit the sweet spot at the top of her spine and she didn't care anymore. There was something to be said for a man who remembered just where and how she liked to be touched.

And as she dropped her head a little, encouraging him to move those magic thumbs up to her hairline, she couldn't help wondering what else he remembered about touching her.

JOE DIDN'T THINK there was anything much sadder than a guy sitting alone, staring into his campfire, and it wasn't long before Kevin ditched them to meander over to Evan's site.

Joe and Mike, being a little more sensitive to Terry and Lisa's disapproval, didn't dare join the guys, though they both looked over when Kevin's laughter reached their ears.

"Go," Terry said.

"Yeah," Mike said. "Go, but be prepared to suffer for it later, right?"

She sighed. "No, just go hang out at Evan's campfire. Like Joe reminded me earlier, you guys have been friends for years. I promise I won't hold it against either of you."

They left on the double-quick, before she could change her mind, but then Joe remembered Keri. "You don't mind, do you, babe?"

Since he was already halfway across the playground, dragging his chair behind him when he yelled it, she couldn't very well say no. Or complain about his calling her babe in front of his family. But he was still relieved when she laughed and waved him away.

The pop and hiss of three cans of Bud—and a Coke for Joe—being opened signaled the commencement of a guy's night out, even if they were only fifty yards from the women and children.

After they ran through sports, politics and an intense debate of Victoria's Secret versus *Sports Illustrated Swimsuit Edition* models, along with the better part of a twelve-pack, the talk inevitably ran to women.

"We've got more women troubles among us four than any dozen men should have to bear," Evan complained, a couple of beers ahead of the rest of them.

"I'm not troubled," Joe protested.

Mike laughed and popped open another. "Man, you got even more troubles than us, because you're still stupid enough to think there's hope."

"That's bullshit. You're married to a great woman. Kevin's got bar bunnies throwing themselves at him and Terry admitted she misses Evan. Hope abounds, my friend."

"You gettin' any yet?" Kevin asked him.

"Hell no." Joe raised his can in a mock toast. "But again, hope abounds."

"You gettin' old or what?" Kevin asked. "You guys are all alone in that cabin and you can't get lucky?"

Mike snorted. "Maybe he was that bad the first time around."

"She's had a real man since then," Evan added, "and she's too worn out from riding to fake a decent orgasm."

Now, that wasn't funny. "I don't know what you've been doing wrong, but my women don't fake a damn thing."

"Hell, Terry doesn't, either. In fact she—"

"Whoa!" all three Kowalskis yelled in unison.

Evan sighed and took another slug of beer. "One of the suck things about being married to your sister right there. You all can share war stories from the sack, but I can't."

"Shit," Joe said. "I'm still trying to scrub the image of you and her on the kitchen table out of my mind."

Kevin groaned and covered his ears, but Mike leaned forward. "That glass thing? No way that would hold you both."

"She wouldn't go for it anyway."

"Which is why you walked out, according to her."

"Seriously? I spill my guts and the only part she hears is how I wanted to do her on the table?"

Joe shrugged. "Women."

"Damn right," Mike said before knocking back the rest of his beer.

When his brother looked over at the cooler, Joe wondered if maybe he should intervene. Whatever the hell was going on between Mike and his wife wouldn't be improved any by a raging case of drunken-ass syndrome.

"Hey, Mike, you want one of my Cokes?"

"Nah, I'll have another brewski."

Well, he'd tried. "We should have nicked some snacks. You got anything, Evan?"

"Three packages of hot dogs and a jar of instant coffee."

"You suck at camping, dude," Kevin said. "You need to go home, because—Terry? She knows how to pack food."

"I'm well versed in Theresa's superiority in all things, thanks."

Ouch. "So how 'bout those Red Sox?"

The standard New England change of awkward subject worked and the conversation drifted into pitching stats and general Yankees-hating.

Until feminine laughter drifting across the playground made them all turn their heads toward the family campfire. The kids and grandparents had all fallen by the wayside at some point, leaving the three women—Keri, Lisa and Terry—illuminated by the fire and a small battery-operated lantern set on a cooler. They'd pulled their chairs together and their heads were all bent over, looking at something on the big Igloo.

"I bet they're playing dirty Scrabble again," Kevin guessed, and he was proven right when Lisa started laying tiles on the board. Another round of laughter, though he could see them trying their best to stifle it.

Mike shook his head. "If Lisa would do half the words in bed she spells out on that board, I'd be one happy son of a bitch."

Joe heard the guys laugh, but his lungs were having some trouble fully inflating and nothing came out.

God, she was beautiful. It was a warm night, so her flannel shirt was unbuttoned over a T-shirt and her hair was tousled a little—not sleek and perfect as usual. But it was more than her looks in the flickering light.

He wanted to stop the world from spinning. To freeze time and hold on to this moment forever.

This was the life he wanted. It was the life that, once upon a time, he'd thought he'd have. Right now, it was as if Keri had never left—as if she'd been a part of his family all along.

She belonged here with him. He was sure of it. The problem was going to be convincing her.

HE KEPT LOOKING OVER AT HER. Keri knew that, of course, because she kept looking at him.

He was in his element over there, kicked back with his brothers and brother-in-law. Though she couldn't hear their conversation, their laughter occasionally drifted across the playground, making her glance over no matter how hard she tried not to.

"He hasn't moved any," Lisa teased after the umpteenth time Keri's head swiveled.

He certainly hadn't. In the glow of Evan's very enthusiastic campfire, she could see his long, denim-clad legs stretched out in front of him. His head was leaning back against the chair and he dangled a can of Coke idly over the arm.

"Ha!" Terry exclaimed, putting all of her tiles on the board. "And since I know neither of you will say that out loud, that's a triple word score for me."

Keri dragged her attention back to the outrageous game of Scrabble she'd gotten sucked into after the kids and grandparents had gone inside. "Umm… yeah, I'm not saying that out loud."

"Is that even a real thing?" Lisa asked.

Terry looked smug, until Keri said, "Yeah, I've done that."

Both women stared at her. "You didn't! But you can't say it?"

They spoke in stereo and when Keri shrugged, they both dissolved into laughter again. It lasted long enough for her to sneak another peek at Joe.

He was on his feet—they all were—and headed her way. "Uh-oh, looks like the party's over."

In the blink of an eye, Lisa had the board tilted, sliding the tiles into the bottom of the box. "If Mike thinks I know some of these words, he might want me to actually *do* some of these words."

Keri laughed, but she noticed Terry didn't. She was too busy watching her husband, who *wasn't* crossing the playground toward them. Evan was heading toward the bathhouse and he didn't even look their way.

Terry probably didn't realize it, but everything she felt was playing out across her face and it all added up to heartbroken longing.

"Later, when it's quiet, you should go talk to him," Keri said quickly, while the guys were still far enough away not to hear.

"Or maybe he should come talk to me."

Keri wanted to say more, but she didn't have time.

Joe was there, sliding his arm around her waist as if it was the most normal thing in the world to do.

"Ready for bed, babe?"

When he said it like that, all husky and hot, she was definitely ready for bed. And maybe for a little of that seven-letter, double word score verb Terry had laid down across the U in Lisa's *pubic.*

"I'd like to take a shower first," she said, but not because she was planning to get naked with him or anything. "Because…umm, bug spray, you know? The DEET's gotta be a half-inch thick by now."

"Sure. We'll grab our stuff and I'll join you."

Wet. Naked. Soapy. Slick. Yes, please.

"Good plan," Terry said. "She won't have to worry about the DEET tomorrow since she won't have any bug spray."

Lisa snickered, but Joe shook his head. "Relax, sis. I meant to join her at the bathhouse. In my own shower."

Well, damn.

No, that was a good thing. There was a reason she wasn't sleeping with Joe. What was it? Oh, yeah. Only everything she'd spent almost the last twenty years working for. "Okay."

Good-nights all around and then she was alone with Joe. Again. He smelled like campfire smoke and bug spray but, then again, so did she.

"Who was winning before Lisa dumped the board so we wouldn't see?" he asked as they turned the corner toward the cabin.

"I was."

He leaned close and bumped her with his shoulder as they walked. "You must know some really good dirty words."

"Oh, I do," she said in a low voice. "Some were so naughty Lisa hadn't even heard of them."

He stumbled, just a little, but enough to merit holding her arm to steady himself. His hand lingered and it seemed like every nerve ending in her body focused on that spot. She was in so much trouble.

"Really? And you know of these things how?"

She smiled at him. "I read a lot."

"Huh. I'd really like to rummage through your library sometime."

They grabbed their bags and made the walk back to the bathhouse, where he naturally chose the bathroom right next to hers so she could hear him moving around. The tap-tap of his razor against the sink between each swipe over his jaw. The clink of the quarters in the metal coin box. The shower running. The shower door closing.

Oh, God, he was naked.

Shaving one's legs in a tiny shower unit was hard enough without the distraction of a naked, sudsy Joe on the other side of the partition, so Keri tried to block out the sounds from next door and focus on what she was doing.

And to focus on the inevitable. She wasn't going to be able to hold out for another week. She'd be lucky if she held out long enough to get back to the cabin, at this rate. If she hadn't been in the process of showering off the bug spray, she would have dragged Joe behind the nearest tree.

The important thing was to make it very clear to him—and to herself, of course—that any little trips down Nostalgia Lane were merely detours. The primary route was still the superhighway to the top of *Spotlight Magazine*'s food chain, and she would hit the on-ramp the second this exercise in blackmail, Kowalski-style, was over.

She could put her professionalism on hold for an hour…or three. Maybe several times over the course of the night, if she was lucky and Joe was aging well, so to speak.

If she was really lucky, they'd find out it wasn't that easy to recapture that Boone's Farm-fueled, first-love magic, the sex would suck and she could get back to focusing on what was really important.

CHAPTER TWELVE

JOE PROPPED HIMSELF AGAINST the big boulder outside the bathhouse and waited for Keri to finish up.

And waited…and waited…and waited.

Either she'd brought an entire pocketful of quarters, or she was taking a shower as cold as his. Not that it had helped. He was pretty sure the water had vaporized the instant it made contact with his skin.

He'd be lucky if he made it through the night, never mind another week.

When Keri finally opened the door and stepped out into the night, the hot, steamy scent of mandarin oranges and something spicy wafted out with her, as if she was a warm dessert waiting to be devoured.

"Feel better?" he managed to ask after clearing his throat a couple of times.

"Much, but I'm a little fruit-scented so let's walk fast before the bugs find me."

She seemed nervous about something, which he found interesting. Very interesting. How many reasons to be nervous were there for a woman who was freshly showered and scented and shaven—the top of her shaving gel can peeked out of her bag—and on her way to being alone in a cabin with a man?

Only one he could think of, but it was a good one. Maybe, while she was mere feet away from him, naked and soapy and slippery, she'd been thinking about the same thing he was.

And, oh, there was a Santa Claus, and he must have thought Joe Kowalski was good enough to get his Christmas present early, because as soon as the cabin door was closed behind them, Keri dropped her bags and said, "I'm going back to Los Angeles next week."

"Okay."

"And I can't take it anymore. The touches. The looks. Let's just do it and get it over with."

She looked so frazzled he almost laughed at her. "Well, when you put it like that…"

"Unless you don't want to," she snapped.

"Oh, I want to, babe." To prove it, he reached out and grabbed her, pulling her so close she could feel just how much he wanted to. "There's really no way you could have phrased that invitation that would make me turn it down."

A blush spread over her cheeks. "Do you have protection?"

"Shit."

"Please tell me that doesn't mean no."

"I left the box in my truck. In the glove box." And he wished like hell he'd remembered that before he'd got his hands on her.

"You carry a whole box of condoms in your glove box?"

"I stopped at the drug store and bought them on

the way up, so I shoved them in there." He wasn't ready when she gave him a little shove, and only grabbing the bunk bedpost kept him from going ass over teakettle.

"You bought them because I was coming? What, you just assumed I'd sleep with you?"

Mentally flailing for what he'd done wrong, he gave her a smile. "Babe, it wasn't like that. Not really."

She gave him a stern look but, thankfully, amusement was playing across her face. "What was it like, then?"

"Okay, it's like this…"

"Ha! It may have been a long time, but I've heard that before. Fairy tales start with *once upon a time* and Kowalski tales start with *okay, it's like this*."

"I wasn't going to do the interview, but I wanted to see you."

"Why didn't you just tell me no over dinner?"

Good question. "It was kind of a joke, and I honestly thought you wouldn't go for it at first. But then, once we were talking and stuff, I thought the chemistry was still there and that you felt it, too. So, when you agreed…"

"You thought I agreed to come up here because I wanted to sleep with you?"

It didn't make any more sense when said out loud than it had in his mind at the time. "No, I thought you agreed to come up here because you wanted an interview, but that you might not be averse to sleeping with me while you were here."

He watched her, dying inside while he waited for her reaction. He'd been so close to the promised land and if she shut him down now, his balls would explode.

She laughed, then gave him another little shove. "Go get 'em."

He'd gotten to the truck and had his hand on the glove box when he heard footsteps behind him. No. *No, no, no.* For the love of his genital well-being, not right now.

"Hey, Joe." It was Kevin. Not so bad, then. He wouldn't stay long. "The satellite's not working on Pop's camper and Ma's gonna miss her show, so we're supposed to go play cable guy."

Shit was the cleanest of the many words Joe managed not to say out loud. "Right now? Are you fucking kidding me?"

"Dude, it's not *that* late."

Keeping his back to his brother, Joe fished out a couple of condoms, which he stuck in his front pocket. Then he grabbed a couple more. Just in case. "It's late enough so people that old should be in bed."

"Yeah, you go tell Ma that. I'll take a picture."

"Fine, goddammit. Just gimme a sec." He slammed the SUV door closed and started for the cabin.

"What the hell's up your ass?"

Joe spun around to glare at his brother. Then he plucked the condoms from his pocket and fanned them out.

Kevin laughed at him. "Cock blocked by Ma's television. Sweet."

"Go away, dickhead. I'll be there in a minute."

Kevin was still chuckling as he walked away, and Joe threw a few more choice curse words into the atmosphere before stepping back into the cabin.

Keri was waiting for him, arms folded across her chest and one eyebrow raised in what didn't look like a *come and get me, big boy* kinda way. "Proud of yourself?"

"What?"

"Did you have to wave the condoms around, for chrissake?"

Oh, that's right. The cabin had windows. "Sorry. I was trying to make a point."

"What point could you possibly be making?"

"That…I'm busy and really don't care if Ma can't watch her show because her satellite's not working?"

The way Keri's shoulders slumped gave him heart. If she was disappointed he had to help his parents instead of bending her over the end of the bed, that meant she still intended to get bent over the end of the bed.

"Right now?" she asked, her mouth a little pouty and begging to be kissed again.

He glanced at the clock. "Her show starts in twenty minutes, so I shouldn't be long. Do not fall asleep before I get back."

WHEN JOE'S FOOTSTEPS practically pounded on the cabin's porch, Keri opened her eyes and peeked out from under the blanket at the alarm clock. He'd been gone closer to forty minutes, but there was no doubt he was back now.

He let the screen door slam behind him, then closed the big door with a bang before turning the overhead light on and jamming the dimmer switch up to full.

"Please don't be asleep," she heard him mutter under his breath, as one shoe and then the other hit the floor with a thump.

She tried not to laugh at him—she wanted to prolong the torture—but she couldn't help it.

"Oh, good, you're awake."

"You made sure of that, didn't you?"

"I hope you're naked under that blanket."

She shook her head, folding back the covers to reveal her pajamas, buttoned up to her chin.

"Oh. Okay." He peeled his T-shirt off and tossed it on the floor. "I can work with that."

"I was cold." That had stopped being a problem, though, about the time he'd taken the shirt off. Now, with the jeans and socks gone, too, it was time to rethink her current state of dress.

But when she reached up to undo at least the top few buttons, Joe shook his head. "I'll do that."

The way he said it made her feel all shivery with anticipation. Not just the normal anticipation that accompanied the knowledge an orgasm was pending, but the thrilling, heart-pounding kind. Eighteen years may have passed, but Joe Kowalski used to rock her world and she was more than ready for him to do it again.

When he slid the dimmer down to low instead of shutting the light off, she felt a little spurt of panic, though. She was almost forty, for heaven's sake. Darkness was her friend.

But then she remembered the hunger in his eyes when she'd stripped down to her underwear in front of him. If there was one thing she could be sure of, it was that Joe didn't have the slightest problem with how she looked mostly naked.

"You nervous?" he asked as he rested a knee on the bed and tossed a few condoms on the bedside table, his dimples visible even in the dim light.

"Of course not. As far as this goes, we've been there, done that."

"Yeah, well…my dick's two decades older than it was the last time we been there, done that."

"So are my breasts."

He grinned as he sank onto the bed next to her. "Good. We can be old and decrepit together."

"Hey! I didn't say anything about decrepit." And judging by the strain on his boxer briefs, no decrepitude lurked there, either.

He slid his arm under her neck and scooped her up, leaving her half-sprawled across his chest, looking down at him. Her hair fell forward, making a curtain around her face, but stopping just short of tickling his nose.

Playful though he seemed, his eyes were serious. "Before we get too far into this, what were you drinking tonight?"

So not the time for a Q&A. "Cranberry-lime seltzer."

"Accept any funny-tasting brownies from strangers?"

"What? Of course not."

"Head injury?"

"No." She scowled down at him, utterly confused. "What are you talking about? Why are you even talking at all?"

He reached up and tucked her hair behind her ears. "Just making sure you're of sound mind, babe. Don't want you to hate me in the morning. Or yourself."

"I'm sober and concussion-free," she promised. "But you totally get brownie points for caring."

"How many points do I have to save up before I can redeem them for a blow job?"

"Oh, I don't even think so, Kowalski."

"At all?"

"How 'bout not right now?"

His smile was slow and sizzling. "I didn't mean right now. I have other plans for tonight."

She trailed her fingertips over his back, loving the feel of his muscles twitching beneath her touch. "Did you lock the door and turn off the porch light?"

"And closed the curtain. Hopefully my family will think we've been sucked into a black hole somewhere."

"Speaking of them…"

"I don't want to speak of them. I want to see what's under these pajamas."

She slapped his hand away from the top button. "Your mother already has ideas where you and I are concerned. This stays just between us."

"Of course," he said, but all his attention was still on the button.

She slapped his hand again. "I'm serious."

With a growl of frustration, Joe rolled until she was pinned under him. Straddling her, he sat up straight and smiled down at her. "I promise I won't announce over breakfast that I spent the night getting my hand slapped for trying to unbutton your damn pajama shirt."

A smart-ass reply would have been nice, but Keri was too aware of how close certain parts of him were to the parts of her most looking forward to getting reacquainted. When he reached down for the top button again, causing the inside of his thighs to squeeze her hips a little, she didn't slap his hand.

"Damn, these are some tiny buttons. Did you bring any other pajamas?"

"Don't you dare rip the buttons off."

"It looks sexy on TV."

"They're not wearing pajamas like these on the television," she said but, judging by the steamy but speculative look on his face, her high-end pj's weren't long for the world.

"They feel nice. How much did you pay for them?"

"Two hundred and eighteen dollars."

"For something you wear to bed?" The lust became incredulity. "Really?"

"One of my few indulgences."

When he ran a finger down the row of buttons, she shivered. "Did I happen to mention during any of the times you've interrogated me that I'm a very rich man. I can buy you more of these."

"Throwing your money around?" She grabbed his wrist and pulled him down until he was stretched out on top of her. "That's kinda hot."

A little of the heat dimmed in his eyes. "You're not the first woman to think so."

She wasn't sure exactly what had changed his mood, but she didn't like it. "These are high-quality pajamas, you know. I'm not sure you *could* rip the buttons off."

That did the trick—the gleam was back. "I work out almost every day. I think I can handle some girly fabric."

"Prove it."

It took three tries, complete with laughter on her part and some masculine grunting on his, but he finally managed to send a few of her buttons flying and she heard them skitter across the hardwood floor.

"Oh, I was hoping it was black," he said as her pajama top parted to reveal another black lace bra.

"You never seemed to mind the white cotton," she reminded him, shivering as Joe's hot gaze and the cool air mingled on her skin.

"Babe, you could be wearing saggy old granny panties and I'd still want in them."

"I might like that flannel shirt a little too much, but I'm not that far gone." She was trying to think of a less clichéd way to say *shut up and kiss me* when he lowered his mouth—and the rest of his body—to hers.

He wasn't the first boy she'd ever kissed, but he'd been one of the best at it and he certainly hadn't forgotten how it was done.

His kisses weren't tentative, but neither did she feel as if he was trying to suck her soul out through her mouth. Perfect pressure. Perfect technique. Just…perfect. She sighed and buried her fingers in his hair as his tongue danced over hers, and when he paused to nip playfully at her bottom lip, she smiled against his mouth.

"I can still remember the taste of Boone's Farm on your lips," she told him, and he lifted his head.

"I remember everything about you," he said.

"Not everything."

"Everything that matters." He reached one hand to her hip and ran it down the back of her thigh until he got to the hollow behind her knee. "I remember where you're ticklish."

"Don't you dare." She tried to jerk her leg away, but she was pinned under his body and couldn't go anywhere.

"And where you're not." His hand left her knee to sneak in between their bodies, and then in between her legs.

She closed her eyes and arched her hips, craving the pressure of his hand through the layers of her panties and pajama bottoms. He pressed a little with the pad of his hand and she whimpered. "Nope, not ticklish there."

"That's cheating," she pointed out, trying not to pant. "That's more of a universal thing, not specific to me."

He laughed and pressed a little more until she couldn't help but squirm. "I know if I stick my tongue in your ear, you'll knee me in the balls."

"That's still true, by the way."

"I know that, unlike most women, you don't like a lot of foreplay."

"Let's not talk about most women," she said, wiggling her hips a little to keep him from forgetting what his hand was supposed to be doing. "And, no, I don't."

"You're more of a down and dirty kinda girl."

"If you don't stop talking and get on with it, I'm going to go be down and dirty by myself in the shower."

"I'll talk all damn night if you'll let me watch. You did once, remember?"

She did remember, and the memory made her cheeks burn. "I was drunk."

"You were hot." He sat back on his heels again, straddling her. "You're still hot."

"I'm still waiting," she pointed out.

With another manly grunt of exertion, he managed to rip the rest of the buttons off her pajama top.

"I've waited almost twenty years to do this again. I won't be rushed."

"I'm sure you've had plenty of sex in the last twenty years, Kowalski."

"Yeah, but not with you." He backed up, dragging her pajama bottoms over her hips. "There was just something about sex with you that stayed with me. Maybe nostalgia. Or maybe it was just that good."

She knew just what he meant, but he wasn't supposed to be waxing philosophical. Or nostalgic. He was supposed to be providing a nonbattery-operated, strings-free orgasm. Analysis was for relationships and they did *not* have a relationship.

Once he got her pajama bottoms untangled from her feet, she decided to give him a kick start by taking off the bra and panties. No striptease or finesse. Just getting the damn clothes out of the way.

"I was going to do that."

"You snooze, you lose, Kowalski. Now yours."

He peeled off the boxer briefs, she grabbed a condom from the bedside table and they met back in the middle of the bed. She hooked her hand behind his neck and dragged him down for another kiss.

By the time they came up for air, her entire body was throbbing in anticipation of the screaming orgasm about to commence, but there was no ripping open of the condom wrapper. Instead Joe's mouth started on a lazy journey down her neck.

He reached that hollow at the base of her throat. Flicked his tongue over it. "I always did like this spot."

"Mmm…that spot always liked you, too."

When his mouth finally reached her breasts and his tongue flicked over her nipple, Keri arched her back, reveling in the zing that shot through her body.

Joe chuckled. "Foreplay's not so bad, now, is it?"

He closed his lips over the nipple and sucked hard before she could say anything, but that was okay. She closed her eyes and sucked in a breath as he turned his attention to her other breast.

She let him linger there a few minutes, then she plucked the condom from his hand and ripped open the package herself. He laughed and took it from her.

"I'd let you put it on me because that's kinda hot, but if you touch me right now, it's all over, babe."

At least he was suffering as badly as she was. Then—*finally*—he hooked his hands under her knees and dragged her down toward him. Her legs draped over his arms as he lifted her hips and knelt between her thighs.

She was so ready for him. Inch by hard, delicious inch he slid into her until she thought the sensation and the anticipation might kill her.

Then he slowly withdrew almost all the way and did it again. "Damn, babe. I hope you're close because this is *not* gonna take long."

He pulled his arms out from under her knees so he could lean down and kiss her, holding himself up on his forearms. She wrapped her legs around his hips, urging him on as he quickened his pace.

Then suddenly he stilled, his breath short and the muscles of his back quivering under her fingertips, just as he used to. The same way he had always done right before he told her he loved her. Those pretty blue eyes met hers and, as the memories of those backseat days became tangled up with the now, she thought *uh-oh*.

"I've missed you, babe."

She'd missed him, too. And not just the sex, though the sex was definitely worth missing. She'd missed his laugh. His conversation. His friendship. "I've missed you, too."

He kissed her again, and then set about proving there was absolutely nothing decrepit about him. The orgasm was worth waiting for, rocking her world so incredibly well she was barely aware of the suddenly jerky rhythm and growling sound that signaled Joe was being rocked himself.

He collapsed on top of her, his breath blowing in sharp bursts over her heated flesh. "Damn. That was… Damn."

"Damn," she echoed, because her brain wasn't ready to engage in conversation just yet.

Slowly their pulse rates returned to normal and Joe got up and wrapped the condom in a paper towel before hiding it in an empty granola-bar box and burying it in the garbage. Then he crawled back into bed and wrapped his arms around her.

Keri snuggled up against him, powerless to stop the smile tugging at her mouth. "We'll have to do that again. Soon."

"I'm going to need a few minutes, babe. I'm not eighteen anymore."

"Well, that wasn't half-bad for an old guy."

"Who you calling old?" he growled against her neck.

"I might call you old, but you're not decrepit yet."

Ten minutes later he set out to show her how right she was.

CHAPTER THIRTEEN

TERRY WOULD KNOW *THAT PROFILE* anywhere, even in the dark. Maybe especially in the dark. Evan had slept on his back and she on her side, facing him. If she'd opened her eyes at night, that was the profile she saw.

God, he looked sad, sitting on the bench by the playground, elbows propped on his knees as he stared off into the dark. His shoulders slumped a little, and he looked somehow defeated.

The smart thing to do? Go back inside and let him wallow in the misery he'd created. If he was sad and lonely, it was his own damn fault.

But her heart ached watching him and there was no master kill-switch for love. She didn't have it in her to turn away from him. Cursing herself for a fool, she made her way to the playground as quietly as possible, not really caring to have any of the family wake up to watch.

"I can't sleep, with you a few sites over," he said when she sat next to him, far enough away that they wouldn't be accidentally brushing body parts. "That whole so-close-and-yet-so-far thing."

"You're the one who walked out."

"Another cliché—couldn't live with you, can't live without you."

Terry leaned back against the bench and folded her arms over her chest. "If you're looking for sympathy, it's between shit and syphilis in the dictionary."

"Sure as hell didn't expect any from you."

Jerk. "Why did you come here?"

"Because you missed me. I tried to get to you before the feeling faded. Guess I was too late."

She didn't know what to say to that, so she let the silence drag on. Crickets chirped. A guy in a tent close by snored so loudly she was surprised his wife didn't smother him in his sleep. She watched a skunk meander from site to site, looking for tidbits of dropped food. If it was smart it would head to Mike and Lisa's site.

"I love you," he said quietly, staring down at the grass.

"Don't. Don't you dare tell me that."

"But I do."

"You told me you loved me before you patted me on the ass and fell asleep one night, then walked out on me the very next morning. Forgive me for thinking the words don't mean shit to you."

"Hey, at least you don't have my dirty socks laying around anymore."

He started to get up, but her hand shot out and stopped him. She knew him too well to miss the pain he was trying to hide with his smart-ass tone. "Why did you really come up here?"

"Like I told you earlier, you said you missed me and I was trying to get here before you stopped."

"You haven't made much of an effort for a guy who cares if I miss him."

"You haven't gone out of your way, either."

"I'm not the one who left."

"Somebody had to."

There was just enough truth in that to keep her from lashing out again. She'd thought herself, more times than she cared to admit, that she had no idea how their marriage would survive Steph going off to college. Or even if it would. Without their daughter to keep them together and giving them a reason for conversation, she wasn't sure they had much left.

"You didn't think talking about it might be the way to go," she said quietly. "Maybe discussing a separation. You thought telling me…what you said, and walking out the door was the best thing for our marriage?"

"Would you have listened?"

Probably not. "You could have tried."

"Then it would have gone on and on and we both would have said a lot of stuff we couldn't take back."

"Instead of just you."

His hand moved in such a way she thought he might put his arm around her, and then he let it fall. "I wouldn't take back what I said even if I could. I meant it. That's how miserable I was, and I won't go back to it."

"Then you should have saved your gas money. I can't magically change because you got pissed off and walked out." She stood up because, no matter how sad he looked sitting alone, this wasn't going to help.

He grabbed her wrist, keeping her from walking away. "I know you're not going to change who you are. But sometimes you could stop worrying about controlling every aspect of everybody's lives and enjoy a few minutes with me. We're not even friends anymore, Terry."

Again, there was more than a grain of truth in what he'd said, but she didn't know how to fix it.

He stood up, too, without letting go of her hand. "I love you, Terry, but I don't like you very much most of the time."

Her breath caught in her throat and she turned her face away so he wouldn't see the shimmer of tears his words had caused.

"I'm sorry," he said softly, "but we can't get through this without admitting where we are now."

"For three months you haven't seemed to give a damn if we got through this or not. Now all of a sudden you think coming up here and dumping on me will save our marriage?"

"I was gonna blow up if I didn't make a change. I was hoping, with some distance, we'd be able to talk things through, but instead we barely talk at all, and it's still about Steph."

She yanked her hand away from his and shook her head. "I don't know what there is to say."

"Let's go out for dinner when you get home," he said. "Someplace nice, like a date, and we can talk about us. Not Stephanie or work or whether or not the garbage disposal sounds funny."

She wanted to tell him she didn't think it would do any good. The things that were wrong with them couldn't be solved with a nice dinner and a bottle of wine. But she made the mistake of looking at him—really looking at him—and it was all there on his face. How hard the past three months had been on him and just how much he wanted that dinner and wine to work.

"Okay," she said. "Dinner."

"A date," he corrected, with just a hint of a smile.

She returned it, much to her surprise, and then walked back to her camper alone. Maybe it wouldn't work. Maybe she'd never be able to get his voice saying hurtful things to her out of her head.

But maybe, if they could remember what it was like to be friends, she wasn't facing the rest of her life alone.

SLAP. "RISE AND SHINE, BABE!"

Keri groaned, swore and burrowed under the covers. "Being slapped on the ass isn't a good way to start the day, you know."

"Beats a bucket of cold water or shaving cream. Having brothers, I know that for a fact. But I have a surprise for you."

"No surprises until after I've wrestled a pancake away from Kevin."

"No wrestling for your food today. The waitress will deliver it right to our table."

The blankets flew and a crazy-haired, sleepy-eyed and deliciously naked Keri emerged. "A restaurant? A real one?"

"Maybe not by your big-city standards, but it's real enough so you don't have to pour your own coffee."

When she flew out of the bed and started yanking on clothes, he wished he'd waited a few minutes to give her the news. "We don't have to run right out. We could—"

"No, we couldn't. I'm starving and I want to... Wait. Who's going?"

"Just you and me, babe."

He appreciated how hard she tried not to let her relief show. She smoothed her hair with her hands and shoved her feet into her sneakers. "I'm ready."

"You want to take a run up to the bathhouse first?"

"No." She draped a hoodie over her arm and went to the door. "We need to go now before your family comes looking for us and sucks us into their vortex. And I'm going to wait and use the restaurant's bathroom. No bugs and no trying to hold the hem of my pants off the muddy floor and sit down at the same time. I'll brush my teeth when we get back, so just don't kiss me, okay?"

He would have tried to kiss her anyway, morning breath or not, but she was already on the porch, heading for the SUV. She was either really hungry or really afraid Kowalskis were going to descend upon them and ruin their plans.

Fifteen minutes later, they were tucked into a corner booth at the local diner, the kind of run-down-looking mom-and-pop operation that always served the best home-cooked meals. The waitress delivered menus and big, steaming mugs of coffee, then left to deliver another order.

"You're ruining me," Keri said after she'd fixed her coffee and taken the first sip.

"How do you figure that?"

"Look at me! I just went from sound asleep to out in public in less than a half hour."

"That's a bad thing why?"

She gave him a look that said *men* and shook her head. "My skin regimen alone takes twenty minutes, never mind hair and makeup and everything else."

"I told you to run up to the bathhouse first if you wanted."

"Oh please," she replied, rolling her eyes. "The bathhouse isn't exactly a day spa, you know. I've been going downhill since the minute I got here."

"Would you kick me under the table if I say you look more beautiful now than you did the last time we were in a restaurant and you were all shiny and polished?"

"Yes."

He laughed. "I'll risk it, because it's the truth."

The waitress returned before Keri could do bodily harm to his shins, and they both ordered more food than they could possibly eat.

"Will your family be mad we left?" she asked

when they were alone again. "They won't worry when we don't show up for breakfast, will they?"

"No. I'm sure they saw us leave and they'll figure it out."

"If your mother comes after us with her wooden spoon, I'm totally throwing you under the bus."

He laughed again, but he hadn't ditched the rest of the Kowalskis and brought her here alone so they could talk about his family. "You didn't ask me a question last night."

Pink tinted the apples of her cheeks. "I was a little busy."

"Maybe we should do the questions in the morning from now on."

She leaned back against the booth, wrapping her hands around her coffee cup. "Implying that I'll be a little busy at night from now on?"

That was the question, yes, regardless of the roundabout way it was asked. While her mad scramble to escape the campground had alleviated any morning-after awkwardness, it had also robbed him of the opportunity to gauge how she felt about the night before. "Hope abounds, babe."

When she seemed to divert a little too much attention into drinking her coffee, he feared hope was about to be squashed, but then she looked him in the eye. "As long as there's no question that, when fun time's over, I'm going back to Los Angeles, where I'll write my article and get my promotion and this little…interlude will join high school in the nostalgia file."

"No question at all." For now. A week was a long time.

"Okay, then. I guess I need to come up with two questions for this morning, since you owe me one."

"Not sure this is the best venue for asking *my* questions, though," he pointed out, and her cheeks were still flushed when their plates arrived.

"Oh, good lord," Keri said when she got an eyeful of the food.

"That's my plan. The full-belly stupor will interfere with your ability to come up with tough questions."

"You made so much of your life off-limits, there aren't any tough questions to come up with. I'm sure *Spotlight* readers will be fascinated by the fact you put ketchup on your scrambled eggs."

"There's always the fact I like mayo on my hot dogs."

"You're a funny guy, Kowalski. I'll remember you fondly when I'm proofreading help-wanted ads for an internet weekly."

It was easy for him to forget this wasn't a game they were playing. When she went back to L.A., she was going to hand an article about his life to Tina Deschanel—a woman his publicist liked to refer to as a boil on the ass of journalism. The stories in the magazine she'd helped build into a supermarket powerhouse were personal, invasive and usually written with a scandalous slant. And, even if Keri used his former drinking problem to hook readers in, there wasn't a lot more than that to spill.

"I'm sorry I'm not a more interesting guy," he said sincerely. "I sit at my desk for hours a day, then I kick back and relax. Hang with the family. Lift some weights. That's about it."

She wanted to bring up Lauren and the lawsuit. He could tell by the set of her mouth how badly she wanted to point out that he did have a very interesting scandal in his past, but she wasn't allowed to bring it up.

Instead she bit the end off a piece of bacon, which transformed her look to one of contentment. "You know, none of my clothes are going to fit me when I get home."

"You can't live on salad alone, babe."

She shrugged and took a sip of her coffee. "Okay, let's see if I can make this all into one question. With the movie premiere looming on the horizon, how much input, if any, did you have in the screenplay, as well as involvement in the filming and, whether you were hands-on or not, how pleased are you with the finished product?"

He laughed and raised his coffee mug in a toast to her. "Such a finely crafted question, so I'm going to let you get away with that. Little, none and I haven't seen it."

Her fork hit her plate with a clatter. "Stop that!"

"Stop what? I answered the question. Or should I say questions, plural, since you snuck three in there?"

"What am I supposed to do with that?"

"Make something up?"

"You're the fiction writer, not me. Could you elaborate a little?"

He hated this stuff. Whatever people thought, he didn't avoid publicity because of some deep, dark secret he feared being revealed, but because he absolutely despised talking about himself or his work or anything else, for that matter.

"Since you really asked three questions, which I answered, if you want me to elaborate, it's gotta count as two questions."

"That's not fair. Those were barely answers." She took a bite of her bagel, but he didn't say anything, just leaving the offer hanging out there. "You may get two for one, but you can still only ask *me* one question in return."

"I'll have to make it a really good one, then." When she looked around, as though to see if anybody was sitting close enough to overhear, he chuckled. He'd have to come up with something really embarrassing if she was that worried about it. "Contractually, nobody had to send the screenplay to me, but the guy they hired to do it happened to be a fan. Because he wanted to respect my work, he sent me drafts as he did them and asked how he was doing. He really seems to get my work, though, and in the end he did pretty damn good all on his own."

Over the course of their meal, which Keri wasn't able to finish despite giving it one hell of a try, he talked about the movie. There wasn't a lot to tell, but he gave her a little insight into how he felt about knowing his words were going to be a major motion picture.

"There's a part of me that's disconnected," he told her over a final coffee refill. "I wrote my book—people can read my book as I envisioned it. The movie's a separate thing. But there's another part of me that's going to want to pick it apart. He wouldn't wear a shirt like that, or that's not what the killer looked like."

"But you'll go see it, right?"

He shrugged. "I promised Joey and Danny I'd take them to see it with Mike and Kevin. I'll go in trying to pretend it's just some random horror flick, but I'm sure as soon as it starts I'll stress over every aspect of it."

She set her empty cup down and leaned back in the booth with a sigh. "I'm stuffed. And that was a lot more interesting than putting ketchup on your eggs. The insight into your conflicted views about the movie will fascinate readers."

"Will it fascinate Tina?"

"Probably not," she admitted reluctantly. "Human interest to her means human drama."

"Scandal."

"Pretty much. But you're just not a scandalous kinda guy."

"Only with the right woman, babe," he said, and when he winked at her, she blushed.

But as he paid the bill and waited for her to emerge again from the ladies' room, he couldn't forget the somewhat defeated look on her face when she acknowledged Tina probably wasn't going to be satisfied with what she was going to hand in.

He couldn't give her what she needed. The only thing even remotely scandalous in his background was the lawsuit with Lauren, and she couldn't print anything about that even if he didn't mind. But in the back of his mind he was a little worried about what would happen when Keri was back in her world, facing off against the woman who could ruin her career. She wasn't exactly seeing his family at their best, and he'd told her things about Kevin even *he* wasn't supposed to know.

And all Joe could do was hope she wouldn't betray his trust.

HE WAITED UNTIL THEY MADE IT back into the cabin without being pounced upon by his family before backing her up against the bunk bed. "I'm still waiting for a good-morning kiss."

She turned her face away. "I told you you have to wait until I go up to the bathroom. Morning breath with a side of bacon and coffee? No, thanks."

"I've thought of a question. A very serious question, as a matter of fact."

Her eyes were wary, but amusement played with the corners of her mouth. "A serious one, huh?"

"Very." Since she wouldn't let him kiss her, he bent his head and nipped at her neck, just below her ear. "After you left for California, did you ever pretend guys you were with were me?"

"Yes," she whispered as he kissed his way down

to the V opening of her shirt. "And sometimes you were even battery operated, too."

And damn if the perennial erection didn't return. "I can't think about that too much or I won't be able to walk."

"How about you? Did you pretend other women were me?"

More than he cared to admit, and not just when it came to sex. "Only the blondes."

"Very funny." She sighed when he flicked his tongue over the hollow at the base of her throat. "Too bad New Hampshire and California are so far apart or we could schedule some booty calls."

He forced a laugh, but on the inside his heart was doing a little flip-flop. It was the first reference she'd made to the possibility of a relationship after the vacation was over and, even though she'd said it as a joke, he got a little hopeful. Maybe a long-distance romance would work until he could talk her into coming home where she belonged.

He was saved from having to answer that by a knock on the door but, on the downside, he had to stop nibbling at her neck. "I knew they'd come after us eventually."

It was Brian, a little out of breath. "You guys have to come down now so the grown-ups can decide what we're doing today."

"Tell them we'll be right there," he told the boy, who nodded and took off running again.

Joe dug into his gym bag, looking for the small toiletry bag so he could clean up a little, too. Keri wasn't the only one with morning and breakfast breath.

"Have you seen the bug spray?" she asked.

"Yeah, it's right there on the…" It wasn't there. "I thought it was on the table."

"I did, too. And there was an extra bottle in my bag. Oh…that *bitch*."

He stopped rummaging through the bags and looked up. Keri had her arms crossed and was literally tapping her foot.

"Terry! She said she'd hide my bug spray if I had sex with you."

"Come on, babe. It's not like she was sneaking around, listening at doors."

She pointed an accusing finger at him. "You were the one waving condoms at Kevin like a winning poker hand."

"Poke 'er." *Heh.* "Get it?"

"Focus, Joe."

He was, just apparently on the wrong thing. "It's probably in the cup holder of one of the chairs."

"All of it? Even the extra bottles and the repellent wipes I don't bother using because the mosquitoes don't seem to be at all deterred by natural tropical scents, which makes sense because why would mosquitoes be afraid of flowers?"

"They're probably not all in the cup holder, no."

"She snuck in here while we were at the restaurant and stole all my bug spray."

"Our bug spray. She took mine, too."

Keri crossed her arms and scowled at him. "You

should write her into your book and do horrible things to her."

He chuckled. "I try not to do horrible things to people I know in my books. They get upset."

"Oh? What about Carrie Danielson?"

Busted. "You were gone, presumably forever."

"Yeah, well now I'm back. And I have no freakin' bug spray."

While he wasn't stupid enough to say it out loud, she was awfully damn cute when she was pissed. "Let's go clean up and then join the crowd. I'll get your bug spray back."

"No."

"No what?" If he and Keri were going to hang out in the cabin all day, he was taking his clothes back off. And hers, too. Bacon breath be damned.

"I'm not going out there. Everybody knows."

"Knows what?"

"That we had sex, Kowalski."

"They didn't think I was a virgin, babe."

"No, they know you had sex with *me*. Because you told Kevin, who probably told everybody, which wasn't supposed to happen. Your mother's probably baking our wedding cake right now, for chrissake."

It was a punch to his gut, the immediate visual of Keri in a wedding dress, walking up the aisle toward him. It superimposed itself over the memory of her on prom night, when she'd worn a pretty navy-blue thing with a long zipper he'd enjoyed pulling down one excruciatingly teasing inch at a time.

Then high school Keri faded, leaving just the

thought of the here-and-now Keri, making her way toward the altar while his brothers fidgeted with their tuxes and their mothers sniffled into crumpled tissues.

He didn't know how the hell it had come to this, but, yeah, he wanted that.

Then she laughed at him. "Oh my God, I said *wedding* and you just totally shut down. You are such a guy, Kowalski."

Let her think that. It was better than confessing he'd been playing wedding planner in his mind. Maybe asking her opinion on a traditional carrot cake. "Nobody cares if we're having sex."

"Tell that to the mosquitoes."

"Come on. Let's go see what the family's up to."

She shook her head, trying to stare him down. "I'm not going out there."

He shrugged and put his hand on the doorknob. "Okay. But you're forfeiting a question."

"Oh, you bastard. You know you haven't given me shit to work with already!"

"You agreed to the terms by showing up, Daniels. You refuse to take part in an activity, you forfeit a question."

"Fine. But if I take a bunch of shit about last night, I'm wiping your hard drive."

"Is that what they're calling it nowadays?" He held the door open and laughed when she slapped him in the stomach as she walked by.

KERI DIDN'T THINK THE BUGS were too bad until she joined the family—minus Stephanie, who was probably off with Evan—on Mike and Lisa's shady site. Mosquitoes apparently liked the shade, or maybe it was her minty fresh breath, and within seconds she was slapping herself like a one-woman Three Stooges impersonator.

"What's the matter with you?" Leo asked, his volume as always attracting everybody's attention.

"I hate mosquitoes."

"Then put on some bug spray, dumbass."

"Leo!" Mary barked. "Don't call Joe's girl a dumbass!"

Joe's girl. She couldn't believe she'd called her that, or the way her stomach started to hurt. It had been a long time since she'd had occasion to remember how much she hated that.

Leo threw his hands up in the air. "What? She can't figure out mosquito repellent repels mosquitoes? That makes her a dumbass in my book."

"All of my bug spray mysteriously disappeared while Joe and I were out to breakfast," she explained, casting an obviously accusing glare Terry's way.

Mary didn't miss it. "Theresa, did you hide Keri's bug spray?"

Put on the spot, she obviously didn't dare lie. "Yup."

"Why?"

Keri saw Lisa's eyes get big and then she focused all her attention on giving Joe an *I told you so* look he couldn't miss.

"Because she…" Terry paused, then gave her

mother a falsely sheepish grin. "It was a practical joke, Ma. That's all."

"Go get it, then, before the mosquitoes eat her alive."

With the rather disappointing show over, everybody went back to talking about where they wanted to ride later, so Keri wandered over to the coffeepot and stole the last cold cup from the bottom. She turned to ask if she should make another pot, but a woman Keri didn't recognize and a little boy were walking up to Lisa.

"Hi, Bobby's mom. I'm Sean's mom." Both women laughed, then launched into a discussion about Bobby going up to their campsite to play trucks for a little while.

But Keri was barely aware of them. *Hi, Terry's mom. I'm Keri's mom.* It was happening again. Hadn't Mary just called her Joe's girl?

She couldn't remember how old she was when she'd realized her mother had no identity of her own. More than likely it was a long-growing awareness rather than a single moment.

Keri's mom. Ed's wife. Mrs. Daniels. Her dad called her hon and Keri called her Mom. She never heard anybody call her Janie. Oh, logically she knew people must have—Mrs. Kowalski, for one. They were friends, so one could assume first names had come into play.

For a while, Keri had even listened for it. And maybe that's why, as they were filing into the gymnasium to "Pomp and Circumstance," she'd been horrified to overhear a woman whisper, "That's the valedictorian's girlfriend."

"Oh, that's right," her companion had responded. "I'd heard Ed's daughter was Joe's girl now."

Keri had made the rest of that long, slow walk cataloguing the ways she'd been referred to lately. Ed's daughter. The Daniels girl. Doll (her father's pet name for her) and Peach (her mother's). Joe's girl. *Babe.*

The index card taped to her folding metal chair had read K. DANIELS.

"Keri," she had whispered to herself. And as she smoothed her gown and adjusted the mortarboard perched atop her big hair, she'd wondered if her mother had ever done the same.

Keri wanted to see her name in lights. On a marquee. Or in an entertainment column. She'd made up her mind before Joe had even started his speech— the world would see the name Keri Daniels somewhere.

Now she was *this* close to seeing it on the masthead of a major weekly magazine.

All she had to do was resharpen her focus— remember she was being granted unprecedented access to Joseph Kowalski.

Flash. "Say cheese!"

And his family.

CHAPTER FOURTEEN

TERRY SAT IN HER CHAIR, not even pretending to read the book in her lap. From there she could see site four, where Stephanie was helping her father break down his tent.

Other than sleeping, Steph had been with her father all weekend and, though she could see them when they were in the campground, Terry hadn't joined in. There was everything and nothing to say and, since she couldn't find the right words, she stayed away. It was his usual time with their daughter, anyway, though she didn't usually have to watch it from a distance.

On a more cheerful note, Keri hadn't spoken to her since the bug spray incident the day before. She didn't have anything to say to her, either. Nothing nice, anyway.

Terry had been on her way to the cabin to deliver a few important emails, which she'd printed out for Joe from the store's computer and then forgotten in the turmoil of Evan's arrival, but Kevin had called to her from his tent site and intercepted her. While he hadn't given her any specifics, his very pointed suggestion she leave Joe and Keri alone had told her all she needed to know.

The dumb son of a bitch had slept with her.

Maybe it wasn't really her business, but she was the one who'd gone off to UNH with Joe after Keri left, and watched him start the slow slide into self-destruction. Terry couldn't help but fear his being hurt by the same girl again would trigger the same coping behavior.

Steph laughed, drawing Terry's attention back to site four. Her husband was trying to stuff the haphazardly balled-up tent back into its storage bag, which would never happen unless he refolded the tent in a tight, methodical way.

As soon as he was done, he'd be leaving and then they'd be right back where they'd started. Actually, no. They would be worse off than when they'd started, because now Terry knew that although they both wanted the marriage to succeed, neither of them knew how to do it. Somehow that seemed worse than believing the marriage was over because he flat-out didn't want to be married to her anymore.

She should say something. Anything. Her sending him away with a cold shoulder would just make it harder for them to communicate when she got home. Before she could second-guess herself out of it, she stood up and started toward his site.

"Mom!" Steph yelled when she saw her coming. "You totally have to help us with this. It's never going to fit."

"It will. You just have to fold it—" she was going to say the *right* way "—a different way."

When a smile tugged just a little at the corners of Evan's mouth, she knew he hadn't missed her self-correction. It wasn't much—not nearly enough—but it was a start, maybe. How long would she last watching everything she said and did, though?

Ten minutes later, the tent was properly packed away and there was nothing for him to do but strap his four-wheeler down and say goodbye.

"Hey, Steph," he said, "would you run down to the store and grab a Coke for me for the ride home?"

He fished a dollar out of his pocket and then she was off, leaving them alone. Terry stuck her hands in her pockets and waited to see what her husband had to say to her that he couldn't say in front of their daughter.

"So, you'll call when you get home?" he asked. "So we can set up a night to have dinner?"

She nodded. "I think it's best if we don't say anything to anybody about it. Especially to Stephanie. I don't want to get her hopes up."

"If that's the way you want it." He stepped closer to her and it was only then she realized they were hidden from view of the campground by his truck and the ATV in the bed of it. "I've got my hopes up, though."

"Me, too," she whispered, not wanting to admit it, but knowing the only way they could come out on the other side of this was to be honest.

When he tipped her chin up and pressed his lips

to hers, her whole body shook. She wanted to throw her arms around him and hold him so tight he could never get away again, but she kept her hands in her pockets. Her heart was too bruised to give him anything more.

He drew back and she heard the footsteps hurrying up the dirt road. Steph was back and Terry turned away to swipe at her eyes while Evan took his Coke and said goodbye to their daughter.

"I'll see you soon, Terry," was all the goodbye she got, and then he climbed into his truck.

She and Steph watched him drive away and pull out onto the main road, and then Terry draped her arm over her daughter's shoulders. For once, Steph didn't pull away.

"Everybody's going riding again," Terry said. "Do you want to go or did riding with your dad tire you out?"

Steph shrugged. "They have that new romantic comedy with Sandra Bullock in it for rent down at the store. We could get it and some ice cream and be lazy bums today."

Terry was more in the mood for pounding out some frustration on the trails, but she squeezed Steph's shoulders. "Sounds like a good plan."

JOE WASN'T VERY HAPPY about the fact that Keri was in the wrong bed. With her back rested against her duffel bag with a pillow over it, she was scribbling away in her notebook on the bottom bunk, probably trying to re-create the conversation they'd had at the restaurant the day before and his lame answer to Thursday morning's question about the team of professionals—editor, agent, publicist and more—involved in making his career a success.

He was working, too, sitting on the big bed with his back against the wall and his laptop on his knees. They'd done almost forty miles on the four-wheelers so, while the family was lazing around recovering, he and Keri had escaped to his cabin on the excuse of squeezing in a little bit of writing before supper.

He'd pictured them snuggled up together on the bed, working side by side, but she'd settled herself on the bottom bunk before he'd even gotten his laptop fired up. Rather than let on how much he wanted to be close to her, he'd taken the big bed and set about trying to choreograph a fight scene in which one of the combatants was invisible. It was harder than he'd anticipated.

A half hour later, Keri set her steno pad and pencil on the nightstand between the beds, and then stretched out on her foam slab. "Totally off the record, between old friends, will you tell me why Lauren Huckins sued you for emotional distress?"

Whoa, where had that come from? He kept his eyes on his computer screen so she couldn't see how the question shook him. "I thought women didn't like hearing about ex-girlfriends."

"No. New girlfriends don't like hearing about ex-girlfriends." She rolled to her side and propped her head on her hand. "I know you met her at a bookstore where she worked and you were signing. You started dating, did some splashy parties and events. Then something happened that made you pay her a rumored-to-be substantial amount of money and turn into a hermit."

"I'm not a hermit," he protested, mostly to buy himself another minute to think.

He didn't like thinking about Lauren and he never, ever talked about her. The few people who needed to know the story, namely his family, already knew what had happened. There was never any reason to bring it up, except for Terry's recent crack about Keri being as bad as Lauren.

"A media hermit, then. I can't imagine you inflicting—reportedly—millions of dollars' worth of emotional damage on any woman. I…I'd really like to know."

A part of Joe wanted to tell her to shut up and leave it alone. It had been one of the more humiliating moments in his life, and definitely not one he wanted to share with the woman he was subtly trying to lure into a real relationship.

But there was no telling what crazy scenarios Keri had built up in her head to explain the lawsuit. He'd rather she think him a sucker than a total asshole.

"I retracted my proposal," he finally said, staring up at the ceiling fan.

"You paid Lauren Huckins a buttload of cash because you broke your engagement?"

"Totally off the record?"

"I swear, Joe. It's a personal question, not a professional one."

He inhaled deeply and then blew out the breath. "Technically there was no engagement because I retracted the proposal before she accepted it. Or rejected it."

When he turned his head to look at her, he wasn't surprised to see she was wearing her annoyed expression. "What...like some kind of practical joke?"

"No."

"You lost me."

He sighed and resigned himself to telling the entire sordid story. "When we started dating, Lauren took quite an interest in my career. She'd been sorority sisters or something with a woman who owned a chain of trendy restaurants in New York and L.A., and she dragged me around, getting our picture taken and my name in the paper. Not really my scene, but whatever. Start hanging with the cool crowd and the world thinks you're a cool kid.

"After a while she started complaining about how much she hated being introduced as my girlfriend, which I took as a sign it was time to propose."

"How utterly romantic."

"I haven't gotten to the romantic part yet. So anyway, I went ring hunting. It took forever, but I finally found one that seemed just right. It had all kinds of fancy, delicate gold work and a real sparkly stone. As soon as I saw it, I thought it would be perfect for her.

"So I did the whole romantic setting thing and gave her the box—"

"Did you get down on one knee?"

He rolled his eyes. "No, I didn't. I don't know why men do that."

"It's romantic."

"It's stupid. So anyway, she opened the box and I was waiting for her to get all teary-eyed and throw her arms around me. Instead she looked like she'd sucked on a lemon." He paused and blew out a deep breath. "Started lecturing me on how she'd expected something a little more substantial and befitting the future Mrs. Joseph Kowalski, and how the wife of a famous, wealthy author shouldn't have jewelry anybody could get at their local flea market."

"That bitch!"

The shocked anger in her voice eased the humiliation that, even though it was but a pale shadow of what he'd felt at the time, still made his gut ache like bad heartburn. "So I took it back. Told her I wasn't the Joseph Kowalski she was looking for. That I was just Joe."

"And she had the nerve to sue you?"

"I guess she felt the amount of *networking* she'd put into my career, along with the so-called emotional investment, entitled her to something."

"I can't believe you paid her. She never would have won that case."

Sometimes he couldn't believe he'd paid her,

either, but most of the time he considered it money well spent. "By paying her off, I was able to tie the money to an ironclad confidentiality agreement. If we'd gone to trial, win or lose, she could say anything to anybody, and everybody would have known what a blind, stupid sap Joe Kowalski was."

"You do realize there are people out there—like Tina, for example—who think you did something horrible or perverted to her."

"Better they think that than think I'm so pathetic I fell for a gold digger."

"Oh, that is such a guy thing to say."

Yeah, it probably was, but maybe Keri had no idea what it was like to feel that stupid. He'd not only been duped by a woman, but a woman he'd been intimate with. A woman he'd asked to be his wife. Even now he couldn't stomach what a moron he'd been.

"So, now you know my deep, dark secret," he said when the silence stretched on.

"You make it sound like you did something to be ashamed of, but at least you tried."

Something in her voice made him look over at her. "Did you ever come close?"

"Mostly just arrangements with fellow career-obsessed singles. Coworkers with benefits. I thought I was close once, but when he started making noises about getting married and starting a family, I realized I didn't love him more than I loved my job."

He wasn't sure what to say to that, so he hit Save and shut down the laptop. "This is depressing. Let's go see what the family's doing."

"A VOLLEYBALL GAME? Are you serious?"

"Not just a volleyball game," Brian protested. "The Annual Kowalski Volleyball Death Match Tournament of *Doom*."

Oh, yeah. Like she really wanted any part of that. "I don't play volleyball. I…don't know how."

"Liar," Terry chirped. "Remember the whole *we all went to high school together* thing? I've seen you play."

"And I suck."

"I didn't say you played well."

"And now I'm not playing at all."

Bobby shot up off the picnic table bench. "Uncle Joe said you were gonna play!"

Or she'd be breaking his dumbass rules and she wouldn't get to ask him a question. "Fine, but I want to be on the same team as Terry."

"That's not how we choose teams," Brian said, shaking his head.

"I'm sorry, but your aunt has a mean spike and I do *not* want to be on the opposite side of the net."

Terry laughed. "My spike isn't all that mean anymore."

"We won't divide evenly this year," Danny pointed out. "There are thirteen of us."

"I'll keep score," Keri was quick to offer. "I don't want to mess up the math."

"We'll count Bobby and Ma as one player," Terry said.

It ended up with Mary, Kevin, Mike, Lisa, Joey, Bobby and Steph on one team and Leo, Danny,

Brian, Terry, Joe and Keri on the other. And the ball was an oversize, inflatable, slightly weighted beach ball designed to look like a volleyball, but smaller, lighter and a lot less painful if you took it in the face.

Keri found that out personally a few minutes later when Mike decided to take his frustrations out on the ball and she didn't duck quick enough. Fortunately, as the ball bounced off her face, Joe dove across the grass and kept it from hitting the ground. Danny sent it over the net and, though Joe did give her a quick glance to make sure she was okay, the play went on.

Until Steph ended up on her uncle Kevin's shoulders, slamming the ball back over the net with ease.

"Hey, that's against the rules," Keri protested.

"No rules in the Annual Kowalski Volleyball Death Match Tournament of *Doom*," Joey yelled at her from across the net. "Whiner!"

"Cheater!" she yelled back, earning boos and hisses from the cheating team.

They tried to offset the advantage by putting Brian on Joe's shoulders, but since Kevin was taller than Joe and Steph was taller than Brian, they remained at a disadvantage.

Until the cheating team scored five unanswered points. Before she realized what was happening, Joe's head popped between her legs and he was hoisting her onto his shoulders.

"Oh my God!" she yelped. "Don't you dare!"

She would have struggled, but Joe was already trying to stand up straight, with Terry's help, and she was afraid she'd fall. This wasn't like playing chicken in the pool, where a big splash was the worst that would happen. Joe was tall and the ground was hard.

"Quit squirming and pay attention," Leo barked as Lisa prepared to serve for the other team.

As the ball came over the net, Joe sidestepped to line her up with it, but the swaying motion caught Keri by surprise and—instead of slamming the ball back over the net—she gripped a handful of Joe's hair to steady herself and watched it sail past.

"Ow! Easy on the scalp, babe."

"Put. Me. Down."

"Hit. The. Ball," Leo ordered.

The next time the ball came over the net, she was ready and, though she kept her left fingers tangled in Joe's hair, she reached out with her right hand to hit it back.

"I did it," she yelled.

Then Steph spiked the ball back over the net, where it hit Joe in the face because he couldn't let go of Keri's legs to defend himself.

"Ow," he said again.

"I've got it this time," she promised.

Almost ten minutes of intense volleyball ensued until, with the score evened up, Keri was pretty sure she could feel Joe's knees trembling through his body.

"Are you going to be able to put me down without dropping me?"

It sounded like he tried to laugh, but the sound

was a little breathless. "Sure. Hey, Pop. Gimme a hand."

In the process of getting her down, Leo's hand inadvertently grabbed her ass, which made everybody laugh, causing her to be unceremoniously dumped on the grass. Joe collapsed beside her, his face red with exertion.

"I'm not twenty years old anymore," he grudgingly admitted.

"Neither is Kevin," she replied.

He turned his head to frown at her. "If we're going for the cheap shot, let me point out Steph's a little lighter than you."

She would have slapped him, but Leo loomed over them, casting a big shadow and pointing at Keri. "Next year, you ride on Kevin's shoulders and Steph can go with Joe. That'll even things out."

Her smile froze in place. *Next year?*

There wasn't going to be a next year and this was exactly what she'd been afraid of before they'd even had sex. His family thought they were a couple. Not only did they think she and Joe were a couple, but his father obviously thought they'd still be together in a year's time.

"I think it's time for a lunch break," Mary declared, and there was a chorus of agreement and a mass exodus in the general direction of shade and the drink coolers.

"He didn't mean anything by it," Joe told her.

So he'd noticed it, too. "I warned you this would happen. They think we're together."

"So what? It's not like they haven't survived my breakups in the past. They survived you leaving. They even survived Lauren. I'm sure they'll be okay this time, too."

Well, he didn't have to make it sound as if she was so easily discarded, either. "By the way, even if I am here next year, I'm never playing volleyball with you people again."

He stood up and then grabbed her hand to haul her to her feet. "Next year? That was only the first match of the day, babe. It's not called the Annual Kowalski Volleyball Death Match Tournament of *Doom* for nothing."

"I hate you."

JOE WAS PONDERING the least obvious way to get Keri untangled from his family and back to the cabin for a little post-lunch dessert when his father toppled off the conversational high wire.

"So what's this I hear about you wanting another baby?" Pop boomed for half the campground to hear.

"Oh, jeez, not another one," Danny muttered.

Mike immediately tensed up and Lisa gave Pop a shaky smile. "Wouldn't it be nice to have another granddaughter to offset all these grandsons?"

His father hadn't even opened his mouth to answer when Mike cut in with a curt no.

"But we have four—"

"No." Mike stood and tossed his paper plate into the fire. "We're done with that, Lisa."

"Maybe we should—"

"I'm done. And since everybody else already knows you've lost your damn mind, they may as well know I haven't."

He started toward his RV, and Joe was surprised when Lisa stood and followed him. They usually stuck pretty close to the Cleaver routine in front of the kids.

"I miss having a baby, Mike. And now that they're older, I…"

"Now that they're older *what?* What part of them getting older and more independent and giving us more freedom are you seeing as a bad thing?"

"You won't have any reason to stay with me."

Joe winced. The fact Mike had married Lisa because she was pregnant with Joey wasn't some deep, dark family secret, but it wasn't exactly lunch conversation, either.

"Are you kidding me?" Mike was getting loud, and their mother stood, ready to intervene. "You think I'll leave if you don't have a baby on your hip?"

"You didn't *want* to marry me. Everybody knows that."

The campsite suddenly became a flurry of activity, and youngster-distracting freeze pops appeared as if by magic in Terry's hands. Their parents were both making a beeline to Lisa and Mike, and it was a toss-up as to who was going to slap whom upside the head first. Keri was working her way out of the group, trying for invisible. And poor Steph was crying silent tears, no doubt traumatized by watching another of the stable, role-model relationships in her life crumble.

But everybody froze when Mike made a frustrated growling sound and plowed his fist into the side of his camper. Joey was on his feet in an instant, freeze pop dropped in the dirt as he stepped in front of Lisa.

Joe watched the boy—so tall, skinny and scared shitless—facing off against his dad, and felt an odd tightening in his chest. Lisa wasn't in any danger. Mike had a bit of a temper, but he'd throw himself under a bus before he raised a hand to his family.

But Joe's oldest nephew had just taken a giant, irreversible step toward the man he'd become, and it was an awesome and yet incredibly sad moment to watch.

Nobody intervened when Mike turned and walked out of the site and up the dirt road. They all knew from years of experience he'd walk it off and in ten minutes be back with an apology and a better attitude.

So Joe had no idea what to say when he heard his own truck start up and then watched it drive past them and exit the campground.

"Where's Daddy going?" Bobby asked, melted freeze pop running down his chin and staining his shirt green. "He didn't give me a kiss goodbye."

Lisa looked totally stricken, so Terry stepped in with a half-assed explanation of Daddy putting himself in time-out for being cranky.

"He should do some timeses."

Lisa, obviously shaken beyond her ability to front for the kids, started to cry. "Is he coming back?" Nobody knew, but they all said yes.

CHAPTER FIFTEEN

MIKE'S LEAVING NOT ONLY derailed any plans to resume the volleyball game from hell, but made Keri keenly aware of her nonfamily status, so she retreated quietly to the cabin and her book.

Cocooned in the pillows and blankets on Joe's bed, she forced herself to turn each stiff, crackling page with the hope of losing herself in the story. It didn't happen. She merely managed to move ahead several chapters without remembering a single page.

She got up and cleaned the cabin, then tried to read some more. The book still didn't grab her, so she took out her steno pad and pencil. She may as well get some work done while the Kowalskis were busy with their family crisis.

Reworking the answers he'd already given into paragraphs that might pacify Tina without violating any of Joe's rules was a grueling, ongoing process. And Keri was still debating whether or not to use the drunken, Carrie Danielson-writing chapter of his life.

Formulating each progressive question was also getting harder, as the questions she wanted to ask Joe were diverging from the kind of questions *Spotlight* readers would want answers to.

With a sigh, she turned to a fresh page and scratched out a throwaway question. Then, disgusted with herself, she leaned back against the pillows and closed her eyes.

When she opened them again, the weak evening sun barely lit the cabin and Joe sat on the edge of the bed, her notebook in his hand.

Keri sat up and scrubbed at her face. That was the first nap she'd taken in years, and she remembered now why she hated them. They left her groggy and disoriented, with no sense of time.

"Is this your next question?" he asked, flashing the page at her.

Why didn't you ask me not to go?

"No. I was playing hangman with myself."

"Where's the gallows?"

"I do that in my head. Makes it easier to cheat."

"Good point. I should try that." He took her pencil and wrote something on the page. "I win."

He tossed the pad on the bed next to her and walked over to turn on the gas fireplace.

Because I wanted you to be a happy zebra. Why didn't you ask me to go with you?

"A happy zebra?"

"I had to get a *Z* in there off the top of my head. Tried to stump myself."

Keri grabbed the pencil. *I couldn't eXpect you to leave your Family, Joe.* "*X, F* and *J.* I win."

He took it and sighed before writing something and handing it back. "I lost a long time ago."

I loved you.

She wrote *I loved you, too* under it, then flipped the cover closed and jammed the pencil through the wire spiral. "How is Lisa?"

"Convinced her husband left her."

"And the boys?"

"Pretending to be distracted just to make the adults feel better."

"Do you think he's coming back?"

"Since he took my keys and stole my truck, he pretty much has to."

"Would it help if we took the kids out for pizza or something?"

"You'd do that?"

Keri laughed. "I know they're a handful, but I've read that children can sense tension, especially in their family, and that it throws them out of whack. As rowdy as your nephews are, I can't imagine them out of whack."

Joe smiled, but it didn't reach his eyes or make his dimples pop. "Do you want kids?"

The question flew at her from left field and she didn't even have time to get her glove up. "I don't know. I guess I stopped thinking about it at some point. By the time I meet the career goals I set for myself and then go daddy shopping, I'll have to deliver in the geriatric ward. How about you?"

"I guess not."

"Why not? Family's always been everything to you, and you'd make a great dad."

He shrugged. "I was pretty self-involved for a while. Drinking and writing were my entire world. And then, after Lauren, I... I've got Steph and the boys, and being Uncle Joe's been good enough for me."

But there was an unhappiness in his eyes that she'd never seen before, and it went deeper than concern for his brother's woes.

"They're growing up," he said abruptly, pacing in front of the fireplace. "Joey tonight...I was so damn proud of him. And it hurt that he's not mine to be proud of. I almost hated Mike right then, for getting to be Joey's dad."

She had no idea what to say to that, and eventually the silence stretched on to the point the moment was gone.

"So, the pizza thing?" she asked after it was obvious no more was forthcoming.

"I appreciate the offer, but I was actually sent here to bring you back for dinner. I got distracted by hangman. Also, I think we covered the fact Mike stole my truck. We won't all fit in your rental and it's a long walk to the pizza place."

Keri stowed her notepad and donned a sweatshirt before following Joe out the door. The extra fabric helped keep the hardiest of the mosquitoes at bay, plus the temperature had a way of going down with the sun.

The entire family—minus Mike—was seated

around the campfire, breaking out the ingredients for s'mores. Clearly the Kowalskis had already inhaled their suppers while she and Joe had been depressing the hell out of each other.

"I made you each a plate," Mary called over. "Hurry and eat before the chocolate's gone."

Keri was licking barbecue sauce from her fingers when a vehicle pulled into the campground. The others must have recognized the sound of Joe's SUV, because their heads all swiveled in that direction and the tension level shot up into the stratosphere again.

Mike parked across the front of the site, then tossed Joe his keys. After lifting the back hatch, he pulled out a gigantic gift box, which he barely managed to carry in Lisa's general direction. Once it became obvious he couldn't see and could feasibly end up in the campfire, Kevin gave him a hand.

"I hid it at Ma's," Mike, a little winded and sounding nervous as hell, told Lisa. "It's your birthday present."

"My birthday's not for two months."

"I know. But I'm giving it to you early."

Bobby dropped his marshmallow into the coals, nearly tumbling in after it in his rush to get to his father. "Can I have mine early, too? Is it a Wii? Can I have it now?"

"No, not telling, and no. Open it, Lisa."

Keri couldn't help inching closer as Lisa painstakingly untied the pink ribbon. Being a paper tearer by nature, Keri itched to reach over and yank hard on the wrapping paper. But she didn't let herself get close enough, because it was, after all, a family moment.

Finally, just about the time Keri was starting to twitch, Lisa sliced through the last piece of tape and ever so carefully folded back the paper and lifted the lid. By standing on her tiptoes and craning her neck, Keri could make out another gaily wrapped and beribboned box, identical to the first, only smaller.

Three boxes later, Bobby had a fresh marshmallow dangling about three feet too high over the fire, Kevin was nodding off in his chair, and Lisa's smile wasn't nearly as bright.

"This was a lot funnier in my head," Mike mumbled.

It only took another two boxes before Lisa started snapping ribbons and shredding paper, much to Keri's relief. By the time she got down to one the size of a shirt box, Lisa had to stop and have a drink.

Inside that box was a navy-blue folder with gold embossed script on the front. Keri edged forward, trying to make it out in the increasingly dim light.

"A travel agency?" Lisa opened the folder, then pressed her hand to her mouth.

"A two-week Caribbean cruise," Mike told everybody who'd managed to hang in there through the unwrapping. Lisa was still speechless, slowly turning the pages. "Our honeymoon. Finally."

Lisa stopped about halfway through the packet and pulled out a sheet of creamy beige paper. "What does this mean?"

"It's a reservation for a sunset wedding ceremony

on the cruise ship. I thought we could get married again, just the two of us. No kids—in utero or otherwise. I've been saving money for three years for this and waiting for Bobby to start first grade, so taking the kids for two weeks wouldn't be too much of a burden on Terry and Ma. That's…that's why I've been so freaked out by you wanting another baby."

"Getting married again? But why?"

"Because I want to. Not because I have to or because it's expected of me. Just because I *want* to."

Almost totally unsupervised at this point, the kids were making monster s'mores and melted marshmallow was congealing on every surface within twenty feet, but Keri didn't care. She was too busy looking for a tissue. It seemed Terry and Mary were hoarding them.

"I wanted to do this a little more privately," Mike continued, "in case you turned me down, but it seemed like the time had come."

Lisa paused in furiously wiping her face to keep her tears from wrecking the papers in her lap. "Turn you down? What are you talking about?"

"Did you ever stop to think if I wondered if you'd only married me because you had to? Or if the only reason you've stayed with me is because it's easier than being a single mother of four kids?"

"I… No. I've always loved you, and I thought you knew that."

"And I thought you knew I've always loved you, too."

"Oh." Lisa clutched the folder to her chest and smiled through her tears. "I'll need a new dress."

Mike rolled his eyes as the guys in the crowd laughed. "Like I can afford one now."

Lisa launched herself into her husband's arms and, while one of the boys made gagging sounds, everybody went back to what they'd been doing before Mike had rolled in.

Except Keri. With everybody laughing at the melted marshmallow on Kevin's ass and the smeared chocolate in Bobby's hair, thankfully nobody noticed her step into the shadows and slip away to the cabin. If Joe wanted to claim she'd forfeited a question by leaving the campfire early, so be it.

Without turning the lights on, she climbed into the bunk and pulled the covers up over her head.

The envy was going to eat her alive. How crazy was that? Never for a second had Keri ever thought she'd be envious of a woman who was a bundle of insecurities—whose career consisted of laundry and carpooling, and who had given birth to four walking, talking weapons of mass destruction.

Hell, right now she was even envious of Terry. Sure, her husband might have walked out on her, but for thirteen years she hadn't slept alone at night. She hadn't stood at her kitchen counter—alone—choking down frozen gourmet meals fresh from the microwave.

Keri could have had all that with Joe. She'd given it all up to make something of herself. To build a career. She was successful, respected, financially comfortable and *this* close to achieving her goal.

It was all Joe's fault. All that talk about love and children earlier had weakened the tick-dampening wall around her biological clock, and now this?

Closing her eyes in a wasted effort to keep the tears from leaking out, Keri hated questioning the path she'd taken, but she couldn't help it. Maybe, when she'd been sitting there so confused in her white cap and gown with the tassel tickling her cheek, she'd made the wrong choice.

JOE TURNED THE DIMMER switch down low before turning on the cabin's overhead light. With the campground wrapped in darkness, his eyes were already adjusted, so he had no trouble picking out the lump of blanket on the bottom bunk.

When Keri snuck away from the campfire, he'd thought about going after her. He could have teased her about bailing on a family activity, or tried to talk her into a short ride. But there had been something about the set of her shoulders and the way she'd held her head that told him she needed a little alone time.

Not that he blamed her. He knew as well as anybody his family could be exhausting. He'd even gone so far, once or twice, as to manufacture a deadline or agent meeting just to get a couple of days to himself.

"You awake?" he whispered. No answer, but she was faking. While Chinese water torture probably couldn't make her admit it, she snored like a chain-saw sucking down its last drop of oil.

She wasn't snoring. She was sniffling.

Shit. He replayed the evening in his mind, but couldn't come up with a single incident that would cause Keri to cry. Things had actually taken a turn for the better, what with Mike and Lisa's tension having been swept away by an overpriced vacation his brother wouldn't let him help pay for. Terry had been engrossed in the familial drama and hadn't even spoken to Keri, that he knew of.

He stripped down to his boxers, then stood in the middle of the room feeling stupid. He couldn't just crawl into his bed and go to sleep. But he couldn't crawl in with her, either. Even if she hadn't been crying, he wasn't sure the bunk would support them.

"Do you need to walk to the bathhouse?" he asked, wishing he'd thought to ask before he'd gotten undressed.

"No," she answered in a squeaky, quiet voice.

"Okay." At a loss, he flipped off the light and sat on the edge of his bed. "Hey, things were so hectic this morning, what with breakfast and Brian skinning his knee and everything, you forgot to ask me a question."

"So?"

"We don't want Tina's winged monkeys reporting back you're going soft."

She didn't laugh. "I don't care."

"Are you sick?"

"No."

Having reached a conversational dead end, Joe punched his pillow into shape and stretched out. To keep from dwelling on the uncommunicative woman lying a few feet from him, Joe turned his thoughts to his manuscript. He'd managed to drop his antagonist into the plot hole from hell, and he had no idea how to get him out. Considering the book was due in less than two months, he needed to start expending some energy in that direction.

"Damn you!" The bunk bedcovers flew back to reveal a fully clothed Keri. "I didn't have to go until you brought it up."

Joe managed not to laugh at her, but it wasn't easy. "Do you want me to walk with you?"

"Yes, you have to walk with me. I think I saw a raccoon trying to hot-wire a four-wheeler the other night."

"If I go with you and protect you from the raccoon gang that rules the campground, will you come back to my bed where you belong?"

She snatched her sweatshirt off the back of the chair so viciously the chair fell over. "Just because we had a little fun under your covers doesn't mean I belong there, Kowalski."

As he watched her pick up the chair and set it right with a thud, he decided to keep his mouth shut and just walk with her before he dug the hole any deeper.

It wasn't easy being single and pushing forty in a big family group, and he guessed that's what was eating at her. He knew how it felt. He slept alone and he ate alone. He watched television alone and, when he was reading a book and came across an exceptionally good passage, he had nobody to share it with.

Most of the time it was okay, but being around a family like Mike and Lisa and the kids had a way of driving the loneliness home like a poison-tipped drill bit.

Joe waited outside the bathroom for Keri, noticing when she came out she'd given her face a good scrubbing. It was still obvious she'd shed a few tears, but he didn't say anything.

"Can I sleep in the big bed even if we don't have sex?" she asked when they were almost back to the cabin.

Maybe *she* could sleep in the big bed if they didn't have sex, but he probably wouldn't sleep all that well. "Sure. We'll call it a rain check."

She didn't laugh, but she did manage a small smile and a big eye roll. He had to turn his back while she changed into pajamas—the same kind as the ones he'd wrecked, but a different color—and then she climbed into his bed and curled on her side.

He stripped back down to his boxer briefs and then, after a moment's hesitation, slipped a pair of sweats over them. Just so she wouldn't worry he was getting ideas. Not that he wasn't getting them, but he wasn't going to act on them.

Fifteen minutes later, with Keri's body limp and warm against his as she slept, he pressed a kiss to the top of her head and closed his eyes. Not sleeping alone, with or without the sex, was nice. So nice, in fact, he wondered how, when she went home, he'd ever sleep again.

CHAPTER SIXTEEN

THE DAY BEFORE IT WAS TIME to pack up and leave, the family always took one last, long ride to close out the vacation. By getting a later start, they could be out until just after dark. Not too late, but enough to give the kids a bit of night-riding thrill.

As they cleaned up the remnants of their hibachi-grilled hot dog dinner, the mood among the adults was melancholy, as was the norm. Nobody wanted to go back to real life and ringing telephones and to-do lists.

Joe was working his ass off putting on a happy face for the family, but inside he was as melancholy as the rest. Maybe more so. The past few days had been a whirl of laughter and lovemaking and enjoying time with the family, but it was almost at an end. Tomorrow Keri was going home to California.

He felt a tightening as he watched her walking across the field, the sunset glinting on the pond behind her, and panicked. It wasn't the same old tightening of the jeans around his crotch he'd come to accept as a constant state of being when Keri was around.

This was a tightening in his chest that made his

heart beat faster and his breath catch in his throat. His palms got a little clammy, and he turned to his machine so nobody could see his face. He probably had a dumbstruck expression he didn't want to have to explain.

He wanted to keep her. It was that simple. He'd stupidly thought he'd drag her up here and spend a couple of weeks together—some of it horizontal— for old time's sake, then send her on her way with a kiss on the cheek and a slap on the ass.

Instead he was getting slapped upside the head with the growing certainty he'd been right the night almost twenty years ago when he'd told his mother she was wrong—he'd never get over Keri Daniels.

He'd tried to hide his pain when she'd dumped him and taken off for California. With two pain-in-the-ass brothers, he couldn't afford to be seen crying over a girl. But then Ma had snuck into his room and sat on the edge of the bed. She'd rubbed his back as she had when he was little and he didn't feel good, and somehow he'd wound up with his head in her lap, sobbing his sorry, broken heart out.

She'd told him he'd get over Keri and someday he'd meet the woman he was meant to spend the rest of his life with. That if he was truly destined to be with Keri forever, she wouldn't have broken up with him and moved as far away as she could without getting her feet wet.

So what did it say about destiny that almost twenty years later his work and her work had conspired to bring them back together? Nothing in his life had ever felt more right than sitting in front of the campfire, holding Keri's hand. Talking to her. Sleeping with her.

Instead of someday meeting the woman he was meant to spend the rest of his life with, maybe he'd simply met her *again*.

"You gonna be okay?" His dad had snuck up behind him and Joe hadn't even noticed.

"Sure, Pop."

"You know your mother's gonna call you every five minutes once we get home, right?"

Joe sighed and nodded. "I know, and I'll try not to take her head off after a couple days of it. But I'm not gonna drink, Pop."

His father wrapped his arm around Joe's shoulders, which made him have to hunch down a little because he was taller than his father but he wanted the embrace. "You don't think you are. But she's still here, isn't she? You might feel different when you're alone in that monster house of yours tomorrow night."

It was a good point, and there was no sense in arguing with him. If there was one thing his twenties had taught him, it was that when you hurt your family as badly as he'd hurt his, the fear was always there he'd become that person again. There was a watchfulness when they knew he was stressed. Family members randomly stopping by for trumped-up reasons. Constant phone calls asking stupid questions, just so they could gauge his sobriety. It didn't matter that he hadn't had a drink since the day he'd hit Kevin. They were afraid one beer would be his undoing.

And while he knew alcohol wasn't a demon he had to battle constantly, he understood where they were coming from.

"If I think I want a beer—I won't, but if I do— I'll call. I promise."

Pop slapped him on the shoulder. "Or you could talk her into staying."

If only it was that simple. "She has to go back. She's got a job and an apartment and a life there."

He'd come to terms with that. She was going to leave tomorrow. It was just that he really wanted the trip to California to be for the purpose of packing up and moving back.

"If she loves you, son, she'll come back."

He shrugged. Maybe that was true. But only if he asked her to stay. He hadn't asked last time. Not because he hadn't wanted her to stay, but because he'd been so stunned he hadn't said much of anything at all.

And it had bothered her, too. She'd even scribbled it in her notepad the night Mike stole his truck to save his marriage. *Why didn't you ask me not to go?*

Somehow he was going to have to find the courage to say the words out loud. And time was running out.

IN THE FADING LIGHT, Keri surreptitiously watched Joe through the corner of her eye having what looked like a private moment with his dad. Since she'd fin-

ished her assigned task of gathering the condiments
and putting them back in the cooler, she'd taken a
walk by the pond and now had time to kill waiting
for Joe and Leo to rejoin the group.

Time she didn't want to spend thinking about
going home tomorrow. Going home meant facing
Tina with a possibly career-ending pile of not much.
She'd asked him about his interaction with fans. No
scandal there. She'd asked him about negative reviews and bloggers who didn't think he lived up to
the hype. No scandal there. Hell, Wednesday night
she'd asked him straight out what the biggest scandal of his career was and…nothing.

Beyond the lawsuit Keri couldn't talk about and
the alcohol, Joe didn't have any bodies buried in the
backyard and Tina only wanted the skeletons. Keri
was screwed. But the last thing she wanted to do was
ruin her last night with Joe, so she just kept telling
herself she'd think about it tomorrow.

With little else to distract her, she focused on
Kevin, who was using bungee cords to strap the
small grill back on Leo's machine. Probably would
have been easier if he hadn't been doing it one-
handed so he wouldn't have to put down his soda,
but maybe it was a guy thing.

He looked so damn well-adjusted for a man who'd
lost his marriage and his career in one blow. Literally one blow, but for the fact that, knowing the
Kowalski temper, there had been a lot more than one
blow exchanged.

So he'd bought a sports bar in New Hampshire's

capital city and seemed pretty content. On the surface. But there was something about him that made her journalistic senses tingle, even though she knew he was totally off-limits where her article was concerned.

"He told you, didn't he?"

Keri blinked, belatedly realizing she'd been staring at him. "About what?"

"My divorce."

"Oh." She did her best not to look guilty. And to not answer his question directly. "I was looking at your nose. It's been broken before, hasn't it?"

"Yeah." He rubbed his finger over the bump on the bridge of his nose. "Joe did that."

"Get a little carried away with the roughhousing?"

"Something like that." He gave her a grin that was a paler version of Joe's, then knocked back a slug of soda.

It was the look in his eyes, also a paler version of Joe's, that gave him away. "You're lying."

"Just a little."

"That happened while he was drinking, didn't it? Not roughhousing."

He took another sip of the soda, watching her over the rim of the can. "He told you about the drinking?"

"He said he had a drinking problem and he quit when the family started liking him less than he liked himself."

"Yeah. I went over one day to see if he had Pop's air compressor and he was just backing out of his

driveway, drunk off his ass and going on a beer run.
I managed to get his keys."

"And he hit you?"

"After the mother of all shouting matches." Kevin
smiled and shrugged. "I wasn't expecting him to
swing, of course, or he never would have gotten the
drop on me."

"Of course not."

"Busted my nose all to shit, complete with the two
black eyes and everything. When Terry showed up
with some stuff for him to sign, we were both sitting
on the grass, crying like a couple of girls."

"Sounds painful."

"Not as painful as watching my brother drink
himself to death."

Even though she knew it was true, she couldn't
picture Joe as a drunk. And Kevin made it sound a
whole lot more serious than Joe had. "That's when
he quit?"

"Just like that. Hasn't had a drop of booze since,
so I figure the nose was a small price to pay." He
wrinkled it at her. "Besides, the chicks dig it."

She'd bet they did. Adding just a touch of the bad
boy to the Kowalski good looks and charm probably
had the women lining up for a shot at him. "So about
your divorce, you—"

"Nice try, Lois Lane." There might have been
humor in the words, but there was none in the tone.

"Can't blame a girl for trying," she said easily.
"You brought it up. All I did was check out the chick
magnet on your face."

"Gear up!" Leo bellowed, and Keri turned to see Joe walking toward her.

He looked a little sad around the eyes and she went to meet him halfway, away from the chaos of five kids scrambling to find their gloves. "You okay?"

"Sure." He smiled, but she could tell his heart wasn't in it.

He looked as if he was going to say something more—something serious, judging by the way he seemed to take a deep breath first—but Steph ran up to them with Keri's helmet and thrust it into her hands.

"Here! I thought it was mine, but it's too big."

Great, not only was Keri heavier than Steph, but she had a bigger head, too. Sure, the kid was only twelve, but still.

"Let's go," Leo called, and whatever Joe was going to say would have to wait.

She jammed her helmet on her head and buckled it as she walked to her ATV, but then she realized Joe hadn't moved. He was still standing there, watching her.

"You okay?" she asked again.

He almost managed a full grin this time. "Really. I'm cool."

But she knew he was lying and as she pulled her ATV into line behind his—truce or not, she wasn't riding behind Terry ever again—she wondered what had prompted what had looked like a heart-to-heart with his dad.

Sadly, she suspected she knew. They were afraid Joe would be upset when she left tomorrow and get drunk. And if he got drunk once, they feared his sliding back to where he'd been before he'd punched Kevin in the face.

She and Joe had discussed the situation, though, and Keri had to trust that Joe was being honest when he agreed to a vacation fling that would be over when she boarded her flight to California. He'd known right up front she wasn't staying.

She had an urge to rub her chest—the damn hot dogs were probably giving her heartburn—but they were going down a rough hill and she had to focus on braking properly and not crashing into Joe.

Would he move to California?

The thought came so suddenly from left field, she almost swerved and ran into a tree.

He'd written that on her notebook. *Why didn't you ask me to go with you?* It was something he'd at least considered, then, even if it had been twenty years ago. Trying to picture Joe in Los Angeles wasn't easy. This was obviously his native habitat.

And, after watching him with his family for a couple of weeks, she couldn't imagine him being separated from them by the span of an entire continent. But that's what frequent flyer miles were for, right?

As much as she tried to remind herself what was at stake—and that it was she who'd implemented the fling-only rule—she couldn't help but wonder if she could have her career and keep Joe, too.

WHEN THEY ARRIVED back at the campground, Joe shut off his machine and just sat there. He didn't want to face sitting around the final campfire yet. And he definitely didn't want to face going back to the cabin with Keri for the last time.

While the family dragged all the gear back to the bins to pack it away, Keri leaned against his fender and put her hand on his knee. "What's wrong with you?"

"There's still another two hours before the trail curfew kicks in," he said. "Why don't you jump up behind me and we'll go out, just the two of us."

She looked for a few seconds as though she wanted to psychoanalyze him, then she shrugged. "Okay. I need to run up to the bathhouse first."

Two weeks in the woods and he'd never managed to convince her to pee over a log, he thought, chuckling as she trotted off toward the closest toilet. She'd done okay for a city girl, though. Other than a lingering paranoia regarding raccoons, she'd acclimated herself to the dirt and the DEET pretty well.

"Going back out?" Kevin asked. He was walking around picking up the stray gloves and goggles the kids had dropped.

"Yeah, just for a little putt."

"Gonna pop the question?"

Joe almost choked. "Jeez, Kevin, it's only been two weeks. Little premature, don't you think?"

When his brother only shrugged, Joe shook his head. It was crazy to think two weeks isolated from day-to-day reality was any basis for believing they could build a life together. Wasn't it? "Do you think I should?"

"Dunno," Kevin said. "But maybe you should wait and see if she sells you down the river to that bitch she works for."

"She won't do that."

"You hope." Kevin looked over Joe's shoulder. "Here she comes. Try not to roll butt naked in the poison ivy."

"Funny."

He leaned forward so Keri could climb onto the seat behind him, then waited until she'd buckled her helmet to turn the machine around and head back for the trails.

The trail was smooth and there was no tension in her body as her thighs hugged his and her hands rested comfortably at his waist. They rode for miles that way, the darkness broken only by their headlights and the occasional glimpse of house lights in the distance.

He took a side trail—one seldom traveled except by the most experienced riders—leading up to a scenic overlook she hadn't seen yet. She fell back into the Heimlich habit a few times while he navigated the ruts and rocks, but it was worth it when they reached the top and he killed the engine. In almost absolute silence and darkness, they looked out over the twinkling lights of the town far below.

"This was worth almost dying on the hill back there," Keri said as she pulled off her helmet.

"You weren't gonna die. I was, if you'd squeezed any harder, but you were safe."

They walked to the edge of the rock jutting out from the ground and stood, hand in hand, just looking.

Was this the moment? The perfect, romantic moment to ask her if she'd consider giving up her life in California and coming back to him? He had to ask. He wouldn't be able to live with himself if he didn't.

But she sighed and leaned against him so his arm wrapped around her and her head nestled under his chin, and he couldn't bear to risk ruining this moment. She would probably say no, and he couldn't spend his last night with her with that between them.

At least if he kept his mouth shut for now, there would still be hope.

"I could stay up here forever," she said with a sigh.

"I wish we could," he said honestly. "But we can't stay long. We're already pushing getting back in the campground before quiet hours kick in."

She only wrapped her arms around his waist and snuggled a little closer. The words were there on the tip of his tongue. *Will you come back to me?*

But he swallowed hard and kept quiet, his eyes on the night sky. He looked up at the stars, wishing one would fall and offer him a wish.

He wasn't sure how long they stood there. At one point he heard Keri let out a shuddery breath and wondered where her thoughts were. Was she thinking about tomorrow? Would leaving him behind be as painful for her as letting her go would be for him?

Eventually he had no choice but to pull away and head back to the four-wheeler. If he didn't get on the throttle a little, he was going to catch hell for breaking the rules, but it had been worth it.

Dangling his helmet from his right hand, he climbed on and waited while Keri took a last look around. But instead of grabbing her helmet and climbing into the seat, she stepped up onto the floorboard and worked her leg between him and the steering column until she was sitting facing him, straddling his lap.

"Gonna be hard steering like this," he joked, but the humor was a little lost in the roughness of his voice.

They were alone. It was dark. And, even if another rider ventured out after hours and headed for the same spot, they'd hear him coming a mile away.

Her teeth flashed white in the dark as she smiled. "Remember when we used to go parking behind the old cemetery?"

"How could I forget?" He slid his hands up her sides until he cupped her breasts, then rubbed his thumbs over her nipples. "It was a little creepy. That time you hit the heel of your foot on the horn almost killed me."

"God, that car was ugly."

He laughed. "I have fond memories of that car, babe."

"Very brown memories, come to think of it. Ugly

brown car. Ugly brown couch in your parents' basement. Brown comforter on your bed."

"Brown shag carpet in your parents' living room."

She yanked the end of her pink riding jersey out of her jeans and pulled it over her head, followed by the sports bra.

Joe had his mouth on her nipple before the clothes hit the ground, and the squirming that commenced on her part was almost his undoing. Straddling the machine's seat tightened the jeans across his erection and, trapped under her, there was no relief.

Not that he was complaining. He switched to her other nipple while his fingers made quick work of undoing her pants.

"God, I wish I had a skirt on," she said, the words dissolving into a moan as he worked his hand into her jeans until he could stroke her.

Joe's thought process deteriorated almost immediately to *hot. Wet. Want.* He sucked harder at her nipple, and her fingers threaded through his hair as she rode his fingers. Her breath quickened, coming in a harsh, rapid pant.

Her hands dropped to his shoulders, her fingernails digging through his T-shirt as she came against his hand.

As soon as the tremors stopped and he withdrew his hand, she tucked her thumbs into her jeans and started to shove them down before realizing that wasn't going to work.

"It'll take me forever to get my boots off." She stood and tried to get her leg free.

Oh, he had a solution for that. Fortunately he'd given this little situation a lot of thought over the past two weeks, and now those sleepless hours imagining would come in handy.

"Kneel in the box, babe," he told her. "Facing backward. And hold on to the back of the seat."

When she did that, he climbed back on, facing backward, too. By standing on the running boards, everything lined up just the way he wanted it to. After fishing a condom out of his back pocket, where he'd been keeping one just in case, he grabbed the waistband of her jeans and panties together and jerked them down over her hips. Then he dropped his pants as far as he could and managed to get the condom on while treated to the best damn view he'd ever seen.

He put one hand on her hip, and she rocked back to meet him as he guided himself into her. Her fingers dug into the padded backrest and she pushed back hard, taking all of him with one hard thrust.

Screw finesse. This was fantasy time. With his hands on her hips to keep her from sliding on the seat, he pounded into her. Harder. Faster. Until she was whimpering *oh, God yes* how much she liked that.

He liked it, too, and as soon as her orgasm hit, he let loose with a few more driving thrusts before giving in to his own with a guttural growl. As the aftershocks rocked him, he leaned over her, resting his forearms on the passenger box's arms so he didn't crush her.

"Holy…shit," she gasped.

He totally agreed. And if he could ever catch his breath he'd tell her so. Instead he nodded his head, figuring she'd feel it, and panted.

Until her body jerked under his. "I think a mosquito just bit my ass."

With a sigh, he reluctantly withdrew and moved so she could pull her pants up. It was then he realized, in his many imaginings of this incredibly hot scenario, he'd left out one little detail. What the hell was he supposed to do with the condom?

One thing the Kowalskis didn't do out on the trails was litter. You carry it in, you carry it out. But he wasn't about to put the damn thing in his pocket. He thought about burying it, but that would be awkward.

In the end he settled for shoving it back in its torn wrapper the best he could and putting it in the machine's storage box. By the time he got that all settled, Keri was fully dressed again, right down to her helmet.

He was a little disappointed. He would have liked to kiss her once or twice or a dozen times before they went back, but it was probably for the best. She climbed into the seat and he climbed on in front of her, only the right way this time. He fired up the engine and turned the ATV around to head back.

When she wrapped her arms around his waist and turned her head to rest her helmet against his back, he smiled. It wouldn't be comfortable long, especially with a rocky stretch coming up, but he'd take what he could get. For as long as he could get it.

CHAPTER SEVENTEEN

JOE WAS AWAKE BEFORE THE SUN. He wasn't sure he'd even slept, if he was honest, but rather had suffered through a series of restless, ineffectual naps.

She was leaving today. The sun would come up and they'd have breakfast and then she'd put her fancy luggage in the trunk of her rental car and drive away.

He slid out of bed, careful not to wake Keri, who didn't seem to be passing a night any more restful than his. After dragging on a pair of sweats, he stood in the middle of the cabin and wondered what he was supposed to do. If he turned the light on, he'd disturb Keri. If he booted up the laptop, he'd stare at the blinking cursor until he lost his mind.

Should have stayed in bed and stared at the ceiling, he decided. But he'd see how quietly he could sneak out the door and water a tree before climbing back under the covers.

When he got closer to the door, however, he heard a scratching sound from the front porch. Quietly, he sidestepped until he could see out the window. By slowly parting the curtains, he could see a raccoon rummaging through the toiletry bag he'd accidentally left on the porch.

A faint creak behind him made him turn to find Keri up, walking toward him. While her nakedness was enough to render him dumb, he managed to put a finger to his lips and then beckon her over.

Her eyes got big when she peeked through the curtains in time to see the raccoon tossing aside the dental floss. He didn't have any interest in disposable razors, either, though he at least sniffed the deodorant before tossing it off the porch and into the dirt.

After a few more seconds he—or she, because who could tell—grew bored with toiletries and turned his attention to the items thrown over the porch railing to dry. In particular, the colorful wrap Keri always wore down to the pool. The raccoon rubbed it against his face, then dragged it off the railing and gathered it into a little ball.

Then he calmly climbed off the porch and started walking down the drive, purloined wrap clutched in his little hands.

"He's stealing my wrap!" Keri exclaimed. "I told you the raccoons were criminals up here!"

"Do you want me to get it back?" He hoped not. There was not a doubt in his mind if he went chasing bare-chested and barefoot after a wrap-stealing rodent, he'd run into one of his brothers and have to hear about it at every campfire for the rest of his life.

She sighed and shook her head. "He can have it.

Or she. Probably a she, and one with very fine taste, I have to admit. That was Dolce & Gabbana."

"She'll be the envy of the entire gang." He looped his arm around her very naked waist and pulled her close. "The family won't be up and making coffee for another hour or so."

"I'm up now. No sense in going back to bed."

"Oh, I don't know about that," he growled, nipping at her earlobe.

A while later, when the sun was peeking through the curtains and they were curled—a little sweaty and a little out of breath—under the covers, Joe felt her silent tears on his chest and his heart breaking.

EVERYTHING WAS PACKED. Keri walked around the cabin, double-checking and looking for any reason not to get in the car and go. But her things were all stowed in her luggage, which was stacked by the door.

"I guess even though you won't be here all day," Joe said, hovering and looking as miserable as she felt, "you should probably get to ask me another question. I've kinda lost track."

So had she because, during the idyllic and slightly surreal past few days, her old life—no, her *real* life, dammit—had seemed to fade away. "I think I've got everything I need. There's really nothing left to ask about that fits within the parameters you set."

As she'd no doubt hear about within two minutes of her piece crossing Tina's desk. Then again, the woman was such a mad fangirl of Joseph Kowalski's, maybe she would find it fascinating he put mayonnaise on his hot dogs.

"Time for my question then, huh?"

"Yes, and it's your final shot, so make it a good one." She braced herself for some outrageous question. Had she ever masturbated in public, or some such ridiculousness. Even Joe would have to think hard to top whether or not she'd ever faked an orgasm, or if she'd pretended past bedmates were him.

But there was no smile, no dimples. "Would you stay if I asked you to?"

Keri felt as if the air had been sucked, if not from the entire room, at least from her lungs. "I don't… What?"

"I'm asking you to come home and give us a chance, babe. A second chance."

"My home is in California," she said in reflex, without thinking first.

Joe sighed and leaned against the bunk bed frame. "Your job is in California. You have a residence there. But the people who love you are here."

People like him? If he was trying to get away with confessing his love without actually saying the words, she wouldn't let him weasel out of it. And, honestly, even if he said those three small and scary words out loud, would it make a difference? Could it?

"There are a ton of newspapers and magazines out of Boston, you know."

"And you can sit in front of your computer anywhere. If you're so sure we have a future, why can't you move to Los Angeles?"

The depth of sorrow in his eyes widened the crack in her breaking heart. "I can't be that far from my family. I love you. There, I said it. I love you, but I can't move to California."

I love you, but... Keri took a deep breath, then stared down at her hands. "And I think I might be in love with you, too, but I can't walk away from the woman I worked my ass off becoming."

Keri was amazed the words coming out of her mouth sounded like those of a reasonably rational adult, while inside she was a teenager again, sobbing into her stuffed animals while Lisa Lisa sang about being all cried out. Even though Keri had done the leaving, she'd thought at the time she'd never be all cried out.

"Well," Joe said in a flat voice, pushing away from the bunks, "at least this time I asked you to stay."

"And I asked you to go with me." In an effort to keep the impending tears at bay, she double-checked the bags waiting to be carried to her midget rental.

"Keri." Joe grabbed her wrist and didn't let go until she looked him in the eye. "I don't *think* we have a future. I *know* we do. I want to marry you and have kids and be a stay-at-home writer dad while you take Boston journalism by storm. I want to wake up beside you every day for the rest of my life."

The tears broke through her will and flowed over her cheeks. Being Mrs. Kowalski and so-and-so's mom and *babe* didn't sound as bad as it had almost twenty years ago. But she wasn't sure she was done with being Keri Daniels yet.

She hadn't been faced with a choice this confusing and potentially devastating since the last time she'd left Joe. And the worst part was not having the slightest clue whether or not she'd made the right choice then. If she hadn't, wouldn't she be an idiot to make the same mistake again? But she'd been pretty happy, more or less, in California, right up until she'd been tossed unceremoniously back into the bosom of the Kowalski family. So how wrong could it have been?

Her temples started throbbing and Keri buried her face in her hands, maybe to stem the tears, or maybe to block out the kicked-puppy look in Joe's eyes.

"I'll put your bags in the car," he finally said, and the moment for choices seemed to have passed. "You should dry your eyes and then say goodbye to the family. We'll be a few hours yet loading everything up."

Saying goodbye to the Kowalskis was excruciating, and it took every ounce of her willpower not to break down again. The hugs and kisses were hard enough, but Bobby not understanding she was going back to Los Angeles almost killed her.

"But I told Mommy to invite you to my birthday party. It's next week."

"I know, sweetie, but you know I live in California. That's all the way on the other side of the country."

"But you're my friend and friends go to birthday parties!"

She was about to dissolve in a puddle of tears when Lisa put her hand on Bobby's shoulder. "We'll send her an invitation and maybe she can try to make it. We'll see."

We'll see. Keri had forgotten that magic maternal phrase from her youth. The noncommittal way to get out of a situation that wasn't going to end the way the child wanted.

She handed Terry one of her business cards and was surprised to find herself wrapped in a fierce hug. Keri wrapped her arms around the woman who'd been her best friend and let a few tears through.

"I'd be so pissed off at you right now," Terry said in her ear, "but you're hurting as bad as he is."

Keri nodded, unable to squeeze any words out of her throat. Then she broke free of Terry's embrace and sent a final wave and a wobbly smile in the family's general direction.

It took her three tries to fasten her seat belt and it was a miracle she kept the car on the road, because she couldn't see a damn thing through the tears.

It would pass, she tried to tell herself. Just as it had before. Once she was back in her chic apartment with a spa day behind her and a promotion ahead of her, the pain would fade into slight, nostalgic longing.

She hoped.

JOE PROBABLY WOULD HAVE been okay if it had been anybody but his mother who finally came looking for him.

He was slumped in one of the chairs, staring off into space, when the cabin door opened and closed behind him. Then he smelled the unique blend of lavender lotion and bug spray and was crumbling inside before she even stepped up behind him and wrapped her arms around his shoulders.

She pressed a kiss to the top of his head. "Joseph."

"I asked her to stay," he said, a little embarrassed by the breaking in his voice.

"What did she say?"

"She asked me to go with her."

"Then why are you still here?"

Did she think they meant so little to him and his life he'd just pack up and move thousands of miles from them? He knew the near future was going to hurt without Keri in it, but he couldn't even conceive of a future isolated from his family.

But he couldn't explain that to Ma. Even if he'd wanted to, the knot in his throat had choked off his voice, and all he could do was sit and shake while tears streamed down his face.

His mother's chin rested on his shoulder so she could press her cheek to his. "I'm so sorry, sweetheart."

He nodded, relieved when she gave him a squeeze and then backed off. "I'll go tell your brothers to start loading the machines up without you."

"No." He stopped to clear his throat, swiping angrily at his face. "Gimme a few minutes and I'll be down."

"We can do this, Joseph. You can pack up and sneak off if you want."

"I know. Not in the mood for being alone right now."

He wasn't surprised when she walked around the chair to peer into his face. Her eyes were soft and warm, but her mouth had that set to it that let him know it didn't matter how big he was or how old he was. He'd get the wooden spoon upside his head if he didn't listen.

"You should come home with us. Stay in your old bedroom for a while."

Now, that would drive anybody to drink. "I don't need a sleepover, Ma. And I don't need kid gloves. I'd just rather move on with things than sit here and sulk."

She kissed his cheek, unmindful of the wetness lingering there. "Fine. I'll tell your brothers you'll be over in a few minutes to help them."

When he finally got his shit together and walked down to help get the four-wheelers onto the trailers, everybody acted more or less normally. As normal as Kowalskis got on leaving day, anyway.

They drove four-wheelers onto trailers, tying them down with ratchet straps, and made sure all the gear was back in the bins. They risked hernias to get the massive grill loaded and spent twenty minutes looking for Brian's left shoe. While the women packed the RVs, the guys took down tarps and folded up awnings.

Finally the Kowalski debris had been stowed or tossed away, and there was nothing left to do but leave behind the place Joe had just spent the happiest two weeks of his life.

CHAPTER EIGHTEEN

KERI RODE THE ELEVATOR up to the top floor of the *Spotlight Magazine* offices, staring at her reflection in the mirrored walls.

She looked like crap. Oh, she'd tried. With her delicious assortment of beauty essentials back at her disposal, she'd put up a good fight. But when a woman tossed and turned half the night before crying herself to sleep, she looked like crap the next day. It was a law of nature.

Only fifteen minutes had passed between emailing the Joseph Kowalski piece to Tina and the summons to the top floor, which didn't bode well for her promotion. The elevator chimed—it was much too classy to merely ding—and the doors swished open.

Taking a deep breath, Keri stepped out and took a right, heading into the mouth of hell. Her heels clicked on the polished marble floor in a steady rhythm, though she faltered a little when Tina's executive assistant wouldn't meet her eyes.

"Go in, Ms. Daniels. She's waiting for you."

And that she was. Perched on the edge of her luxurious leather chair, tension emanating from her like a toxic cloud. Keri closed the door behind her. There wasn't much she could do about the puffy eyes, but she could try not to look as though her stomach was tumbling like a Laundromat dryer.

Tina held up what looked like a hard copy of the interview. "You spent two weeks with the man and all you give me is this Stock Interview 101 shit?"

"You told me to get an exclusive interview with Joseph Kowalski. You got one."

Tina threw the pages in her direction, but they fluttered harmlessly to the ground. She must have been really pissed if she'd printed the article just to throw it in Keri's face. "Do you honestly think anybody gives a flying fuck that he puts mayonnaise on his hot dogs?"

"A lot of people find that disgusting. And did you skip right over his struggle to write alcohol-free?"

Tina leaned back in her chair and ran her tongue over freshly whitened teeth. "I've read FBI most-wanted posters with more personal dirt than you handed me. I want to know who he sleeps with, whose picture's in his wallet. What laws he's breaking. Boxers or briefs."

That would be Keri and Keri again. The only thing being broken was her heart. And boxer briefs. "That's all he approved."

"You know those sharks in the legal department we feed fresh interns once a week? That's why we pay them the big bucks." Tina sat upright again, her glare trying to burn a hole through Keri. "And speaking of the big bucks, you have two hours. Go sit in that cushy office that's just one of the many perks I choose to give you, think back over the last two weeks and write me shit I can use. If you don't have the balls for this job anymore, Daniels, then get the fuck out of my building."

Two minutes later, Keri tried to slam the door to said cushy office, but it caught on the plush ivory carpet and stopped an inch short. She was halfway to her desk and didn't bother going back to close it.

Tina thought she didn't have the balls for the job anymore? That was bullshit, plain and simple. Keri slapped her mouse to wake her computer up and pulled out the keyboard drawer.

She didn't even have to close her eyes for the Kowalski family dramas to replay in her mind. Terry's marital problems and Stephanie's tears. Mike's fist denting the side of his RV. Danny's writing aspirations. The story of Joe's relationship with Lauren. Kevin was a gold mine of violence, sex and politics. She'd seen the family at their best and at their worst.

Swiping the tears from her eyes so she could see the screen, Keri opened a new document file and started to type.

JOE REALLY WANTED A BEER. Just one.

The problem with wanting one beer, of course, was that they came most readily in packs of six and he wasn't likely to pour the other five down the drain. That would be wasteful.

It was the ticking of the clock getting to him. Or it would have been if his clocks weren't all digital.

He'd told himself he'd wait thirty-four hours before he called her. He'd started with twenty-four, but then realized that would be smack-dab in the middle of her first morning back at work. Another twelve tacked on made it probably too late to call, so he'd gone with thirty-four.

Seemed very logical at the time. Now it seemed like some stupid, random number that did nothing but fuck with his head.

So here he was at two o'clock in the afternoon of his first full day back at home and he'd spent the past who knew how many hours staring out the window and wanting a beer.

He hadn't slept for shit. He missed Keri's body next to him. He missed her warmth. Even her snoring. His nerves were shot and his mood was as sour as the milk he'd forgotten to throw away before heading north.

A cold, foaming brewski would take the edge off. Just one.

The phone rang and he picked it up without looking at the caller ID, because if it wasn't Keri he wouldn't answer it, and then he'd continue to sit there and think about beer. "Hello?"

"Joseph," his mother said, "it's your mother."

As if it was necessary to tell him that, despite her being the only person on the planet who called him Joseph on a regular basis.

"If you're working, I can call back later, but I was hoping you'd—"

"I want a beer, Ma."

That rendered her speechless for a couple of seconds but, as was her way, she rallied quickly. "Have you had one?"

"No. But I've been thinking about it. A lot."

"Well, you're not going to have one. You're going to write down the list of things we need at the hardware store and then, after you stop and pick them up, you're going to come over here and help your father change the garbage disposal thing in the sink."

"What happened to it?"

"My youngest grandson."

Joe laughed and rummaged around for a pen on his desk. He really needed to declutter it. Again. "Give me the list, Ma."

Two hours later, Ma had a new garbage disposal unit and it still wasn't time to call Keri. But he'd decided against having a beer.

"We should have stretched this out a little longer," Pop said. "God only knows what your mother's going to come up with for us to do now."

"I was thinking about taking a ride down to see Kevin."

"Your brother owns a bar. You think anybody in this family will have a moment's peace if your mother finds out you went to a bar?"

"I'm at Jasper's all the time." The place had been called Jasper's Bar & Grille when Kevin bought it and, rather than pay for a new sign, Jasper's it had remained.

"Not today."

Joe sighed. "I'll probably go home and try to call Keri."

"You got your cell. Call her from here and if it doesn't go well, we'll find something else to do around here." Pop walked away to give him some privacy.

He got her voice mail. "Hi, babe. It's me. Joe. I was just…checking to make sure you got home okay. So…gimme a call, okay?"

He'd helped his Pop do the maintenance on the lawn tractor and put in a few hours cleaning the garage before he finally gave up on her and crashed in his old room—in the twin-size bed with the brown comforter.

EVAN WAS ALREADY SEATED at a back corner table when Terry walked into the restaurant, three nights after she'd gotten home, and she had to admit watching him watch her walk across the room made her feel pretty damn special. He only had eyes for her, as the saying went, and, for the first time in a very long time, she appreciated the old sappy lyrics.

He even stood as she reached the table, and when he handed her a single pink rose she didn't know whether to laugh or cry. Sure, it was sweet, but a romantic gesture on one date wasn't enough to save a floundering marriage. It was the day-to-day crap they were drowning in.

She did crack a smile, though, when he pulled her chair out for her. Corny, but he was trying. "Thank you."

"Steph get off to her sleepover okay?"

"There was some matinee they wanted to see, I guess, so I dropped her off earlier this afternoon."

Turning his water glass around in his hands, he gave her a sheepish smile. "Sorry. We're supposed to talk about something besides parent stuff."

"There's no sense in pretending to be people we're not." She flipped open the menu, trying not to look for the obvious comfort foods. She'd struggled enough keeping the weight off during the recent months of stress and loneliness. "If we can't be together for an hour without acting, there's no point in even being here."

"I don't think not talking about our daughter or our work or whatever is pretending to be somebody we're not. We should have been having a night out alone for years, with no worrying about anything but us."

She took a sip of water. "So what are we going to talk about, then? No Steph and no work doesn't leave a wide-open field."

"Did you know if you wash your jeans with tissues left in the pockets, you never see them coming out of the washer, but it takes three hours to pick all the shredded tissue off after the dryer cycle?"

The perplexed look on his face made her laugh loudly enough to make the hostess look in her direction. "You didn't know that?"

"I don't remember ever doing laundry before in my life."

It would have been easy to point out it was his

own damn fault he had to do it now, but ruining the mood before they'd even gotten their drinks probably wouldn't be a good thing. "You only pick shredded tissues off your clothes a few times before you start remembering to check the pockets before you wash them."

He leaned forward suddenly, amusement fading into seriousness as he rested his elbows on the table. "I want to come home, Theresa."

The time it took for her to register the sudden change in his tone was just long enough to allow her to resist sliding to the floor in a sobbing puddle of relief. Even as she drew in what seemed like her first full breath in three months, she knew she couldn't make it that easy for him.

He'd hurt her. Badly. And he was going to do a little groveling before he parked his car in her garage again.

"Pretty drastic measures to get out of doing laundry," she replied, making sure her voice didn't reveal any of the hope that was fluttering in her heart like a moth against glass.

"It's not that and you—" He broke off when their server appeared.

Terry ordered a coffee and the chicken Alfredo special in a fog, not caring in the least what food was going to be set in front of her. What was important was why Evan suddenly wanted back in and whether or not she could risk opening that door. Lord knew she wanted to. But if he changed his mind and she had to stand there while he left her again, she wasn't sure she could survive it. Being strong for her daughter—putting on a good face for the family—only stretched so far. She could only take so much pain.

They were both silent while the server went and poured their coffees. It wouldn't take long and Terry doubted Evan would want to be interrupted again. She spent those few minutes steadying her nerves and trying to harden her heart against whatever proclamations and promises her husband was about to throw in her direction. Steph, she thought. She'd focus on just how devastating it would be for her daughter to have parents who separated and reunited, only to separate again. Heading into her teenage years, Stephanie didn't need the emotional upheaval. She couldn't take any more pain, either.

"If I hated doing laundry that much, I'd pay the laundry service downstairs," Evan said when their coffees had been delivered and they were alone again. "You may not believe it, but there's nothing I'm not capable of either doing for myself or paying somebody to do."

"Well, gee, when you segue from your laundry woes to wanting to come home, what am I supposed to think?"

"I didn't mean for it to pop out like that," he said, and there was a hint of a blush on his cheeks. "I'm not very good at this, I guess. The whole date night thing, I mean."

Probably because neither of them had dated in

almost a decade and a half. That she knew of. "Have you been seeing anybody else?"

"No." The way he said it, and the look on his face when he did, made her believe he was telling the truth. "I don't want anybody else."

But he hadn't wanted her anymore, either. He'd made that pretty damn clear. "Nothing's changed, Evan. Everything's the same, so the stuff that made you unhappy enough to leave will just make you unhappy enough to leave again. I'm not putting myself—or our daughter—through that."

"Everything has changed. The pretense is over and if we spend the rest of our lives together it'll be because we both want to, not because neither of us had the guts to walk out the door."

She ripped open a third packet of sugar and dumped it into her coffee, just because she deserved it. "What if we both want to, but we still can't make it work?"

"Do you love me?" The question came at her so fast, she nodded in reflex before she could think about whether she was ready to give him that much power. "Then we can make it work."

"I loved you three months ago and it wasn't enough." Why couldn't he understand that it wasn't as simple as deciding he was ready to come home? "And you just think it will magically be enough now?"

"Not magically. But now that we've dragged our baggage out from under the bed, we can start dealing with it. It'll take time, but our marriage is worth it."

He sounded sincere enough, but he'd lost her with that last bit. He'd gone straight from *A* to *Z* by walking out on her that morning with no warning. Now he wanted to go back and sort through *B* through *Y*? They could have tried rummaging through some of the baggage before he'd packed his.

When she didn't say anything, Evan drank some of his coffee. Fidgeted with his silverware. Buttered and ate a slice of the bread that had arrived with their coffees. The silence stretched on long enough to grow awkward, but she still couldn't find the right words to fill it.

"You don't think so?" he finally asked.

"I don't know." She buttered a slice of the home-made bread, but then just stared at it. "Why didn't you tell me you were so miserable you were thinking about leaving?"

"Because you're a control freak and if you think something's okay, it must be okay. I had to do it quick, like ripping off a Band-Aid, or you were going to keep telling yourself it was all in my head."

She set the buttered bread on her napkin and pressed her fingertips to her eyes, trying to stem the tears. She was tired. She was sad and confused and angry and heartbroken and she didn't want to be anymore. "I'm scared, Evan. It hurt. It still hurts."

"I know you don't believe me, but it hurt me, too. It hurts a lot more, though, being without you."

And that was the bottom line. It had hurt so much

when he left and the thought of risking that again hurt, too. But the thought of living the rest of her life without this man hurt in a way that tightened her throat and robbed her of rational thought.

"Not tonight," she whispered. "I'm not ready yet."

"But you'll try?"

She nodded and he reached across the table for her hand. She let him hold it. "We need a little more time…to talk. But I want to work toward you coming home, too. See if we can be friends again."

"I love you, Terry."

Squeezing his fingers, she smiled at him through the sheen of tears. "I love you, too."

IN THE FIRST THREE DAYS of her unemployed state, Keri let her voice mail collect four job offers. They were flattering, especially the call from *Spotlight*'s primary rival, but it was the numerous calls from Joe that had her wrist-deep in a bucket of chocolate gelato.

Answering the phone wasn't an option. She didn't have it in her to tell him she'd left him and broken both their hearts for a job she'd walked out on her first day back.

But she also couldn't say, "Hey, since I don't have a job anymore, maybe I'm willing to give us a shot, even though I let you believe the job was more important."

She was going to need more gelato.

Lazing around in yoga pants and a flannel shirt, plowing through frozen comfort foods for three days left plenty of time for two things—crying and reflection.

Of course, the common theme of her chocolate-fueled reflections was the shitty state of her life now and how it hadn't been shitty before she'd boarded the plane in Boston.

The problem was, how much of the fortnight of nonshittiness was Joe, and how much was taking what had passed for her first real vacation since she'd started at *Spotlight*. Instead of wearing heels that made her feet throb and making sure everything, right down to her eyebrows, was impeccably groomed. Smartphone. Laptop. Bluetooth device stuck in her ear.

Even if she removed Joe from the equation, it was no surprise she'd been happy in New Hampshire. S'mores. Volleyball. Tandem cannonballs of doom. What wasn't to love?

But her gut didn't ache at the thought of never playing volleyball again. Or trying to get melted marshmallow out of her hair. The thought of never seeing Joe again…

Another crying jag left her emotionally wrung out, hiccupping and trying to lick the last drops of chocolate from the gelato bucket.

She couldn't keep going on like this. The freezer was almost empty, for one thing. And she'd dehydrate if she didn't stop crying so damn much. It was time to decide where she'd be happy.

And there was only one way she could think of to do that.

CHAPTER NINETEEN

AFTER LISTENING TO KERI's generic voice-mail greeting for the umpteenth time of the umpteenth day, Joe dialed a different number and said the magic words.

"This is Joseph Kowalski, calling for Tina Deschanel."

He wasn't on hold long enough to identify the music.

"Mr. Kowalski, what a pleasant surprise!"

He didn't even like her voice. "Your reporter's dodging my calls, Miss Deschanel."

There was a rather heavy pause. "Keri Daniels is no longer with *Spotlight Magazine,* Mr. Kowalski, but I'll be happy to take care of your needs personally."

"Good. The first thing I need to know is why she's no longer there."

"I'm not in the habit of discussing—"

"Hey, Bob, you still have the number for that guy from *People?*" he called to the potted fern on his windowsill.

Joe had never heard anybody grind their teeth over the phone before. It echoed a little. "If you must know, Miss Daniels submitted an interview with you that didn't contain the sort of in-depth details *Spotlight* readers have come to expect. When I asked her to rework the piece, she resigned."

"You asked her to betray my trust and that of my family and she walked instead."

"In a nutshell, yes."

"When?"

"She came into the office the morning after she flew in and she was gone two hours later."

Joe sank back in his leather office chair, disbelief robbing him of coherent words. She'd quit the day after she'd left him but she still wouldn't return his calls. Did she blame him?

"Mr. Kowalski, if I could just ask you a few follow-up ques—"

He hung up on her. Then he wished he hadn't. Not only because it was incredibly rude, which he tried not to be as a rule, but because he should have asked her if she knew where Keri had gone.

It had been a week. A whole damn week since she'd walked out on what she'd claimed she wanted more than anything, and he hadn't even rated a phone call. An email. Hell, even a fax would've worked.

That pretty much told him everything he needed to know about where he stood with Keri Daniels.

He picked up a pencil just so he could tap it against the edge of his desk. A couple of phone calls and he could be in California in time for supper. The problem was finding her when he got there.

"Hey."

Joe almost fell out of his chair, but he recovered well. "Hey, Kevin. I didn't hear you come in."

"Probably the drum solo. I knocked but you never answer the door when you're working. Or pretending to be working."

"Keri quit her job the day after she flew back to California."

Kevin walked over to the sofa and perched on the arm of it—something he did no matter how often Joe told him not to. "You found this out how?"

"I called the magazine."

"Dude," Kevin said, shaking his head. "I know you don't have as much experience with the ladies as I do, but when a woman won't return a week's worth of phone calls, she's not that into you."

"She's into me." He didn't know where she was or what she was doing or why she wouldn't answer her goddamn phone, but he knew she was into him. "Go away. I need to call the airport."

"You don't wanna do that."

"I'm thinking about moving to Los Angeles." There. He'd said it.

"To be with a woman who doesn't want to talk to you? Think about it."

"I've done nothing *but* think about it all week. I'll rack up some serious frequent-flyer miles, so it's not like you'll never see me again."

"The question is if *she* wants to see you again." Kevin threw his leg over the arm of the couch and slid his butt down onto the cushion. "Have you told anybody else about this?"

"No. Now I need to call the airlines and pack a bag and figure out how to find her when I get there. So you can go now and tell the family you checked on me and I'm still sober."

"I'm not here to check on you."

Joe snorted. They'd been finding less-than-inconspicuous ways to check on him all week. It was as if they had a rotation schedule of who was going to stop by or call, and when, and what their excuses for needing to talk to him would be. "Whatever. Hey, do you have any contacts that could run a check on Keri through the system? Maybe get her home address for me?"

Kevin sighed and folded his arms across his chest. "Pop sent me over to tell you he got a call from the campground. She's there."

"Who's there?" Joe started tapping the pencil again, anxious for his brother to leave so he could start making arrangements. He'd fly out and talk to her and, if all went well, he'd fly home to pack some stuff and get his house on the market.

"Keri."

The pencil froze in midtap. "Keri's where? At the campground?"

"Yeah, she's been there a few days, from what he said. Staying in the cabin."

He heard the words coming out of Kevin's mouth, but they didn't make any sense. Why would Keri be back in New Hampshire? Not only back in the state, but back at the one place he would have thought she'd never want to see again. "Why?"

Kevin shrugged. "Nobody knows. He only called Pop because he said she seemed pretty sad. Thought something might be going on we should know about."

"Why didn't she call me?" He hadn't meant to say that out loud, but his brother only shrugged, skipping the manly mocking of a less than manly question.

"For the last few days, she hasn't had cell reception," Kevin pointed out. "Before that…maybe she needed some space to figure out what she's going to do. Or…"

"Or what?" When Kevin just shrugged and refused to finish the thought, Joe tossed the pencil onto the desk. "You think she blames me for losing her job, don't you?"

"You said she quit."

"She quit because Tina was going to fire her if she didn't spill all our family secrets. So, quit or fired, my refusing to give her decent material to work with killed not only her promotion, but her whole freakin' job."

"She had plenty of material to work with," Kevin said. "All she had to do was use it and then let Tina worry about your lawyer having a fit *after* the magazine published it."

He had a point. If she'd had her fun and didn't have any intention of seeing him or his family again, what did she care if *Spotlight Magazine* and Kowalski Inc. were embroiled in a legal rumble after the article was published and she had her new office?

"Look," Kevin said, "there's nothing you can—"

"I'm going up there." The only way he could find out what was going through Keri's head was to ask her, and it seemed the only way he would get to talk to her was to go up to the campground and find her.

"Let me remind you she's given no sign she even wants to talk to you."

"She'll talk to me. She came back to New Hampshire for a reason, and I intend to find out what it is."

TERRY SUCKED IN A DEEP BREATH as Evan walked through their back door and tossed his keys on the phone table, as he had every weekday afternoon he lived in the house. The phone table was gone now, however, so the key ring skittered across the tile floor and came to rest in front of the dishwasher. He didn't seem to notice. He was too busy staring at her.

She knew what he saw—a middle-age woman with sad eyes, a few unshakable extra pounds and a hopeful half smile, perched on one of the most hideous pieces of furniture ever manufactured. The table was a thick slab of maple set on four posts as massive as elephant legs. Covering the surface was a beveled layer of faux-marble tiles. Not surprisingly, the set had been in the clearance barn, deeply discounted. Honestly, the thing was as big, brown and ugly as Joe's first car.

"Most beautiful thing I've ever seen in my life," her prodigal husband said.

That gave some weight to the theory he'd left her because he was freaking crazy. "I don't know about beautiful, but they said it would support…just about anything. And the top can be bleached. You know, for disinfecting."

God, she sounded like an idiot. Her plan to be suggestive and sultry and subtle was misfiring badly.

"I meant you."

Maybe it was the nightgown. She'd gone all the way to the mall for it, paying way too much for an above-the-knee drape of black satin held up by two spaghetti straps that precluded a bra. With her breasts in their natural, gravity-weary state and her thighs too exposed for comfort, she didn't feel quite as sexy as she had in the fitting room with the subtle lighting and lack of an audience.

Her audience didn't seem to mind the bodily wear and tear, though, judging by the look on his face as he walked across the kitchen.

Take off your shoes. She started to open her mouth, then snapped it closed. So he had his shoes on. So what? It wasn't raining and the path from the driveway to the door was paved, but…

Evan put a hand on each of her knees and pushed them apart so he could stand between her thighs.

He smelled different. It was subtle, but he didn't smell like her Evan—the Evan who used the laundry detergent and the soap and the shampoo she kept in the house.

After hooking his finger under a spaghetti strap and sliding it over her shoulder, he leaned forward and kissed that spot on her collarbone halfway between her throat and shoulder. It was a spot that never failed to make her shiver.

Then he brushed her hair back so he could nuzzle his lips against her ear and whisper, "It's killing you I didn't take off my shoes, isn't it?"

A burst of laughter surprised her and she couldn't hold it back. At least he smiled with her.

"I heard your laugh before I ever saw your face," he told her. "I heard you laugh and thought to myself I'd really love to spend some time with you—make you laugh some more."

"As if I could ever forget all those god-awful jokes you told while we were dating."

"Most women would have dumped me, but you loved to laugh just as much as I loved hearing it." He reached up and tucked a few stray strands of hair behind her ear. "We used to laugh all the time, Terry. When did we stop? Why did we stop?"

Would've been nice if the sight of his wife in a slinky nightgown had robbed the man of the ability to form a coherent sentence, never mind the desire to stand around between her legs analyzing what had gone wrong with their marriage. "I laugh."

"At sitcoms, but not at life. Not…just to laugh."

Deflating like a cold balloon, Terry put her hand on her husband's shoulder and pushed at him. "Now I'm sorry I called you and asked you to come over."

He captured her wrist and raised her hand to his mouth. When he drew her finger into his mouth and sucked lightly, the little twinge of sexual need at the small of her back flared into a full-blown ache. He locked gazes with her and she felt the heated flush climbing her neck and spreading into her face.

"I'm not," he told her.

"That's because we're not talking about what's wrong with you."

"There's nothing wrong with you. There's been something wrong with *us.*" He let go of her hand and grabbed her hips, sliding her to the edge of the table so his denim-covered erection was pressed against her and her legs wrapped around his waist. "But right now, let's focus on what's right with us."

"I'm having a little trouble focusing at all."

"I'm going to fix your fixation on my shoes, too," he said, running his hands up over her ribs until he was cupping her breasts.

"How are you going to do that?" she asked, surprised she had enough breath left in her lungs to make words.

"I'm going to unzip my pants and then I'm going to do you just like this on the table, with my shoes on," he said, and her entire body started celebrating when his hand left her breast and reached down between them to unbutton his fly. "And from now on, every time I walk into this house with my shoes on, you're going to remember this day and all the things I'm about to do to you and the last thing on your mind will be footprints on the linoleum."

It was a struggle not to pant in the face of such delicious anticipation. "I don't know. Clean floors are pretty important to me."

"Screw clean," he told her and she heard the rasp of his zipper. "Right now I want to be dirty."

Twenty minutes later, Evan could have tracked

cow manure across the linoleum, over the living room hardwood and up the carpeted stairs for all Terry cared. The ugly table wasn't the most comfortable piece of furniture she'd ever been sprawled across, but it was definitely her new favorite.

At some point he'd ended up on the tiled surface with her and now his pants were around his knees. Still had his shoes on. Thank goodness she'd been so paranoid about being in the kitchen in her skimpy nightgown she'd pulled every blind in the house.

He shifted onto his side, flopping his arm across her and planting a kiss on her shoulder. "I like this table."

"Me, too," she murmured, too wiped out to care that the hard surface wasn't the best mattress for middle-age bones.

"Wonder if there's a matching coffee table version."

She laughed, a breathy sound, as she was still a little winded. "We could just get a bigger couch."

"We could get a leather one," he agreed.

We.

"Steph won't be home for another three hours." Maybe it was the great sex or maybe it was the fact that this was her life—the one she wanted back— but she took a deep breath and stepped off the ledge. "We could get dressed and go pack up some of your stuff. Bring it home."

The arm across her tightened and she felt his sigh against her heated skin. "That sounds like a plan."

"I love you," she told him, because it seemed important that she say it first this time.

"I love you, too. And you better hurry if you're going to get dressed. Lucky for me, I've still got my shoes on."

KERI WASN'T SURPRISED to turn the corner to the cabin and see Joe's SUV parked in front of it, but the way her heart seemed to seize up in her chest was a bit of a shock.

She stopped walking, her mind racing as she tried to guess why he was here. It had only been a matter of time before the owner called the Kowalskis—she'd known it from the time she'd arrived—but she hadn't been sure Joe would come. She'd hurt him when she left and then she'd ignored his calls for days. And who knew how many times he'd called since she'd left the land of cell phone reception.

"You gonna stand there all day?"

She hadn't even seen him, sitting on the picnic table in the shade. With his elbows resting on his knees, hands hanging between his legs, he looked totally relaxed. Forcing her feet to move, she continued toward the cabin.

"I see somebody finally ratted me out," she said, trying to keep her tone light.

"They were worried about you being here alone." He pushed himself off the bench and met her at the cabin door. "They didn't know what else to do for you, so they called Pop. Said you looked sad."

She went through the door first and dropped into a chair. "I've been happier."

Like last week and the week before, when she and Joe had stayed in this same cabin together. Sometimes it seemed as if it had been a dream, so separated was it from her usual day-to-day life, but it had been a really good dream.

He dragged the other chair close to hers and turned it around to sit on it backward, like guys usually did. "What happened, babe?"

She managed a one-shoulder shrug. "I guess Tina was right. I don't have the balls for the job anymore."

"While the mere mention of you having balls gives me a serious case of the heebie-jeebies, I think it takes more nut to walk away from everything you've worked for rather than hurt people you care about."

"Well, me and my impressive nut are currently unemployed."

"Why didn't you call me? I'd have come up and stayed with you."

"I didn't know what to do. But I was happier here than I've been in years, so I came here to figure it out." It didn't sound any more logical now than it had when she'd packed a bag and headed for the airport. "I wasn't sure if it was being here with you that made me happy, or if it was just being totally out of the rat race—no phones, no email, no meetings—for two weeks."

He folded his arms across the back of the chair

so he could rest his chin on them. "The owner said you've been here a few days."

"Yup, with no phone, no email, no meetings."

"And?"

She sighed. "I think it's you."

Joe laughed. "You don't have to say it like that— like I'm the plague. I think it's a good thing you were happy with me."

"That's because you don't have to sacrifice anything to be with me."

"You're right. I don't have to change jobs in exchange for spending the rest of my life with the person I love."

"Don't do that, Joe. It's not like I'm exchanging one fast-food hat for another. I've dedicated years to—"

"I'm sorry. You're right about that." He got up off the chair and paced a tight circuit for a few seconds. "But don't downplay what I've had to ante up, either. You left me once and it almost ruined me. Do you know how hard it was for me to ask you to stay? And then you left me for the second time. Yet here I am again, pride checked at the door."

"But, Joe—"

"And if you'd answered your freakin' phone before leaving California I could have told you I was willing to come to you. It's not like I can't afford to fly across the country a few times a year. But by the time I got desperate enough to call Tina, you were gone."

She didn't know what to say. He was willing to

leave his family and move to the opposite end of the country to be with her, but was that what she really wanted? Even without the promise of Joe, she'd breathed a sigh of relief when she disembarked at Logan.

"So you'd go back with me?" she asked, just because she could barely believe it. "There are a half dozen L.A.-based magazines who'd be interested in me."

His jaw tightened, but he nodded. "If that's what it takes."

"It took me a few days to realize why I was so miserable after I got home. Part of it was missing you, but part of me felt like I'd put a costume back on and it no longer fit right. It's like I was being who I thought I wanted to be, but when I was here I was who I really am."

"I'm confused."

"So was I."

"No, I mean about us. Is there an us? Are you going back to California? Did that costume include black fishnet stockings?"

"Yes, no, and they chafed too much so I took them off."

It took him a second to match the answers to the questions, then he grinned. "Did you take them off slowly, unrolling them a little bit at a time?"

"Focus, Joe."

"Oh, I am, babe. Believe me."

She had to look away from his dimples before her

train of thought jumped the tracks to follow his. "On our future."

"Does our future include black fishnet stockings?"

"At the rate we're going, our future includes support hose."

Joe withdrew a clenched fist from his jeans pocket and, after giving her a highly dramatic rolling of the eyes, got down on one knee.

She thought the little squeaking sound she heard might have been the strangled panic rising in her throat. This was a big leap from maybe having a future. "I didn't mean you had to hit the warp-drive button."

"You said this shit was romantic."

"Well, yeah, but—"

He unfolded his fingers to reveal his bulky class ring, a not-so-delicate gold chain already strung through it. "Keri Daniels, will you go steady with me?"

The relief—and okay, maybe just a tinge of disappointment—made her laugh. "Tell me you didn't drive here in a Ford Granada."

"I almost got one on eBay, but some guy snuck in a high bid at the last second."

"You're kidding."

"Yes, and you're not answering my question."

"I was going to slip a note through your locker vent later."

With a grunt he tried to hide from her, he pushed himself back to his feet. "You're killing me, babe."

"Yes, Kowalski, I'll go steady with you. Does that still mean making out in the backseat and watching really dumb action movies?"

"Yeah, pretty much."

"Good. And my dad gave up golf, so you're safe there."

"Oh, well, going steady also now means living in sin with me until I find the perfect ring and propose properly."

She snorted. "Keri Kowalski?"

"At least Terry's last name is Porter now, so you won't be too ridiculous out in public together."

"She sent me an email about her and Evan. That's really great. And Bobby sent me about sixty pictures of his Wii, including close-ups of the control buttons, which would have been a lot more fun to look at if I wasn't up here in the land of dial-up. Plus I get about six emails an hour updating his high scores."

Joe arched an eyebrow. "Emails?"

"Okay, so I cheated. Charlie lets me use his computer when I go down to the store for my daily chocolate fix. And Danny and I have exchanged a few emails about short story markets."

"You're just going steady with me for my nephews."

She smiled and shrugged. "Don't forget Steph. She sent me some pictures, too."

"Any other secrets?"

"I've also been in touch with a former colleague who relocated to New York. She set me up with a job freelance editing from home—or wherever my computer access may be. It's not a lot of money—*really* not a lot of money, but it sounds less stressful than trying to rebuild my career out here. I don't want to commute to Boston." Saying it out loud helped cement how right her decision was.

"I'm sure Kowalski Inc. could throw a little free-lance work your way, too. And if you're good in bed, the boss will give you nice bonuses."

"I don't care about Kowalski Inc. I want you. Just Joe."

He stuck a finger through the belt loop on either side of her waist and hauled her into his arms. "I can't wait to be married to you."

"I'd suggest we elope, but the idea of your mother stalking around Las Vegas with her wooden spoon looking for us scares me."

"Plus that would deny me the satisfaction of giving any magazine but *Spotlight* exclusive photos of the Daniels-Kowalski wedding."

"The Daniels-Kowalski Wedding of Doom," she corrected him, making him laugh.

"I suppose," he said, sliding his hands down to cup her ass, "that with both of us being writers, you'll expect me to write my own vows."

"Um, you write sick, twisted horror, so probably not." She wrapped her arms around his neck and gazed into the face of the man she was going to spend the rest of her life with. "Just promise to love me forever."

"This is one story that's going to have a happy

ending," he told her, and he lowered his mouth to hers.

Keri Daniels-Kowalski, she thought as she surrendered to his kiss. *Joe's wife.* Had a nice ring to it.

* * * * *

Next month, don't miss
UNDENIABLY YOURS
By Shannon Stacey
This fun, sexy, family-centric contemporary
romance continues the story of the family you fell
in love with in EXCLUSIVELY YOURS.

CHAPTER ONE

October

EVERY TIME THE New England Patriots chalked one up in the win column, Kevin Kowalski got laid.

A score for them was a score for him. Not that he was always looking for a companion on a Sunday night, but the offers weren't scarce. As he slid a foaming mug of Sam Adams down the polished surface of the best damn sports bar in New Hampshire's capital city—which just happened to list his name as proprietor—he caught a blonde watching him. The Pats were lining up at first and goal on the bigscreen, but her eyes were on him, letting him know the New England quarterback wasn't the only guy in scoring position.

But tonight he was having a hard time concentrating on the blonde with the chemically enhanced lips, surgically enhanced boobs and alcohol-enhanced sex drive giving him the *you could go all the way* look.

He was too busy keeping his eye on the brunette at the other end of the bar. It wasn't just the fact she was pretty, with a mess of dark brown hair falling to her shoulders and eyes to match. Or that her fisherman's sweater and jeans hugged her body in all the right places, though that certainly didn't hurt.

Mostly he was keeping an eye on her because her date was going downhill in a hurry. Either the guy in the uptight, button-down shirt and khakis had had a couple before he walked into the bar or he had the alcohol tolerance of a high-school freshman, because it had only taken a couple shots of scotch for drunken-asshole syndrome to kick in.

Now there was some body language going on between the couple and her body wanted away from his body. His fingers would start looking for a soft place to land. She'd deflect. Rinse and repeat.

Jasper's Bar & Grille had three rules. No smoking. No throwing beer mugs, even at the Jets fans. And when a lady said no, it meant no.

The Patriots scored and the glasses shook on the shelves as a triumphant roar filled Jasper's. The blonde hopped up and down on her barstool, her boobs testing the bungee ability of her bra straps. And the jerk with the wandering hands raised his empty glass to wave it in Kevin's general direction.

He made his way down to the couple, but ignored the glass. "We won't be serving you any more alcohol, but you're welcome to a coffee or a soda, on the house."

Uptight Guy's face turned as red as a Budweiser label and Kevin sighed. He was going to be one of *those* guys. Jasper's had a zero-tolerance policy, so as the guy's ass lifted off the stool, Kevin gave

Paulie the signal and watched her roll her eyes as she reached for the phone.

"I'm not drunk and I want another goddamn scotch!"

The woman put her hand on the guy's arm, as if to push him back onto his seat. "Derek, let's—"

"Who the hell are you to tell me I can't have another goddamn scotch?"

Uptight Guy's bad-ass act was diluted a bit by the weaving. "I'm the guy who reserves the right to refuse you service."

"Beth, tell this asshole to gimme another drink."

Kevin shook his head. "You're cut off."

It happened fast. Kevin wasn't sure if the guy was throwing a punch or reaching in to grab him by the shirt, but his elbow hit his date and knocked her backward. She didn't fall, thanks to the guy sitting next to her, who was pleasantly surprised to find himself with an armful of brunette, but it distracted Kevin enough to allow the guy to land a weak, glancing blow to his jaw.

Uptight Guy, who the woman had called Derek, sucked in a breath, as if he just realized what he'd done. Kevin watched as the guy's fight-or-flight instinct kicked in and wasn't surprised when he chose flight. Sadly for him, Kevin was six-two and had some experience collaring yahoos, whether they were crooks back when he wore a badge or his four rowdy nephews. He reached across the bar, grabbed the guy by the scruff of the neck and yanked him back.

Derek was struggling like a pickerel on a hook

and, when Kevin's grip almost slipped off the guy's collar, he jerked his left arm hard. Derek's head snapped around and his nose exploded on the edge of the bar. Oops.

The guy screamed like a girl…and the crowd went wild. Jasper's didn't attract a real rough crowd, but everybody loved a good fight.

"Good fight" being relative, of course. Derek cupped his hands over his face, trying to stanch the blood, and made a high-pitched keening sound that made more than a few of his patrons wince.

"Shut up or I'll knock your ass out," Kevin yelled at the guy which, of course, got everybody in the bar chanting. *Do it…do it…do it…*

"Oh my God, his nose!" Derek's date untangled herself from her neighbor and grabbed a couple of napkins off the bar. She tried to get to Derek's nose, but he kept pushing her away.

The crowd quieted when a couple of police officers walked through the front door. Derek's keening changed pitch when he saw them, from a pain-filled squeal to an *oh, shit* desperation.

"Hey, Kowalski," the older of the two cops said.

"Hey, Jonesy. Your old man like those tickets?"

"Are you kidding me? Tenth row, fifty-yard line? He was in heaven. Said to tell you thanks and give you his best."

"Glad to do it," he said easily, still holding on to Derek's collar. He fostered a friendly relationship with the local P.D., not only because he'd been on the job once down in Boston, but because any good businessman did. Especially businessmen who served alcohol. "Got a live one here."

"What happened to him?"

"Hit his face on the bar. You know how it is."

In the split second between Kevin releasing him and Jonesy grabbing for his wrists, Derek stupidly decided to make a break for the door.

The rookie made a move to stop him at the same time Beth did. She accidentally—at least it *looked* accidental—tripped him and the young cop fell on his face. Jonesy jumped over his partner and did the nearing-retirement version of a sprint after Derek.

Beth was practically hyperventilating.

The rookie scrambled to his feet as Jonesy took down his prey in a half-ass diving tackle that made the crowd roar in approval. Rookie had his handcuffs out, but it looked like Uptight Guy was going all in on a resisting charge.

"Why are you doing this to him?"

Kevin's gaze swiveled to the woman, who looked almost as pissed as her date. "I didn't do jack to him, lady. Did you forgot the part where he hit you?"

"He didn't hit me. He bumped me trying to hit *you*."

Yeah, that was so much better. "How about the groping? How many times were you going to tell him no?"

She actually rolled her eyes at him. "I had it all under control."

"No, now it's all under control."

"Look, it's not what you… Forget it. You have to help him, though."

Since Derek had two hundred pounds of veteran cop kneeling on his head while the rookie tried to secure the cuffs, there wasn't much Kevin could do for him, even if he wanted to. Which he didn't.

"It's not what you think," she insisted.

"I'm going to sue you for everything you've got, asshole," Derek screamed over his shoulder. "And you, you dumb bitch, you're fired!"

Oops. Kevin looked at Beth. "I thought he was just a bad date."

She climbed onto a stool and dropped her forehead to the bar with a thunk. "You just cost me my job."

Only several years of fine-tuning his brain-to-mouth filter behind the bar kept him from pointing out she was maybe better off without it. "Want a beer?"

A BEER? RAMBO THE BARTENDER here thought a beer was going to fix the mess he'd gotten her into? Beth Hansen curled her hands into fists to keep from reaching across the bar and shaking him like a martini.

So Derek was a drunken ass. So what else was new? It was nothing she couldn't handle. She handled it once a week or so, as a matter of fact, and had been for three months.

After work, Derek would leave the office and walk down the street to have a drink. He'd call his

secretary—that would be her—with some bogus
excuse requiring her to stop by the bar. A paper that
needed signing. A fax he'd forgotten to read but absolutely had to before he went home. She'd show up,
he'd try to get in her pants, she'd put him in a cab
and the next day they'd pretend it didn't happen.

Maybe not ideal working conditions, but she'd
suffered worse.

But this time Derek's usual bar was closed for
renovations so he'd kept on walking until he came
to Jasper's Bar & Grille. Now her boss had a broken
nose and she had no job.

A beer wasn't going to help.

She lifted her head and propped her chin on her
hand. "Did you have to call the police?"

"Yup."

"You could have let it go."

He rested his palms on the edge of the bar and
looked her in the eye. God, he was tall. And that
wasn't all he had going for him. Besides the height
and the blue eyes and the dimples, he had broad
shoulders straining the seams of an ancient Red Sox
T-shirt and thick brown hair that had that careless
style of a man who didn't want to fuss with it. Probably mid-thirties.

"Lady, he punched me in the face."

"It wasn't much of a punch," she muttered, since
she couldn't deny it. "I almost had him talked into a
cab, but you had to go and make it a big deal."

"Hey, Kevin," a younger guy called out. "Can we
make a mimosa?"

"This is a sports bar, not Easter brunch." He turned back to her, shaking his head. "All I did was tell him he was cut off. Not only do I have the right but, when a patron's visibly intoxicated, I have the obligation. And I ain't exactly a turn-the-other-cheek guy when it comes to getting punched in the face."

Kevin had a point. It wasn't his fault her boss was a jerk, so blaming him was probably a little unreasonable. But the only difference between the previous times and this time was him. "You didn't have to break his nose."

"*That* I didn't really mean to do. He slipped. Kind of." The sheepish, dimpled grin he gave her was so irresistible she could feel aggravation's hold on her temper loosening.

She was about to respond when he reached his arms up to a high shelf. Muscles rippled under his T-shirt and, when he stretched for a stack of folded towels, a gap opened between its hem and the waistband of his low-slung jeans. The tantalizing glimpse of abs made her mouth go dry, which was okay because she'd forgotten what she was going to say, anyway.

When he moved out from behind the bar to mop at Derek's blood, she grimaced and moved over a stool. Not that she was queasy, but because Kevin smelled as good as he looked. And the closer he got to her, the better he looked.

Then, without warning, her view was blocked by a busty blonde whose outfit made Daisy Duke's look like going-to-church clothes. The woman handed Kevin what looked like a Jasper's napkin with lipstick smeared on it. The same shade painted on the woman's plumped and puckered-up mouth.

"Hi, Kevin," the blonde said in pretty much the same breathless, baby-doll voice Marilyn Monroe had used to wish President Kennedy a very, very happy birthday. "Here's my number. You know…in case you want to call me…or something."

He winked at her as he took the napkin. "Thanks, doll. I just might do that."

Beth managed to hold it in until Hooters-wanna-be Barbie had simpered out the front door, then she rolled her eyes. "Doll? Smooth line, Mickey Spillane."

"Hey, makin' the ladies happy is good for business."

"Yeah, and I bet you're just the man for the job. You should go after her. She seems just your type."

That wiped the naughty-boy charm off his face. "What makes you think you know anything about my type?"

She shrugged, making it clear she didn't really give a damn. "Careful you don't smear your napkin. And speaking of business, I need to go find another job now."

"I feel bad about that, even though it wasn't really my fault."

"I'll get over it." She slid off the stool and started toward the door. "Have a nice life. *Doll*."

KEVIN SMILED FOR THE CAMERA. Then he smiled again. And again and again and again.

"Okay," the bossy photographer said. "Now a few of the bride and her ladies, and then we'll do the groom and his brothers."

With matching sighs of relief, Kevin and his brothers Joe and Mike, along with their brother-in-law, Evan, moved away from the gaggle of women. They'd been at the picture-taking thing for twenty minutes already and, early October or not, it was hot in a tux.

Joe's reception was at some swanky hotel-slash-banquet center that specialized in wedding receptions. As far as Kevin could tell, that meant they had a shitload of places to take pictures. In front of the garden. In front of the rock waterfall. Under the gazebo thing in front of the pond. His cheeks were starting to ache.

Mike tugged at his collar, but not so much the drill sergeant with the camera would bark at him. "I'm ready to hit the bar."

Kevin nodded, though he didn't fidget because their mother was giving them the *I'm watching you* look. "Joe, I swear, if they don't hurry up, your wedding photos are going to look more like a Chippendale's photo shoot."

"If I'd known you two were going to whine like a couple of girls, I would have had you be bridesmaids instead of my best men. You'd look good in a dress."

Kevin snorted. "Don't make me kick your ass on your wedding day."

"Terry sure looks good in her dress," Evan said. "Kinda makes you want to—"

"No," Terry's three brothers said in unison.

Their brother-in-law scowled. "I hate that. I never get to share the good stuff."

Mike laughed. "Joey and Danny are old enough to watch the younger two in a room of their own. I'll be doing the good stuff to Lisa later."

Must be nice. After the wedding, they'd all be heading upstairs to their rooms to do the good stuff. Joe and his gorgeous new bride, Keri. Mike and Lisa. Evan and Terry.

He, on the other hand, was stag at his own brother's wedding so the only good stuff he had to look forward to was losing the cummerbund and penguin shoes.

It had been a couple of years since Kevin's marriage had exploded in a cloud of toxic flames, torching his career along with the relationship, and since then his libido had survived on a steady diet of bar bunnies. Less satisfying, but also a lot less risk, like eating a microwave meal instead of preparing a five-course meal. A lot less painful to throw away if it sucked.

He'd gone through his share of willing companions after the divorce, when he bought the bar, but lately he'd been making the trip upstairs to his apartment alone more often than not. The kind of women willing to spend one night with a guy they didn't know just because he filled out his shirts well, or so he was told, and owned the bar weren't the kind of women he wanted to have breakfast with the next morning.

And definitely not the kind of women you brought to your brother's wedding.

Unfortunately, thoughts of his type of woman led to thoughts of Beth, the pretty brunette who'd passed judgment on his type and been totally wrong. It had been two days since he busted her boss's nose and it irked him he kept thinking about her. It also irked him she'd left with the impression he was some kind of player.

If she wasn't so prickly—and if he knew her last name or where she lived—he'd probably like an opportunity to show her she was wrong about his type. He wasn't sure why he cared, but it bugged him she'd left with such a bad opinion of him. He wasn't used to that.

"Almost our turn," Joe said, jerking him out of his thoughts. "And then we should be able to go inside. And do more…girly wedding stuff. Whatever. Keri's so happy she's gonna bust, so it's worth it."

"So are you," Mike pointed out. "I still don't know how you pulled this all off."

Joe snorted. "It's called a blank check, my friend. Keri wanted fall foliage and I wasn't waiting a year for her to be my wife, so I said the magic words—*money's no object.*"

His brother didn't usually make a big deal about the money the sick horror novels he wrote earned, but a blank check from him was a pretty big blank check.

The drill sergeant bellowed for them. "Okay, I want groomsmen lined up behind the groom, four inches between you and slightly angled away from the camera. You, the tall one—you're in the back."

Screw that. Kevin threw his arm around Joe's shoulders and pulled him into a headlock. Joe jerked to the right, trying to escape, but he moved right into Mike's waiting noogie. Evan laughed and added rabbit ears to the back of Joe's head.

The photographer almost dropped her big, fancy camera, but the mothers of the bride and groom were hitting the shutter button as fast as their compact digital numbers would fire.

"Kowalski Wedding Photo of Doom," the bride shouted and Mike's four boys and Terry's almost-teenage daughter joined the pig pile.

They were all still laughing, a little breathless and more than a little sweaty when the wedding planner finally pulled them apart and ushered them inside. Thankfully the black tuxedos hid the grass stains, but Stephanie's dress was missing some lace around the hem.

They were supposed to go to the head table, but there were still toasts and formal dances and more freaking pictures to survive before the party could begin and he wasn't getting through all that with nothing but a sissy glass of champagne. With beer on his mind and a possible redheaded dance partner in his peripheral vision, he made a quick detour to the open bar.

And came face-to-face with Beth.

CHAPTER TWO

OF ALL THE WEDDINGS in all the world, she just had to be working this one. Beth took one look at Kevin in his tuxedo and knew it was going to be a very long night.

Tuxedo meant wedding party, which meant he was not only going to be there for the entire event, but he was a VIP. That meant she had to smile and make nice with the pain in the ass whose fault it was—kind of—that she was manning an open bar from six in the evening until one in the morning instead of sitting with her feet up after a fairly mild day answering Derek's phones and syncing his calendar.

She felt the hot flush spread across her chest as his blue eyes met hers. She'd been kind of bitchy the day they met and she felt bad about that. But mostly the hot flush came from the memory of what he'd done to her in her dreams last night.

This morning she'd blamed it on the microwave burritos she'd devoured too close to bedtime, but now, with the man once again in arm's reach, she had to reluctantly admit—but only to herself—she might be attracted to him. Just a little. Since, even if she *was* looking for a relationship, it wouldn't be with a guy who collected numbers on napkins, she'd prefer to blame the hot and sweaty night on nuked pseudo-Mexican food.

"What can I get you, sir?" she asked, hoping he wouldn't remember her.

The way his dimples flirted with the corners of his mouth said no such luck. "Sam Adams."

She grabbed a chilled bottle and popped the cap. "Glass?"

"Bottle's good." Instead of letting her set it down, then picking it up, he took it out of her hand, which caused his fingers to brush hers and her to shiver. "Glad to see you found another job."

She shrugged and tried not to make too big a deal about pulling her hand away. "Part-time and temporary, but better than nothing."

"Gimme your cell phone for a sec."

"Don't have one." Not that she'd hand it over to him. She didn't need him punching his number into it because she wouldn't be calling him.

"You don't have—"

"Uncle Kevin!" A teenage boy in a tux rushed over and took hold of Kevin's elbow. "If you're not sitting down in ten seconds, Grammy said she'll drag you over by your earlobe and make you cry."

Kevin laughed, then winked at Beth. "I'll be back."

That's what she was afraid of. Unfortunately, things would be slow at the bar until the toasts were done and people felt free to get up and move around, so she had plenty of time to watch the goings-on.

When the DJ announced it was time for the best man's toast, she saw Kevin laugh, which made the groom look nervous. Intrigued, she stood on tiptoe, trying to see around the guests jostling for videotaping space. Kevin accepted the microphone from his dad and a few people snickered when a guy she assumed, based on family resemblance, was another brother was handed one, too.

"Did I ever tell you you're my hero?" Kevin asked Joe, and then he got down on one knee in front of him. The other brother stood behind him with his four sons—or so she assumed after watching them—gathered around.

Then they started to sing and laughter rippled through the crowd. It seemed that besides blue eyes and dimples, not being able to carry a tune was a strong family trait for the Kowalskis.

But watching Kevin sing the worst off-key rendition ever of "Wind Beneath My Wings" to his brother, with his other brother and nephews singing backup, Beth felt the first alarming stir of a bad case of the warm and fuzzies.

It just got worse watching him interact with his family, especially dancing with his mom and a teenage girl Beth thought might be his niece. It was a big, affectionate, loud family and their laughter was the soundtrack of the night.

Once the duty dances were over and then the dinner dishes cleared away, Beth lost track of time handing out mimosas to the women and mostly beer to the men. Once the older folks and kids went off to bed, the drinks would get stronger, but for now it was easy work.

"So you really don't have a cell phone?"

Or it would be easy work if her body wasn't tuned in like a quivering antenna to the vibe Kevin was broadcasting. "I really don't. Another Sam Adams?"

He held up a half-full bottle. "I'm set. Mike grabbed me one."

Then why are you over here? "Okay."

"Even my mom has a cell phone and she can't figure out how to check her email."

"Why are you so hung up on my not having a cell phone?"

"Hung up?" He laughed. "Hung up. Cell phone. Get it?"

She rolled her eyes, but couldn't stop herself from laughing with him. "That was bad. And I washed my cell with my jeans and haven't gotten around to replacing it yet."

"Got a phone at home?"

"Yup." She turned away to make another mimosa for the beaming woman she'd figured out was the mother of the bride.

When she was done, Kevin slid a cocktail napkin toward her. "Got a pen?"

There was one next to the register, but when she held it out to him, he ignored it. He just grinned at her, with the pretty blue eyes and the oh-so-charming dimples.

"Oh, hell no," she said. "I'm not writing my number on a napkin so you can add it to your collection."

"I don't have a collection because I don't want their numbers. I want yours."

Before she could respond, another of the boys ran up and yanked on his arm. "Uncle Kevin, it's time for the cake!"

Beth used the blank napkin to wipe down the bar, then tossed it in the trash. She was there to work, not dodge advances from a guy who thought his dimples would make her throw herself at him.

The dimples wouldn't. The whole package might—the looks and the sense of humor and the very sweet way he was with his family, along with the steamy way he looked at her—but she wasn't going to be a number on anybody's napkin.

It was almost two in the morning before the staff got the go-ahead to call it a night and Beth sighed in relief as she yanked out the elastic holding her hair back and tossed it into the trash. It had been one hell of a night.

Kevin Kowalski was persistent, she'd give him that. She'd sucked it up and presented him with nothing but bland professionalism until he'd seemed to catch the hint. Still, every time her gaze landed on him—which was a lot more often than she cared to admit—he'd been watching her. When they dropped the lights, signaling to the stragglers the party was over and it was time to get the hell out, he'd given her one last inviting look. She'd turned her back, making busy with a bus pan, and when she turned around, he was gone.

The payphone beckoned, waiting for her to call a cab to take her home to her bed, but first she snuck out the back door and walked down toward the water. The grounds were beautiful and now, with the twinkling party lights off, the moon dancing across the water beckoned. It was quiet, soothing her frazzled nerves.

"You look beautiful in the moonlight."

She didn't scream, but her heart seized in her chest like a blown engine. Because he startled her, of course, not because of the words Kevin said in a voice a man usually used with a woman who was naked under him.

He was sitting on one of the stone walls with a half-empty bottle of beer, his long legs stretched out in front of him and crossed at the ankles. The jacket, bow tie and cummerbund had been abandoned somewhere and the white dress shirt was unbuttoned, baring his chest to the chilly night air. She tried not to give him the satisfaction of looking, but the expanse of chest led to taut abs she'd have to be dead not to want to run her hands over.

To his credit, he didn't gloat at being so obviously ogled. He reached down under his legs and picked up an unopened beer. After twisting off the top, he held it out to her.

She shouldn't. Even though she was off the clock, she was an employee and he was a guest. But there was something so lonely about the way he looked—

unlike his usual life-of-the-party self—she couldn't bring herself to refuse and walk away.

"Thanks." She sat farther down the wall and took a sip of the ice-cold beer. Cloaked in the shadows, watching the moonlight ripple across the water, she had no idea what to say.

Then he grinned at her and, even in the dark, she could see those impish dimples. "Did your boss tell you we tried to get you free for a dance?"

"Oh my God, what did you do?" Though it wasn't *really* his fault she'd lost her last job, if she got fired again because he stuck his nose in her business, she might need a restraining order just to stay employed.

"Joe—the groom and my oldest brother—asked your boss if you could leave the bar long enough for a dance. She refused, so he offered to pay extra. Then she got really snooty and informed us this isn't a dance hall and the young ladies in her employ are not for private hire."

His fake, snooty old-lady voice made her laugh, despite her utter disbelief at what they'd done. "And why would Joe do that?"

"Because I wanted to dance with you."

The stark simplicity of his response made her shiver, and the tingle of desire mixed with leftover warm and fuzzies made for a dangerous combination. "I counted at least a dozen women who would have danced with you free of charge."

His eyes were serious when he looked at her again. "I'm not that guy."

"What guy?"

"The guy you think I am."

The only thing she knew for sure about him was that she was trying like hell not to want him and doing a piss-poor job of it. "I don't think anything. I barely know you."

"Dance with me now."

She laughed and it sounded loud in the still night. "I haven't danced in years."

He put down his beer, then took her hand and pulled her into his arms. She set her bottle on the wall so she wouldn't spill it down his back. She'd tried resisting him, but it was a lost cause and wrapping her arms around those broad shoulders was inevitable.

As her hands clasped behind his neck, his arms circled her waist and pulled her close. "You don't dance in your kitchen? You know, when you're all alone?"

"No. I don't dance in my kitchen, even when nobody's looking."

"You should. It's good for the soul."

No, good for the soul was swaying in his arms to the rustling, chirping music of the night as the water-reflected moonlight rippled over them. Okay, maybe not good for the soul, but it sure as hell was good for her body.

"Are you going to get all prickly on me if I try to kiss you?"

She tilted her head back so she could see his face. "I guess that depends on how well you kiss."

Kevin's eyes smoldered at the challenge—and

invitation—and he threaded his fingers through her hair so he could tilt her head to just the right angle. Her eyes slid closed and she sighed—a soft, breathy sound she couldn't believe she'd made—as he touched his mouth to hers.

The man could kiss and, as the aching desire of the present wrapped up with the steamy memory of her dreams, her body practically trembled with need.

"Stay with me tonight," he whispered against her mouth.

Some logical voice in the back of her mind wanted to argue against staying, but she didn't want to hear it. "Yes."

He took her by the hand and, after they grabbed their beer bottles, they raced across the manicured lawn. They slowed down in the hall, where she hoped they wouldn't run into any of the staff as they dumped the bottles in the trash, and then tried their best to behave in the elevator.

Kevin managed to unlock and open the door to his room one-handed, his other hand still holding hers, then he closed it behind them and pressed her up against the wood.

"Watching you tonight and not being able to touch you was killing me," he said, and then lowered his mouth to hers.

She wrapped her arms around his neck and lost herself in the kiss, aware that even as his tongue danced over hers, he was slowly and not so stealthily trying to unbutton her shirt one-handed. It had been way too long since she'd been kissed, never mind had a man's hand on her, so she pushed his hand aside to hurry it along. As his tongue brushed hers and their breath mingled, she unbuttoned her shirt and then slid her fingertips under his, feeling the solid muscles twitch under her touch.

Then his hands were on her shoulders, sliding her shirt off, and she let him go so it could drop to the floor. She dropped her bra after it. His gaze raked over her, the look in his eyes as smoldering hot as his touch.

His shirt joined hers at their feet as he stripped down to just his pants and then, before she was quite finished admiring the broad expanse of naked chest, his hands and mouth were on her again. When he lifted her off the ground, she wrapped her legs around his waist and held on to his neck.

His kiss grew more urgent and she couldn't stop her moan when he backed her up against the door. With the cool wood against her skin and his hips between her thighs, her body trembled in anticipation.

Kevin licked his way down to her breasts, where his tongue flicked across one nipple, and then the other. "You are so…freakin'…hot."

She didn't want to talk. She wanted those hips moving against hers as they had while they danced in the moonlight, but without any clothes between them.

As if he could read her thoughts, he turned and started toward the bed. She laughed when he dropped her onto the mattress, but the sound died in her throat when he dropped his pants and boxer briefs in one smooth motion.

Oh, yes, staying was *definitely* the right decision.

Ten minutes later, he had her naked, too, and so desperate she was horrified when a frustrated growling sound tore from her throat. He only chuckled and kept right on teasing her—kissing and licking and touching her, but never quite enough to give her what her body yearned for.

Finally, just about the time she was sure she'd go mad, Beth heard the telltale crinkle of a condom wrapper being torn open.

He settled himself between her thighs and rested his weight on his forearms so he could look down at her. His smile was warm, but his face was flushed and naughtiness lurked in his gaze.

For a second she thought he was going to tease her some more, which might make her scream, but he kissed her instead. Beth threaded her fingers through his hair as he reached one hand down between their bodies and finally gave her what she wanted.

They both moaned as he slid into her, the sound mingling on their joined lips. He moved slowly, with short, gentle strokes and she raised her hips to meet them. She savored the sweet friction of every thrust as he murmured in her ear—telling her how hot she was and how amazing it felt and how he never wanted it to end.

As his pace quickened, Beth ran her hands over his back, reveling in the light sheen of sweat and the way his muscles rippled under her touch. She was drowning in the intensity of his blue eyes and she closed her eyes as the long-awaited orgasm took hold. He thrust harder and she heard him groan as he found his own release.

As the tremors faded, he lowered himself on top of her, a hot, heavy weight she didn't mind at all. He kissed the side of her neck and she smiled, stroking his hair. They lay like that a few minutes, catching their breath, before Kevin rolled away. She felt the bed shift under his weight, and then he was back, pulling her against his body.

"I'm glad you stayed," he said into her hair.

"Me, too." Very, very glad.

A night on her feet followed by a night on her back under Kevin without sustenance had Beth awake at too-early o'clock, her stomach rumbling in protest. Doughnuts, she thought. She'd sneak down to the continental breakfast nook, filch some doughnuts and coffee, and be back before Kevin woke.

It took her a few minutes of rummaging to find her clothes and, when she was dressed, she went digging through Kevin's clothes for his hotel key card.

And found napkins. The cocktail napkins she'd handed out with drinks, though they hadn't had names and phone numbers scrawled on them at the time. Oh, and fun notes, too. *I'm a former gymnast and I can still hook my ankles behind my head. Call me!*

When she snorted, Kevin rolled over, barely

cracking his eyes open, and muttered, "Make sure you lock the door when you leave."

Beth froze as all the warm afterglow left her body in a disappointed whoosh. So much for him not being *that* guy.

She didn't waste any more time hunting for his key card. Slipping into the hallway—and making sure the door locked behind her—she told herself she'd never see the man again.

And this time she meant it.

* * * * *

**He must choose between the life he forgot and
the life he never knew existed....**

From acclaimed author

DELILAH MARVELLE

Roderick Gideon Tremayne, the recently appointed Duke of Wentworth,
never expected to find himself in New York City, tracking down
a mysterious map important to his late mother. And he certainly never
expected to be injured, only to wake up with no memory of who he is.
But when he sees the fiery-haired beauty who's taken it upon herself
to rescue him, suddenly his memory is the last thing on his mind.

Available now!

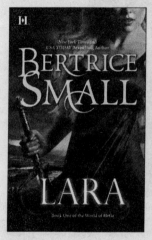

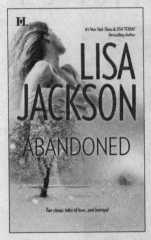

**When seduction becomes betrayal
and betrayal becomes love....**

A new tale of scandal and intrigue from
New York Times **and** *USA TODAY* **bestselling author**

BRENDA JOYCE

Seduction

Available now!

"Joyce's tale of the dangers and delights of passion
fulfilled will enchant."
—*Publishers Weekly* on *The Masquerade*

A new generation of cowboys stake claims to their land—and the women they love....

A classic tale from
New York Times **and** *USA TODAY* **bestselling author**

LINDA·LAEL MILLER

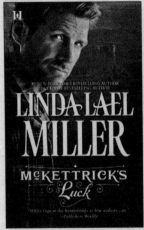

Like those of his celebrated ancestors, who tamed the wilds of Arizona, Jesse McKettrick's Indian Rock ties run deep. The Triple M Ranch is in his blood, along with the thrill of risk. But with his land at stake, this world-class poker player won't be dealt into Cheyenne Bridges's gamble—despite the temptation she brings.

Available now!

Husband of convenience. Lover by choice.

**A tale of betrayal, redemption and desire
from national bestselling author**

SARAH McCARTY

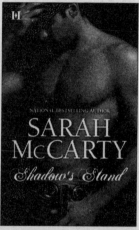

Former Texas Ranger Shadow Ochoa is lying low in the western Kansas
Territory waiting for his brothers in Hell's Eight to clear his name. That is,
until he's unjustly strung up for horse thieving...and pretty Fei Yen intervenes.
Invoking a seldom-used law, the exotic lady prospector claims Shadow as her
husband and rides off with the bridegroom shackled to her buckboard.

Savvy, fearless Fei Yen is devoted to her small claim and all it promises—
wealth, security and freedom for her and her cousin Lin. A husband is just a
necessary inconvenience for a woman alone on the frontier. Shadow isn't a
man to take orders, especially from Fei—except that the friction between
them ignites into an all-consuming passion.

Shadow's Stand

Coming in February 2012!

PHSM705CS